THE DEFENDANT'S FATHER

A MICHAEL GRESHAM NOVEL

JOHN ELLSWORTH

COPYRIGHT

PROLOGUE

Amy Tanenbaum had attended a bar mitzvah in a special new outfit given to her by her helicopter mom. Thursday night, she wore that same outfit to the Wendover High football game: black tights, black watch skirt, and a loose black sweater over a white blouse. It was October 12th and chilly in Chicago with frost in the forecast. Her mother made Amy take along her North Face jacket when she left home that evening. Amy complied, intending to leave it behind in the car along with her mother's admonitions about boys, drugs, strangers, and gentiles. Mothers were impossible, especially Jewish mothers with their uncanny ability to sniff out snowflakes and boys from miles away.

Nancy Jewell's mom had driven Nancy, Erin, and Amy to the game, dropping them at Wendover Field. The field was nothing more than recently painted bleachers and gridiron. The high-school girls met up with other friends and played musical bleacher seats as pair-offs began. Amy found herself sitting beside a boy she didn't know, a senior, and she was a little scared and a little excited all at once.

The boy left and returned with Pepsi's and nachos. They drank cola and shared the snack. Under the bleachers, a sea of popcorn boxes and soft drink cups deepened. Late in the second quarter, following a home-team touchdown, neither Amy nor her new friend noticed the boy's red wool scarf fell from his shoulders to the ground beneath the bleachers when the two students rose to their feet to clap and cheer.

Midway through the third quarter, Amy excused herself and headed for the ladies' room, courtesy of the 32-ounce soft drink. Her new friend remained seated. Amy stopped once to turn and smile at him. He flicked his hair away from his face and smiled back at her. She blushed and moved along.

Amy stopped at the snack bar to give her ex-boyfriend his ring back. The other girls in her group kept moving for the restroom while Amy dawdled with her ex.

A small block building on the visitor's side of the field housed the restrooms. The building was just beyond the end zone lights, which left it mostly hidden from the bleachers. As Amy made her way along the path, the lights became a distant glow until she could no longer see her feet. She shivered and forced herself to continue, at the same time wishing a friend had accompanied her or they had waited for her. At last, she made it to the block building. A single halogen lamp burned at its far end. Amy hurried inside, failing to see the dark form following at a distance, keeping to the shadows, treading along, casting nervous glances back over his shoulder.

She found herself alone in the restroom. It unnerved her. She realized her hands were shaking and her mouth was dry. Still, the need to relieve herself was greater than ever. So she locked herself in the far stall and straddled the commode so she could urinate without the porcelain contacting her body. Relief was instantaneous; she closed her eyes and shivered. She didn't see the shadow come into the restroom and proceed to her stall where he paused inches from the door. The intruder pulled a guitar string from his pocket and unwound it. He took a single wrap at each end around the gloves he wore.

Amy saw movement through the back-lit crack in the door. She heard panted inhalations and exhalations as the intruder prepared.

"Is someone waiting to use this stall?" she said in a small voice. "I'll be done in a minute."

The man reached out with both hands and rapped his knuckles on the door. "We're waiting!" he said.

"Please don't do that!" the girl cried. "You're scaring me!"

Again the rapping and again, "We're waiting!"

"Dammit, please. Just go away. Please, I'm hurrying." Tears washed into her eyes. Her hands shook as she unwound toilet paper. "Are you watching me through the crack?" she asked. "Please just go away. My friends are coming."

The man felt his power growing with every word the girl uttered. He held her very life in his hands, the final moments, and they both knew it. He lowered his hands and pressed his groin against the door to the stall. Then he was rigid and ready.

He leaned his forehead against the cool metal and sighed.

And then... "Meow!" he cried. He stepped back and swung his foot at the door with all his weight behind it, kick-boxer style.

When it was over, the killer grabbed a wheelbarrow near the adjacent maintenance shed and loaded the girl's body into it. He kept to the shadows off the trail and wheeled the cart underneath the bleachers where the killer found himself and his prize shielded from most of the game's ambient light. Which was good since his ministrations required secrecy.

He proceeded with his plan, posing her just so.

There was an explosion overhead as the home team scored a touchdown. The bleachers shuddered as hundreds of fans stomped their feet.

The sudden maelstrom shocked the killer back to reality.

He crept away. The ticket booth was empty and dark as he passed into the dimly lit parking area just off Gordon Street. He was within two miles of Chicago's Upper Loop.

He rolled out of the parking lot and onto Gordon Avenue fourteen minutes after he had first watched Amy go alone into the ladies' room. Fourteen minutes to experience his fantasy at long last.

He already remembered the calendar of home games. He thought the next home football game was a couple weeks away. And if not that, basketball would soon follow.

By Friday morning, the police had turned over many rocks. They had arrested the senior boy Amy left sitting in the stands. Initial statements were fuzzy: some spectators claimed to have seen him leave with Amy for the restrooms; some claimed to have seen him in the vicinity of the restrooms; some claimed he remained behind in the stands. But one thing was sure—they were together the last time someone saw her alive. He was new in the school, and no one knew much about him. Nancy Jewell identified the red scarf found under the bleachers as belonging to Amy's new friend.

The police had their lead.

1

Outside U.S. Grand Jury Room 204 in Chicago, in the nook just beyond the elevators, is a black leather bench where I practice law. That's how much the federal judiciary thinks of me and other defense lawyers who wait outside the grand jury room to help our clients plan their answers to questions posited by the U.S. Attorney. The U.S. Attorneys, the prosecutors, get offices in this court building with windows that offer a lordly view, where they may look down upon the mere mortals below. We defense attorneys are given a public bench—one to share among us—maybe leather, probably Naugahyde. Which is how the justice system treats criminal defendants and their attorneys. The worst of the worst, the crummiest of the crummiest, always second-rate for second-rate citizens. Even the cops get their own office. But am I bitter? You're damn right I am.

Here's another thing as long as I'm making my case. I feel I am representing my client in the most half-assed way possible. He's under subpoena so he has to be inside the grand jury room with the grand jury. But I'm defense counsel so

I'm not allowed to enter that sanctum. However, he has the right to come out into the hall and discuss questions and plan answers with me. Which we're doing, one question at a time, which is also his right. Then he goes back inside and tells them what I think. How, you might wonder, would this be any different from me, Michael Gresham, being inside the grand jury room with him? The answer is that the identity of the grand jury is secret. If I were allowed inside, the rationale goes, it might compromise the grand jury's anonymity. So here I sit, tearing up the New York Times crossword, trying to flash on a four-letter word that means forlorn. Down? Might it be down? Surely, it's not that simple. It's from New York, for the love of God.

My client is Thomas A. Meekins. He is the thrice-elected sheriff of Mackenzie County. Meekins is under investigation by the grand jury for embezzlement of public funds, money they say he ripped off from the sheriff's office with phony invoices and real checks. One $54,000 check to Glock, Inc. was cashed at Imperial Casino in Wisconsin, ninety minutes north of Chicago. Was it my guy who presented the check to the cashier? Or did someone else? To solve such mysteries, grand juries are hatched, defendants are subpoenaed to appear and encouraged to give testimony against themselves, and lawyers like me make camp on a sun-faded bench surrounded by crazies who look like they stepped off some Martin Scorsese soundstage. They're waiting for their grand juries, too, and they don't mind standing close by where they might pick up a gem of legal wisdom as I advise my sheriff.

I whisper to him, but he frowns at me, stone deaf in his right ear from too many hours at the gun range and two tours as a tank commander in Iraq. Did he hear I told him to take the

Fifth in answer to whether he'd ever been to the Imperial Casino? Or did he think I told him to pay the rent before playing bingo? I have no idea. My growing audience is getting more out of my admonitions than my client if his troubled face is any indicator.

Here he is again. The tenth question in an hour.

"Is that my signature on the check?" he asks. His face is ashen, and I don't like that. Fear is one thing; self-incrimination by skin tone is something else.

I motion for him to sit. "Well, is it?"

He scrutinizes me. The crowd steps forward. "I endorsed it," he whispers.

"Have they asked that?" I whisper.

"Not yet."

"Well, let's talk about that. If you admit you endorsed it, then bam, you're indicted. If you deny endorsing it, then bam, you're guilty of perjury. Perjury is the lesser of the two charges."

"Isn't there any other way?"

"Do you remember what I told you about the Fifth Amendment, Tom?"

"You told me if I'm unsure of something to take the Fifth."

"Right. This is one of those times."

"So take the Fifth?"

"Definitely."

"How long can they keep me in there?"

"All day. Days. A week."

"State grand juries take maybe an hour, tops," he says from experience.

"This is federal. No need for the prosecutors to get back to campaigning year-round like the state boys. These guys are full-time, professional prosecutors. They get to stay on for life if they want. So they don't give a damn if you're inside an hour or a month. It's all the same rate of pay to them. Now, knowing how the cards are stacked, is there any reason you would ever want to give the grand jury any answer other than your name, address, and employer's name?"

"No—no—no."

"But you argued with me this morning when I told you that. You wanted to come here and clear your name. Remember that?"

"Yes, I did. It was damn stupid advice I gave myself."

"Yes. So let's agree that from now on, you do nothing but take the Fifth. Understand?"

"I understand. All right," he says and pushes up from the bench. The crowd takes a step away to give him room. He's wearing a uniform and a big black gun and scares the bejesus out of them. He goes back inside, and the pneumatic door whooshes behind him.

"Why don't we do this?" I say to the crowd at large. "Why don't you come up one at a time and ask your questions? I'm a lawyer, I'm already paid, and I don't mind pitching in." Better use of my time than the New York Times crossword and the damned four-letter word for forlorn.

They form a line along the bulletin board and watch as the first-in-line approaches me.

She is maybe twenty-five years old, wearing gray pleated slacks and a red blouse with a pink and white tie. She's still wearing her peacoat, unbuttoned and flopping around her, like it might be the property of someone much larger. She moves close and says in a low, rueful voice, "They want to ask me about shooting the president."

I look into her eyes and see this is no joke. I keep my voice low. "Someone's saying you want to shoot the president?"

"Secret Service arrested me. Kept me in jail for three months before my dad found me. He called Senator Armstrong, and the Senator raised hell. Then they released me, but I have to appear today. A subpoena." She holds out her subpoena.

It's the real thing and lists the witness's name as Phun Loc.

"Phun Loc, that's you?"

"Yes. Everyone calls me Fun Luck. That's my American name."

"Okay. Well, have you spoken to a lawyer?"

"No. We can't afford a lawyer."

"Did you try to shoot the president?"

Her eyes wander off to one side then jerk back to the other. "I don't want to say in here. It's a long story."

"Well, look, you're under subpoena, so let me try something." I say to the queue, "Folks, would you all mind moving to the other side of the elevators? I need a little more privacy here, and then it'll go faster for everyone."

Other than minor grousing, they assemble themselves on the far side of the elevator. Now Phun Loc and I can speak in normal voices.

"So, tell me a little about what happened."

"My grandfather is American, and he's a Vietnam veteran. He has PTSD and won't sleep inside. So he sleeps in the streets and begs for food. We bring him home, but he always runs away again. The VA has a ninety-day waiting period. If he doesn't show up on the exact date of his counseling appointment, he goes back to the bottom of the list."

"And so you're mad at the VA?"

"They're inflexible. We get him in there finally, and they say he doesn't have an appointment."

"You're young. Where were you born?"

"In Chicago. But I don't see what that's got to do with anything. I'm as American as you are, sir."

"No, no, I wasn't implying anything. But I get it. You're angry as hell, so you wrote a letter to the president. Is that it?"

"Yes, I wrote a letter. I said they need to be careful before someone gets shot. Can you help me?"

"I'm a criminal lawyer, but I need more facts. Now, what else did you do?"

"The president lives in Chicago. Sometimes. I watched his house whenever he was in town. The Secret Service found out and connected the letter to me and searched our home.

They found guns, and now they want to indict me. I have to testify."

"You've been watching the president's house. That's not a good idea."

"Why not? It's a public sidewalk. If I want to stand on public property and look at that damn house why not? Nobody can stop me, can they?"

I must admit it is public property in front of the president's house. Maybe he'll move elsewhere when he finishes up in office.

"Who did the guns belong to?"

"My grandfather. He brought them here from Vietnam."

"Do you know what kind of guns they are?"

"One's an M-something."

I know enough to ask, "M-16?"

"Yes. M-16. They confiscated grandfather's guns. That was one."

"Had you ever handled those guns?"

"Sure. I moved them every time I cleaned his room."

"He has a room in your house? Anyone else living in that room?"

"My grandma. She's old-country Vietnamese and won't speak English. She watches American TV but refuses to speak English. But she knows how. She laughs in all the right places."

"Okay. Look, will you come back and talk to me after you're

done in there?"

"Can't you help me?"

"I can't go in with you, no. The law won't allow me inside the grand jury room."

"What if I take the Fifth?"

At last, someone after my heart. "I would suggest you do that. Make them do their job without you."

"Okay. I'll be back."

Phun Loc turns on her heel and walks to the grand jury room entrance. She presses her back against the wall and waits.

The queue moves up a notch as the next client heads my way. He is a slight, weather-beaten man of about sixty. As we're about to shake hands, my client Tom Meekins comes out of the room and scurries over to my bench. It's late in the day on a Friday, and I can guarantee the grand jury won't get to these other poor saps who have been waiting all day. They'll be rescheduled to come in on Monday after the weekend.

I sigh, but I don't show my frustration. I am a professional, and I've done this song and dance for a long time. "Now what?"

"Can you wait over there?" he asks my newest customer. He indicates the bulletin board. The old man nods and backs away.

"Here's what. They're telling me they've done an audit of the sheriff's books. My books. I had no idea."

"So what are they asking about?"

He blanches. "They're saying the missing funds total up to over a million dollars."

"Do they?"

"I don't know. I didn't think so."

"So what's the question, Tom? What's pending right now?"

"They want me to admit I bought my lakeside property with the money."

Lakeside property—real estate right on Lake Michigan—is horribly expensive in Chicago. Only the Richie Riches of the world can touch that inventory.

"Did you?"

Meekins darts his eyes around. "Actually? Yes."

"So you took money from the sheriff's budget and bought real estate?"

"A condo. It's a third-floor condo on the south side, so not all that great a view."

"Sure. Well, you want to take the Fifth again."

"But they wanted to know the address and asked about the deed. I think they're getting ready to seize it."

"Which they have a right to do if you used embezzled funds to buy it. Get used to it, Tom. RICO seizures happen every day." The Racketeer Influenced and Corrupt Organizations Act, referred to as RICO, was originally passed to help against organized crime, but today, it's mostly about corrupt

CEOs or trust holders that abuse their positions. Something named even the Catholic Church as a RICO defendant.

"Carol will murder me, Michael."

"Carol would be who?"

"My girlfriend."

"I thought you were married."

"I am. I keep Carol on the side. My wife doesn't know."

"Tom, you and I need to talk when we're done here. You haven't been entirely forthcoming with me."

"You never asked me about a property."

There it is, the red flag. He's right. I never specifically asked him whether he had used embezzled money to buy a condo. I've been down this road with criminal minds before. Not that I'm making a diagnosis or anything, but I can see a malpractice claim nibbling around the edges of the case because I did not ask germane questions. My office has three or four such malcontents just waiting to sue me for malpractice. People unwilling to accept responsibility. So they want me to co-sign their bullshit, like I'm responsible. Sorry, but no thanks.

"I asked whether you had embezzled funds, and you told me no. Why would I ask about fruits of the crime?"

He holds his face in his hands. "God, oh God, what have I got myself into?"

I put my hand on his shoulder. "Just take the Fifth on every-thing. Any and everything incriminates you so just let them know you're not answering any further questions."

He stands and wheels on me, pointing and accusatory. He shouts, "I paid you to defend me, Gresham! And you can't even go in there with me! Why didn't you tell me that?"

"Calm down, Tom, please."

He reaches and touches the big black gun on his hip. "I'm going—"

"Wait, Tom. Please sit down."

He ignores me, heading back to the grand jury room. There, at the entrance, Phun Loc is waiting to be called inside. Without warning, Sheriff Meekins wraps his arm around the Vietnamese girl, whips his gun out, and disappears back inside. The door whooshes shut, and I can hear muffled, excited voices. I can only imagine the pandemonium inside, and I'm wondering what I might do to help when the door flies back open, and the sheriff comes out into the hallway, still dragging his hostage, and orders a man in a gray suit to press the elevator down button. The man holds up his hands and averts his head from the muzzle of the gun but keeps enough presence of mind to press the button as ordered. He shrinks back away from the sheriff.

"Tom," I call out, "this isn't right! Let the girl go! Let's talk. Nobody's hurt, and we can end this peacefully and get you some help!"

He ignores me. The elevator door slides open, and gunman and hostage disappear inside. Just as quickly, they come right back out. Sheriff Meekins again drags Phun Loc into the grand jury room, and the door again whooshes closed.

Seconds later, the building's alarm system erupts with a god-awful clanging and lights flashing.

I stand up from my bench. The legal clinic is at an end. They look at me like I might have something to say. "Please go to another floor," I tell them, "but wait around. You're all witnesses, and the FBI will want to speak with you."

I sit back down on my bench. The group stares at me as if unsure, but when the elevator door opens, they are cramming themselves in as tight as sardines.

The second set of elevator doors whooshes open, and a rush of armed law enforcement officers unload onto the floor. I've been sitting on the same Naugahyde bench for two hours when I realize I have given away so much advice this morning I have none left for myself. So I walk over to the grand jury room and its closed door.

With two knocks and a cry of "Coming in!" I push through the door.

2

Six months ago, I inked an agreement with the local Chicago police union, Long Blue Line. I agreed to defend the city's police officers who faced criminal charges. It was a great honor and an enormous burden at the same time. Cop crimes are serious cases for two reasons. One, they put a police officer's entire career on the line. Two, a guilty verdict is a guarantee there will be money damages against the city. So the union looked high and low for the right law firm for the job, and it so happened my firm fit the bill. My trial record is outstanding (I'm talking statistics, not self-flattery), and my rates are reasonable. Plus, I make clients feel like I care—which I do. I understand criminal clients, and I can empathize with a police officer accused of a crime.

How does it work? Well, there isn't a more difficult client than a cop on the wrong end of an indictment. They are often bitter, angry as hell, and ready to strike out. Their favored targets are the system and, all too often, me, for no other reason than I am part of that system. So it's my job to temper the negative feelings and to lead the client into using his anger in a positive way. Which means, bottom line, if I can turn them away from spewing hate about the system and move them to helping me investigate their case by using their experience catching and prosecuting bad guys, then I have the best assistant working alongside me that any lawyer could hope for.

Which is how I happened to meet Tom Meekins. Sheriff Tom Meekins that is. He didn't show up on my doorstep through the Long Blue Line contract per se; he contacted me for help because a friend of a friend (both cops) knew about me and trusted me. We had two meetings before he hired me. The first meeting was a getting-to-know-you moment. A half hour of who and what we were. A week later, we had our second meeting. This time around we talked case specifics. I was introduced to a series of high-value thefts by embezzlement, perpetrated by the head of a department, the elected sheriff himself. It would be very challenging and almost impossible to defend. Still, that's how I earned my spurs—making the impossible possible.

Tom Meekins is an Ironman athlete. He is just five-eleven, 177 pounds, steely blue eyes and a whipsaw attitude that's very offsetting to bad guys: friendly one moment and demanding the next. He moves with the grace of a leopard, always occupying his space with confidence and an extroverted familiarity that swings votes and sways juries whenever he's testifying to put a bad guy away. The question is, will these same characteristics help him in the trial he's now facing? Probably not. Here, the evidence is compelling, and his future looks bleak.

I enter the grand jury room to confront the man who won the 2014 Police Pistol Combat Shooting Championship for law enforcement officers in the Midwest. In fact, Tom won it with a score of 850 points, which was fifty points more than any previous shooter had ever scored.

So Tom has deadly skills and, as I step through the door, I know that he can drop me with a single shot if he decides I'm in his way.

3

"Glad you could make it!" Tom shouts as I enter the room.

Immediately, I'm relieved. He holds his gun down at his side, its muzzle pointing at the floor. But then Tom swings it up and points it at the clutch of people positioned at the back. He turns to me and winks.

I recognize two marshals from previous court appearances. The marshals stand there with empty waistband holsters and stupid looks on their faces. I look again at Tom. He has their semiautomatic pistols stuck in the waistband of his trousers. Apparently, when Tom dragged Phun Loc into the room, the threat he made on her life compelled the marshals to turn over their weapons to him. Since then, they have cowered with the other two dozen souls. Also, frozen in place is the Assistant U.S. Attorney commissioned to prosecute Tom. I know her; she doesn't lift her eyes to meet mine. Tom has corralled them into a corner of the back of the room where they sit bunched on the floor along with the court reporter and jurors. Most of them look nervous, afraid, but some sit there casually, as if their life wasn't held in the palm of this sheriff's hand.

"Have a seat, Michael," Tom says, indicating a front-row seat. "I'm going to need your help."

I sit in the first row of visitor seats where he directs me, keeping my eyes fastened on the gun. The last thing I want is that thing roaring to life. My agenda is clear: help bring this to a safe and sane conclusion, no bullets fired and nobody hurt. Following that, I will help Tom get the psychological care he needs. The man is temporarily insane compared to the précis of the man I knew before today. So who is this new and nutzoid Tom Meekins?

He takes a seat facing me across the aisle, the hostages at my back. Phun Loc stands just on the inside of the swinging doors that lead to the lectern and counsel chairs. It's obvious he gave her orders, and she means to comply by staying at his side.

"What I need, counselor," he says to me, "is an airplane and one million dollars in cash. I also want a hundred feet of rope. Get them delivered, and I will let these people go."

"So you're telling me I'm your negotiator?" I ask.

He smiles and waves the gun across the crowd. "These folks are counting on you, counselor. Your job is to keep them alive."

I lean forward in my seat, closing the space between us. "Tom, what happened? We were going to handle this. I was going to find a way out."

He laughs. "A way out of dozens of confirmed thefts? I don't think so, counselor. Not even the Great Houdini could get out of that mess. No, this is the easier, softer way for me to conclude the case."

"Let's think this through. Where will you go that the FBI can't come get you?"

He smiles and raises his free hand. "Michael, Michael, Michael. You're my lawyer and my friend, but you will also help the cops just as soon as I'm in the air. There's no possible way I can divulge my plan to you. So please"—the gun is pointing at my head—"don't insult me like this. Hold your questions, and we'll all get through this alive."

"They'll never let you go, Tom."

"Then they'll end up with thirty dead citizens on their hands. It will be a stinkfest of bad publicity, a mess of wrongful death cases, and lost jobs for the idiots who bring down my wrath on these folks. Think about it. Would you like your name associated with mass murder? Didn't think so, counselor. Now, here's what I need you to do."

I'm noticing that his speech has picked up speed and is forced like he's on something. There's that to think about, too, that he might be drug-addled.

"A jet airplane at Midway Airport. One that can cross an ocean. One million in cash. One hundred feet of clothesline rope. All 'ones,' Michael. You can remember that. Now go. Tell them I will shoot my first hostage at noon if I'm not sitting in my first-class seat by then."

"I will. I'll tell them."

There is pounding at the door. Voices are demanding Tom throw down his weapon and come out with his hands in the air. He smiles and shakes his head. "Can you imagine?

These cowboys will need to be educated, Michael. That's your job." Tom's face morphs into a cornered wolverine, his teeth bared and spittle on his lower lip. He pounds the railing. "Let them know I'm goddamn serious about all this!"

"Okay."

"Now! Get out there now! Make your opening statement, counselor. Convince them their only option is meeting my demands. Go!"

I'm up and out of my chair and headed for the door in a heartbeat.

"Tell them you're coming out alone!" Tom shouts at me as my hand touches the door. "If even one of them steps inside, I shoot."

"Hold your fire!" I shout at the door. "This is Attorney Michael Gresham, and I'm coming out!"

I push the door, and a dozen cops step back, their sidearms leveled at me.

"Identify yourself!" commands a fat plain-clothes cop. He has a bad comb-over, a belly that protrudes over his belted pants, and a bulbous nose. He looks like a walking cliché.

"Michael Gresham. I'm the lawyer for the man who has taken the hostages. He's sent me out here to talk."

"ID, sir."

I pull my wallet and flash my bar card. The fat man takes it and compares it to my driver's license.

At that moment, two other uniforms step up and frisk me. I raise my arms and let them have at it.

"What's going on in there?" asks another cop wearing a suit. This man is thin to his partner's girth with a wide mouth and heavyset brows over beady eyes.

"Whoa, who are you guys?"

"We're the U.S. Marshals in charge. We have jurisdiction over this court building. I'm Marshal Hanover and my colleague"—he gestures to fat man—" is Marshal Stewart."

I browse the crowd of gun-toting lawman. "Where's the FBI hostage negotiator?"

A third man in casual gear, khaki pants, a polo shirt, and FBI cap nudges his way through a few of the cops and steps up. "I'm Rahman Smart. I'm the negotiator. Who is that in there?"

"Tom Meekins, Sheriff of Mackenzie County. He's under investigation on embezzlement charges."

"I think I read about that. And he's armed?"

"Big black gun."

"What kind of gun is it?" interrupts Marshal Stewart.

"I don't know. Some semi-automatic," I tell him from my limited experience.

"Any other weapons?"

"He's disarmed two marshals. He has their guns in his waistband."

The first cop and the negotiator trade looks. *He has enough bullets to execute everyone in there* is what their faces say.

"He has a message for me to give you. A demand. One airplane, one million dollars, one hundred feet of rope. Clothesline rope."

The hostage negotiator shakes his head and holds out a cell phone. "Knock on the door and pass this phone to your client, counselor."

He says it in an almost accusatory tone as if I am to blame for my client's actions.

I shake my head, too. "I can try, but let me be clear. I know Tom Meekins. That guy in there... that's not any Tom Meekins I know. He's walking a tightrope, and he's about to fall off and shoot lots of innocent people. So why not just meet his demands and chalk it up?"

"We'll make those decisions as we go, counselor," says the FBI negotiator. "Please pass him the phone, now."

I accept the phone and head back to the door. I knock four times and shout, "Tom! It's Michael! Open up and take this phone! They want to talk to you!"

"No talking, Michael! Tell them I shoot at noon!"

I turn back to the crowd of cops. All eyes are on me. "Now what?"

They look at each other. FBI Agent Smart is frowning, and then he is on his cell phone, speaking to his supervisor. Then he ends the call.

"Our policy is not to capitulate. Please step aside, counselor. We'll take it from here."

"Wait!" I say. "You don't know this guy. He's a combat shooter. If you're thinking of storming the room, you will lose cops and innocent people before you take him. Is that really what you want?"

At that moment, the door opens a crack and Tom shouts, "Michael! Come back here!"

The cops look at me and nod. I disappear back inside with Tom and his entourage.

We retake our seats away from the rest of the hostages.

Tom leans into me and asks me under his breath, "The cops are getting ready to take me out, aren't they?"

"I don't know. They're saying they don't negotiate."

"I won't give up. I've got nowhere to hide. I'm looking at the entire rest of my life in prison. I can't do that."

"Well, let's talk about that."

At that moment, my smartphone buzzes. Tom looks at me. I shrug.

"Answer it. They probably want to talk."

I pull the phone and hit TALK. "Michael Gresham."

A familiar voice reaches out, "Michael, are you okay? Father Bjorn here."

"It's Father Bjorn," I tell Tom. "My priest."

A knowing look crosses Tom's face, and he smiles. "Cute. They've done their homework. They know I'm Catholic."

"Father, did the police tell you to call me?"

"They did. Put me on speaker, please."

I do as he says.

"Tom Meekins? Father Frederic Bjorn is speaking. I hope you'll talk."

"Go ahead, Father," says the sheriff. "Can you speak sense to these cops?"

"That's just it, Tom. These people will not negotiate. They asked me to call you before they rush in and take your life."

"That's what they said?"

"Exactly that. Which makes me very sad. There's no need for anyone to die. Are you Catholic, Tom?"

"Yes."

"This would be an evil thing for you to take innocent blood. Terrible."

"What are you saying?"

"I'm saying I'm not sure you would be forgiven."

"God forgives everything, Father. We only have to ask."

"Not necessarily. Trust me, you don't want to spill innocent blood because of your sin. That's an evil that isn't easily forgiven."

Tom's eyes fall to the floor. He wipes the sleeve of his sheriff's shirt across his eyes. I am astonished. Something has touched him, and I don't know why. For me, it's almost always negotiable with God. But this man sees it differently.

"I don't want to die. I want to live. But I don't want to spend my life in prison."

"I've talked to the U.S. Attorney," says Father Bjorn. "He's willing to reduce your embezzlement case to one count. And he's ready to charge you with only one count of kidnapping because of what's happened here today. Trust me, Tom, this is the easier way. This is the way to atone for your sins here today and receive forgiveness."

Tom looks at me. I offer a smile and meet his eyes. "That's better than where we were an hour ago," I tell my client. "This is the deal you want. Take it."

Tom nods and asks me, "Do we need it in writing?"

"No, the word of a third person, a priest, will be enough. Why don't you hand me the guns, Tom? Let me tell them you accept."

Tom's eyes dart to the terrified people along the back wall. Their anxious looks are pleading with him. Phun Loc steps up. "Do it," she whispers.

Without another word, Tom snaps the magazine out of the gun and works the slide, ejecting the round in the chamber and locking back the slide. All cop style. He hands me the gun, then repeats the process with the seized guns. Then he sits back and says into the phone, "Thank you, Father."

The marshal hostages rush forward and spread-eagle my client on the floor. He is frisked and cuffed. Then they stand him up. They take back their weapons, one at a time, then relieve me of Tom's pistol.

"Coming out! Don't shoot! U.S. Marshal Johnson! The suspect is disarmed and cuffed!"

The door bursts open before Marshal Johnson can push it open. A horde of cops surrounds my client and takes him away.

Father Bjorn's voice blares from the phone. "I heard that. All's well that ends well, Michael."

"Honest to God, Father, thank you."

"God has his hand in it. That's all I can say."

"Thank you, anyway."

"Michael, take me off speakerphone but don't hang up, please."

I do as he says and raise the phone to my ear. "Okay. I'm listening, Father."

"I got a call last night. I need to see you immediately. Can you come by the church?"

My hands are still shaking, but I cannot refuse the man who just saved us all. "What time?"

"Can you come tonight after you are done there?"

"What's up?"

"There's been a murder, and they have contacted me."

"A parishioner? Do they need a lawyer?"

"They need a lawyer. But they're not a parishioner."

"Then what?"

"I'll explain when I see you. Please hurry, Michael."

We hang up. Phun Loc has hung behind. Off to my right, the cops have formed in a circle and are taking names and addresses of witnesses and hostages. It's a mess, so Phun Loc asks me to step to the back of the room. I follow her there.

"Yes?"

Tears have filled her eyes. She blinks hard. Again. "I am terrified."

"Sure you are. Do you want my help?"

"Would you? But I have no money to pay you."

"We won't worry about money for now." I hand her my card. "Call this number. Tell Mrs. Lingscheit you need an appointment right away. No later than Monday. Will you do that?"

"Yes."

"Okay. I have to get going now. We'll talk later."

She nods and leans against the wall.

There is no hurry, but will the cops allow me through? They already have my particulars, and the FBI will most likely drop in and take my statement at some point. Trauma counselors will work with the hostages themselves.

It has been a long morning. But to the criminal practitioner, it has been productive.

How many times do you get to plead out a case before the grand jury has even indicted?

It's a win.

In so many ways.

In the men's room at the end of the hall, I throw up into the toilet of the first cubicle. After I purge, I cup cold water to my face at the sink. Then the tears come, and I am shaking. I cry silently, but violently. When I finish, I stand upright and smile at myself in the mirror. The smile does little to help. I look depressed and forlorn.

"You did it," I say to encourage my reflection. "You didn't die."

Then the air goes out of me, and I am down on the floor, shuddering and trying to stand. With all muscles flexed, I stand and lean against the porcelain sink to steady myself. I peer into the mirror a second time.

The tears come again, and my hands shake. I didn't die, but I could have.

At times such as this, I always expect to hear God's voice whispering to the good son, "Good job, Michael."

Instead, a crossword puzzle jumps randomly to mind. That four-letter word meaning forlorn? *Down.* Four letters for *forlorn*, no matter what they say in New York.

4

The fire crackles and pops in the church office fireplace. It is a cold October 13th in Chicago after midnight. It is the kind of cold that makes the old-timers say, "The hawk flies!" Chicago can go both ways in October, warm days where you can still don shorts and go for a sail, other days, like today, when you need to wrap up in hats and gloves.

As agreed, I am meeting with my priest. We have discussed today's courthouse drama, and now Father Bjorn is telling me about a new case. I lean toward the fireplace and warm my hands. Then I turn my face to him, waiting.

"Who is he to you?" I ask.

The priest draws himself up in the chair in which he sits in his diocese office and confesses, "Jana is my son."

I have followed this priest my entire life. A son? "You're a priest. I thought priests didn't have sons."

"I have a son. It's a long story, Michael."

As he speaks, Father Frederic Bjorn looks small and frightened. He seems to have aged ten years since I saw him last
Sunday. But it wasn't always this way. In my youth, his words
terrified me. He told our catechism class that certain sins
were an affront to God for which there could be no forgiveness. It was never clear to me how that worked and why
those were the worst-of-all sins. But it scared me to no end
since there were several I committed at least once a day. It
was in his presence I learned to speak only after the utmost
deliberation, and the lawyer was born. Still, I stayed close to
Father Bjorn's hem as I served at the altar, assisting in Mass
while knowing I was unfit to serve, unfit to consume the
Host.

It has taken half a lifetime and tens of thousands of dollars
of therapy for me to move beyond those notions. And while
I revile the sins of the recent church, I love the sinners—
especially the priests. And especially this one, the head of
All Saints-St. Thomas Catholic Church, the largest Catholic
church in downtown Chicago. They know father Bjorn
throughout our city as a great humanitarian, healer, and
politician-maker. His ability to sway elections is unrivaled.
Ward healers bow down to him and aldermen call upon
him for prayer and favors. But now he confides to me he has
a son. This is huge and will so inflame the diocese it might
arise and expel him. We must keep the lid on.

"A son?" I say, but I don't want to give the information too
much weight, so I add, "It happens."

Indeed.

I lurch ahead. "And you say they have arrested him?"

Father Bjorn's eyes cloud over. "His mother called me. That's why I begged you to come by tonight, Michael."

My hands have quit their shaking since my run-in with death at the federal court. Sheriff Tom Meekins is in a private cell in the Cook County Jail and awaits evaluation by a psychiatrist. So that turned out well enough. After all the excitement, I had returned to the office to deal with several emergencies until nine p.m. A late dinner followed and then my trip here to All Saints.

"Do you know what he's charged with?"

"They say he killed a classmate."

We sit for a minute or more in the hollow carved out of the air by these words. Then I follow up. "Is he even capable of that?"

Now the tears overflow down his cheeks. He chokes down a sob, and I think, *he really is a father.*

"Is he capable?" Father raises his hands in the air as if he will give the benediction. "That's just it! I have no idea! I know nothing about him!"

"Why not? You haven't been involved?"

"Now there's an understatement. I've never even seen him. There are all kinds of child abuse, Michael. Like never seeing your son!" He slaps the desk hard, and I startle. Sometimes, even after therapy, I get flashbacks.

"No need to trouble yourself with all that just now. Why don't we talk about what needs to be done?"

"He's waiting for my visit. He's hoping for something from me at long last."

"Does he know his father is a priest?"

"His mother always told him I had vanished. But last night she told him the truth. How she became pregnant, moved in shame from Chicago to Los Angeles, and raised my son in the shadow of the Santa Monica Pier. She says he is waiting for my help. She says he believes I have God's ear, that I can make the sign of the cross and this will all disappear."

"Wait. If he grew up in California why is he in a Chicago jail?"

"He came here to stay with his mother's brother, my son's Uncle Tim. Do his senior year here, away from the influences in California that had him smoking pot and devil worship."

"Devil worship? Seriously?"

He spreads his hands and looks into the fire. He slumps forward, the white collar cramping his jaw shut as if to silence him. His hands twitch as they seek warmth from the blaze, and his legs, crossed at the ankles, jitter up and down like a sewing machine. In all of our years of coming together, I have never seen my priest like this before. He has never been in this situation before. While the priesthood can be difficult, where Father Bjorn was involved, I always thought the struggle was with the other guy, never the man of the cloth. Now it appears I was wrong about Father Bjorn and am running to catch up.

The cloth, it appears, has its human enticements. In that instant, I know I will help.

Father Bjorn repeats, "They are saying he killed a classmate. A girl."

"Do you know where they say he killed this classmate?"

"They found her body at the football game. Wendover Field."

I check my watch. Maybe we can still see the scene before the techs take it down.

"Let's get over to the school at sunrise and look around. Then we'll swing by and see your boy."

"Why the school? Shouldn't we go see Jana first?"

"Jana isn't going anyplace. We'll visit the scene first. I'll be back to pick you up in about five hours. Right now, I'm headed back to the office and my couch and pillow."

I leave the church the same way I came in: the secret back door.

Every church has one.

5

We take Clark north to South State Street, then jag over west, then north again for several blocks until we reach Wendover Field. On the way over, I receive a call from the Cook County Jail. They have booked Tom Meekins, and he is under medical watch. The jail psychiatrist and physician saw him last evening. I am relieved and end the call.

At Wendover Field, we pull into the parking lot. Police cars and crime scene vans are everywhere. I can see photographers and CSI's working in the bright light under the stands where portable lights are arranged in a circle. Father Bjorn and I walk up to the east end of the stands where we encounter crisscrossing yellow crime scene tape and two uniformed officers checking IDs for those seeking entrance to the crime scene. We're given rude once-overs by the cops.

"Hey," I say to the biggest cop, "we're here to check out the crime scene. Can that happen?"

He continues to scowl at me. I look beyond him at the activity under the bleachers.

There are no ambulances and no vehicles from the M.E.'s office, so it's a safe bet that they have removed her body. The M.E.'s group is a tight-knit, proud staff, and I guess we will get little out of them. In a 1972 referendum, they established the Office of the Medical Examiner of Cook County while they abolished the Office of the Coroner. The Office is the only Medical Examiner system in Illinois and covers half the population of the state. Of all state agencies, it is the most close-mouthed.

I remove my state bar ID and flip open my wallet. The nearest cop looks over my proffering.

"What is this, counselor," he asks, "some kind of joke?"

I flip my wallet and slip it back inside my suit coat. "No joke. I'm Michael Gresham. I would like an opportunity to view the scene."

The cop elbows his buddy, and they share a laugh.

"Didja hear the one about the lawyer who goes into the bar and asks for a cup of coffee?" says Cop One.

"No," says Cop Two, the stooge.

"Bartender asks him what he orders when he goes into a coffee shop. Lawyer says he orders coffee. The bartender asks him why he's ordering coffee in a bar. Lawyer says—"

"Wait," I break in. "Is this the one about the lawyers on the bottom of the sea? Or is it the one about how many lawyers it takes to change a light bulb? Is your supervisor around, officer?"

Cop One scowls at me. "Move it back, sir, please. You're impeding the investigation standing there."

"Please use your shoulder mic and get your supervisor over here. I just want to view the crime scene. It's my client who's been arrested. That's all I'm asking."

He rolls his eyes and speaks into his radio. He thanks his sergeant and turns back. "He's on his way."

Moments later, a man in a uniform with a slash of stripes on his sleeve emerges from under the bleachers. He's holding a Jungle Bob coffee cup and smoking a cigarette down to the filter.

"Sarge," says Cop One, "this guy's claiming to be a lawyer. I don't know why he has a priest with him since the kid's already dead. They demand to be admitted into our crime scene."

The sergeant is not in a good mood. His eyes are alcohol-rheumy, and his uniform is rumpled. My best guess has him sleeping anywhere but home last night.

"Sergeant," I say, extending my hand, "my name is Michael Gresham. I've been contacted by the boy that CPD arrested. I only want to look at the crime scene."

"Mr. Gresham, your request is denied. This is a murder scene, and nobody but department personnel and medical examiner staff gets in. What else can I do for you?"

I raise my cell phone and snap his picture, all in one quick movement.

"You can give me your name so I can tell the jury in four months how you refused to cooperate with a simple request to view the murder scene, so I can tell them you refused to allow me to prepare to defend my client, so I can tell the reporters at the *Tribune* how you blocked me." I pause for dramatic effect, just like in court. "Your name? Oh, that's right, I already have your name on the name tag with your picture. So, Sarge, let me ask again, still politely. I'd like to just have a quick look around at the crime scene. I promise not to touch anything, not to step on anything, not to take any pictures you don't want me to."

The sergeant removes his hat and runs his right hand back over his closely shaved skull.

"Fuck it, let 'em in," he says to Cop One and abruptly turns and heads back under the seats.

Cop One disengages from us and stands to the side. Father Bjorn and I follow the sergeant's path.

We've made it under the bleachers about twenty yards when we arrive at a cordoned-off area where the CSI's are still working. There are photo tags with numbers scattered throughout the trash and spectator detritus in abundance. Techs are on their knees, combing through the grass, plastic, and cardboard with colored lights and special brushes. They snap close-ups—always the pictures—at every conceivable square inch near where the dead girl was found.

"How long was she dead before they found her?" I ask the CSI's.

"M.E. put the death between eight and ten," says one tech without turning around to see who she's speaking to. "Someone found the body just after, at ten-thirty."

"Who found the body?"

"Groundskeeper. A Mexican national on the payroll of our taxpayer-supported public school system."

"That sounds bad for the school," I offer, keeping up my end of the conversation. She still doesn't know she's talking with a civilian.

"It's a big joke. Hell, we've got cops working CPD who aren't even Americans. Go figure."

"How was she killed?"

The CSI turns to look at me. "Who are you?" she asks.

"I'm Michael Gresham. I'm an attorney assigned to the case."

Never mind that I self-assigned. In a way, it's true what I'm telling her. Of course, it might sound like I'm with the DA's office. One could always get that confused if they were on their hands and knees combing through grass with a magnifying glass. Father Bjorn, shaking his head at my deceit, wanders off.

The red-haired woman is back looking at the grass, blade by blade. "She was garroted."

"Was the strangulation device found?"

She turns again. "Who did you say you're with? The DA?"

"I'm an attorney on the case."

"Who sent you here?"

"I sent myself. My client is Jana Emerich."

"I don't know her. Or him. Tell you what. If you have any

more questions why don't you go on over to those two guys by the evidence cart? They're the dicks who caught the case assignment."

I turn to follow her line of sight. Of the two detectives, one is short and one is very tall. The shorter one looks Hispanic. He's chewing a cigar and spitting. The tall one looks of African descent—very black skin, long neck, and maybe six-ten. He's pulling at his necktie and giving me the stink eye. I approach and keep my hand extended to shake. I tell them my name and introduce Father Bjorn, who's back with me now.

"You are who?" says the short man.

"Michael Gresham. I represent Jana Emerich."

"What the hell?" exclaims the tall man. "Who let you clowns in here? Hey!" he calls to the same sergeant who cleared the way for us to enter. "Enzo! What the hell are these civilians doing in my crime scene?"

"I just have a couple quick questions," I say, hurrying my words as Enzo comes toward us from the far end of the stands.

"I know your questions. We'll cover those in court," says the black man.

"At least give me your card so I can call you," I protest as Enzo steps into our circle.

The black man rolls his eyes but pulls a business card from his shield case. He passes it to me, and I see that his name is Edward Ngo.

"Thank you, Detective," I say to him.

"Clear off my scene, sir," he says. "You're trespassing, and I could run you in."

I don't tell him that Sergeant Enzo allowed us inside. No point in getting that guy in bad with the dicks.

"Please," I say, "please allow me to ask one question. What evidence do you have connecting Jana Emerich to this death? Please just answer that, and I'll be on my way."

As if the collar might help, Father Bjorn adds, "Detective, I'm Jana's father. It would be a tremendous service if you would answer this one question."

The detective's lips part in a sneer. "You think that collar works on me, Father? I'm a protestant. We kicked the pope's ass out of Nigeria before you were even born. Take that crapola elsewhere, Father."

"So," says Father Bjorn, "you're Nigerian? I served for a year in Niger."

The detective's eyes narrow. He doesn't know whether he should buy it. "You served in Niger? Doing what?"

"Orphanage. We were trying to locate parents of children abandoned when the warlords came into the villages and killed all the adults."

The detective's face softens. The sneer is replaced by an honest expression that approaches appreciation for the priest's service.

"I was one of those children," says the detective. "The church brought me here."

Father Bjorn beams from ear to ear. "I probably knew you way back when. I might even have processed you, Detective Ngo." He pronounces it "Go."

The detective catches himself. "Maybe. But I will have to ask you two gentlemen to leave us now. We've got hours of work here on a crime scene that must be kept sterile from civilians. I'm sorry, but that's my job, and I must enforce departmental rules. Sergeant Enzo? Please show our guests the fastest way out of here."

Two minutes later, we find ourselves ejected and standing outside the bleacher crime scene.

Oh, well.

We can and will continue this interview at the preliminary hearing.

After Father Bjorn left me talking to the red-headed tech on the ground, he'd sidled up to two first-line supervisors at the scene. Unlike with Detective Ngo, the collar helped loosen lips and Father Bjorn could learn the identification of the dead girl's father.

His name is Abraham Tanenbaum.

"That would be the mayor?"

"That's right," says Father Bjorn. "Trumps my diocese."

It means there will be no plea offers.

Jana is headed to trial.

6

Father and I arrive at the jail before noon. A cold rain sprinkles on us as we walk the sidewalk along California Avenue from Parking Lot A to the Cook County Jail. Jana is somewhere inside this ninety-acre facility with concrete walls and doors that buzz.

Father Bjorn wears a black suit and shirt, white collar, and a black overcoat down to his ankles that I'm guessing was a gift since the material is cashmere. It makes me happy that he is warm. I cannot say how much I love this man. He has meant so much to me throughout my life. As he walks along beside me, I want to scoop him up and save him from a world about to inflict so much pain on him. There is a son, and there is a murder. Either one alone would be heart-wrenching from his perspective. Together, they must be unbearable. But I continue walking, leading him in to meet his offspring. I am tall, and my long gait's hard for him to pace. He double-times every fifth step to stay even with me. It is like our roles are reversed: I am the father guiding his son past the world of jails and dead children. It is an uneasy, harsh path.

"It's weather like this," he says, "that makes me want to shelter away from the world, stay inside by a toasty fire and read Thomas Merton."

I vaguely remember the reference from some college course long ago. So I don't know whether reading Merton would be a good thing or a bad thing. I wish I'd done the outside reading I'd confirmed I'd done but really hadn't.

"So your son is about seventeen years old?"

"I guess that's about right." I can see his gloved fingers curl as he counts years. "Yes, just seventeen in August."

"Has he ever been in trouble before?"

The priest shrugs. "Don't know. Haven't asked, I'm ashamed to say. Only what his mother told me about the drugs and devil worship."

We push through the double doors and approach the glassed-in deputy. We show our IDs, and she asks our business. I'm easy; I'm the attorney. Father Bjorn gets a little more hassle but convinces the gatekeeper he is, in fact, a priest the prisoner has asked to see.

We are shown into a conference room by a deputy wearing the liver and chocolate outfit of the Cook County Jail staff. She is polite and silent as she pushes open the heavy steel door and stands to the side. The furnishings are bleak: a metal table bolted to the floor surrounded by four backless metal chairs. Everything is painted a mint color that threatens to swallow you up.

The prisoner enters five minutes later. Jana Emerich is a wide-eyed boy—young man—who enters the conference room with a bewildered look on his face. He is average height, very thin, very angular in body and face, and he reminds me of the kids who operated the movie projectors back when I was in high school. He stops just inside the door and looks from Father Bjorn to me and back again. I can see the connection as his brain makes it. *This is my father*, his face says, and he almost looks embarrassed. Then there is a look of disbelief that comes into his eyes as he realizes he is seeing his father for the first time in his life. And that his father is seeing him in that same light.

He steps forward and takes the seat across from Father Bjorn and me.

"Let's introduce everyone," I say and reach out to shake.

He offers me his hand. It is warm and moist, and we shake. Then he takes his father's hand and shakes again. *Flesh of my flesh* says the priest's eyes as their hands grip. Like the son, his look is one of bewilderment. They both fall silent and look to me.

That's when I realize Jana thinks I'm his father; a priest wouldn't be his father. The new age of enlightenment falls to me to begin.

"Okay," I say with a friendly sigh, "Jana, this is Father Bjorn. He is your father. Notice I didn't say he's your dad. He's not. But he's your father, and I want you to get to know him as I do. When you have, you will know you can trust him with any secret. You can even trust him with your life."

"Let me write that down," says Jana. "Do you have paper and a pen?" he asks me with full-blown sarcasm.

"Just try to work with me here," I tell him. "Right now you need us a hell of a lot more than we need you. Don't forget that."

He sits bolt upright on his stool and gives me a second appraisal.

Both men turn their eyes on each other and then flee back to me.

"A priest fucked my mother? How's that work?"

Father Bjorn's gaze seeks the tabletop.

I start in again. "We're here because your mother called your father."

Father Bjorn nods, and the boy sits there mute, frozen in disbelief now that the sarcasm has left him wordless. It is surreal to him, and he blinks hard several times.

"My name is Michael Gresham, and I'm a lawyer. Your father asked me to visit with you today. Is it okay I'm here?"

"I guess."

"Now. You've been arrested, and we've heard a bit about maybe why you're here. So I will ask you some questions. At first, my questions can be answered yes or no. I'm doing this so you can feel as comfortable as possible."

He nods weakly, but I see he has heard and understood.

"Now. Is it true they have arrested you?"

"Yes."

"Were you picked up yesterday?"

"Yes."

"And have they told you why you were arrested?"

"Yes."

"Has someone died or been killed?"

"Yes."

Damn multiple-choice questions.

"Killed?"

"Yes."

"Did you kill someone?"

He looks at his father but then drops his gaze. He shakes his head as a child might in trying to avoid a spoonful of medicine. "No."

"Did the police say you killed someone?"

"Yes."

"Why don't you tell me the name of the person they're saying you killed. If you know."

"A freshman, I guess. Her name's Amy Tanenbaum."

"Does Amy go to your school?"

"Yes."

"Do you know her?"

"No. I know who she is. But I'm a senior."

The implication being that senior boys have little truck with freshman girls. Fair enough.

"Have you told the police you killed someone?"

"No."

"All right. Now I'll change the rules for a question or two. Try to answer my next question as thoroughly as you can. Here we go—please tell us what you know about her death."

He swallows hard and then belches. He looks up at the ceiling and then takes a darting look at his father, who is sitting erect, his hands folded in front of him. Father Bjorn's face says he's holding four and drawing for an inside straight, hoping his son pulls through all this. He's all heart. I can tell by the shallow breath and the soft eyes. He loves this kid. "See?" I want to say to them. "This isn't so hard."

"After the football game, someone told me they found her under the bleachers. They said someone choked her and rolled her on her back. I heard they put something in her mouth."

"Who told you these things? Do you remember?"

"Bobby Knupp. He's my best friend. We're partners in physics lab."

"Taking physics your senior year? Do you plan on studying science in college?"

For the first time, there is the slightest recognition of irony in the question. A small smile. "If I'm not in jail, I might."

"What else did Bobby tell you?"

"That's about all I know. But someone put something in her mouth. The police leaked that out."

"Why have the police arrested you in connection with Amy's death?"

"I don't know. They didn't tell me that."

"Now I need to ask you the hardest question you will be asked today. Please answer completely if you want help."

"Okay."

"Were you at the football game with Amy?"

"No. Not with Amy. But I was at the game."

"Did you go under the bleachers with her?"

"No."

"Did you take her body under the bleachers?"

"What?"

"Did you kill her under the bleachers?"

"Hell no."

"Did you kill her somewhere else and take her body there?"

"Hell no."

"Do you know who killed Amy?"

"Probably Rudy Gomez. He's the queerest guy in our school. He loves zombies and vampire shit, and he's always doing drawings of people getting whacked."

"Gomez? Spell it, please."

"I don't know. The usual way, I guess."

I file the name away for future reference. "Was Rudy at the game Thursday night?"

"I don't know. Probably not. He won't even dress out for P.E."

"All right. Now let's switch gears. You can ask me or your father questions. We're here to answer, too."

He wrinkles his forehead. "How come you never called me?" he says to Father Bjorn.

The priest shakes his head. "I don't know. I am sorry—"

"Didn't you know I was asking to meet you?"

"No. When?"

"Jesus. When I was a little kid, man. I wanted a dad like everyone else."

"Nobody told me."

"So, what, they had to tell you for you to call me?"

Father Bjorn shuffles his feet under the table. He inches down in his chair, and his son realizes the man is trying to disappear, to transubstantiate into the steel chair.

"I have failed you in every way possible, Jana. But I'm here to change that. If you'll let me."

"I don't think so. I don't need that father-son shit anymore. Let's say that train left the station long ago."

"I'm sorry to hear—"

"Please. Don't lay the sorry routine on me. If you were sorry, you wouldn't have broken a little kid's heart. So no bullshit, okay? Sorry, shit. You sucked as a dad. Own it."

"I do own it. I've prayed and asked God—"

"Whoa! Save the god shit. That's the last shit you want to lay on me. You might believe in those fairy tales, but I don't want to hear it. Save that for someone who cares!"

Father Bjorn nods. Then he holds out both hands to his son. "I want you to know I'm here for you. From now on. I will be your father and will fight to be a good one if you'll just let me in."

"Fuck that, man. Mr. Gresher, do I have to take this shit for you to help me?"

"Mr. Gresham, and no, Jana, I will help you regardless. There's no requirement for anything with your father."

The boy shakes his head. "That, I can live with. But get this piece of shit out of here before we go ahead."

Father Bjorn heaves himself upright. He struggles to pull on his topcoat that he had draped over the back of the chair.

"Sit down, Father," I tell him. "I want you to look your son in the eye first. Tell him what's in your heart. And Jana, I need you to hear this."

Father Bjorn nods and fixes his gaze on his son's eyes. "Jana, I am your father, and I love you. I have acted shamelessly, and I have hurt you. I am sorry for that, and it will never happen again. I only pray you'll allow me in your life now. I only pray you can find it within yourself to forgive me."

"Now. Jana?"

"God forgives, dude. Ask him about that."

"I will. I'm sorry."

"Now get your candy ass out of here before I throw up all over that shiny black suit. All right, Dad?"

Father Bjorn stands and hammers his fist on the steel door. It swiftly opens, and he exits the room.

The jailer sticks her head inside. "Everything cool in here?"

"We're okay," I tell her. "Another ten, please."

"I'll check back. But we're gonna need the room in five minutes. By the way, staff has refused your request to see Sheriff Meekins. Your client is under medical watch and won't be available for attorney visits today. Please hurry along now."

"Fine. I'll hurry."

She leaves, the door shuts, and the electric bolts hammer home. We're locked away.

I explain to Jana about not speaking to his cellmates or the police. I explain what will happen next, both in court and in jail. I answer several questions about clothes and books. Evidently, he's an avid reader and wants someone to bring his book bag to him. When I tell him that is impossible, he slams the table with the palm of his hand.

Finally, he says, "Keep that piece of shit priest away from me, Mr. Gresham. Please don't bring him back here."

"I won't. As long as you're sure."

"What's not to be sure? He's way late to this party, man."

"All right."

We agree without words that our meeting is over. I will next see him in court at his initial appearance, according to the papers he has produced from the pocket of his orange jumpsuit.

I slap the door with my hand, and it opens.

"Come with me," the jailer says to Jana.

We step outside.

Father Bjorn is nowhere nearby.

I cannot say I blame him. His heart is pierced, and I'm sure he feels like he has been exposed.

"Wait," Jana tells his jailer. He turns back. "Who's paying you?"

"That has yet to be arranged."

"Don't look to me. I'm a kid, and I'm broke. My mom doesn't even have a job."

"I won't look to you. I imagine your father will be the responsible one."

"Him? That fucking priest? He doesn't have two nickels to rub together, dude. You'd better get it up front, okay?"

"Okay."

"Okay, well, look, thanks for coming by. I'll see you."

"Yes, we'll talk just before court."

The kid turns and follows his jailer, and the scene reminds me of a young colt following a mare across a pasture just because she's his mother and he hasn't started thinking for himself.

That's right. He's not even thinking yet.

So how in the world could he ever murder someone?

A sudden chill rolls across the floor as the outside door opens into the staging area. I pull my overcoat across my shoulders and slide my arms into the sleeves. It's freezing outside; winter has come early.

What a terrible day to be seventeen and in jail. What a terrible day to be a sheriff under arrest and locked up.

Now my work begins.

7

I don't like driving in Chicago traffic on Saturday afternoons. The traffic angst is already underway when Father Bjorn and I pull away from Cook County Jail. Weekdays are hellacious, a mix between a solar storm and an Indy 500. Given the opportunity, Chicago drivers will run you off the road with glee. Or tailgate you at eighty if you linger in the fast lane. But Saturdays are just as bad. The roads are full of tourists trying to navigate the city streets, and unfamiliar with their destinations, causing havoc and delays. Normal business trips like mine should be avoided. Today, that isn't happening.

Dania asked me to run by the grocery on the way home, but I'll be damned if I can remember what for. Carrots? Pot roast? I'm guessing at her Sunday menu in hopes something jogs my memory.

"What are you thinking, Michael?" inquires Father Bjorn as we turn south. "Did he do it?"

I tap the steering wheel with my fingers. "That's hard to say. So far we don't know why the investigation has narrowed down to Jana. We don't know why they picked him up. My gut says we need to talk to Uncle Tim. He surely must have talked to the police when they came for Jana. What do you say we drop by and ask a few questions?"

Father Bjorn dials up Jana's mother and gets the uncle's address. He lives only three miles away, so it's an easy decision.

The house is an ugly duplex with two doors on the front porch. Uncle Tim is the one on the right. The curtains are closed, and the Tribune is waiting outside. I ring the door- bell. The curtains move where a large yellow tabby cat has sprung onto the windowsill to greet us. The cat looks at us with total disinterest. It arches its back and turns away.

I ring a second time. We hear footsteps, and then the door swings open. A round, barrel-chested man wearing a T-shirt and black jeans stands and blinks at us. He does not try to open the storm door.

"I'm Jana's dad!" Father Bjorn shouts through the glass.

The man's face relaxes as he understands. He reaches and pushes at the handle. "Come in." He backs away from the door.

"I'm Michael Gresham," I say, extending my hand. "I'm Jana's lawyer."

The man ignores my hand. "He has a lawyer? How does he afford a lawyer? He has no money."

"I'm his father's parishioner. I'm here because I want to help my priest and his son."

"Well, I'm Tim. Uncle Tim. I don't have coffee to offer. We ran out last night. Come in, sit down."

Just then a thin, tired-looking woman comes in wearing a chenille bathrobe. Her eyes are red-rimmed, and she's smoking a long black cigarette. She pats the side of her head as if arranging the poof of hair that winds out like a corkscrew. "Didja tell them we ain't got coffee?" she says to Uncle Tim.

"They know. They don't want no coffee. They're here about Jana."

"You're the priest. You're his dad, am I right?"

Father Bjorn gives a quick nod. "I'm his father. I've never been much of a dad."

"Not to be mean, Father, but you ain't been any part of a dad," says Uncle Tim. "I mean no calls, no visits, no Christmas presents, no letters, no nothing."

"I wanted to speak with you," I say to the couple. "I have a few questions, if I may."

"Knock yourself out," says the woman. "I'm gonna put on my face, but Tim can answer."

When she leaves us there, Uncle Tim backs himself up to the couch and plops down. There are two mismatched stuffed chairs on either side, all facing a glass coffee table. Father Bjorn takes the one on the far side of the room, a plaid print with cat scratches all along both arms. I take the one nearest the door, a dirty beige recliner, but I sit on the edge of the seat. There is cat hair everywhere.

I jump right in. "First, Tim, were you present when the police arrested Jana?"

"Yep."

"Did they tell you why they thought he was involved in the girl's death?"

Tim's face turns to concrete. "Did you say 'girl's death'? Is that what this is about?" Tim finally asks.

"It looks that way. What did they say when they came for him?"

"They said there had been a problem at the school. I thought they meant like vandalism. They didn't say nothing about a girl dying."

"He's been arrested for murdering a student at his school. No one told you that?"

He rubs his belly and rolls his eyes. "Nothing like that. As I said, they was very low-key. Just something about school."

"What time were they here?"

"Early yesterday morning before I went to work."

"Who answered the door?"

"I always get the door. This ain't the best neighborhood, Mister—Mister—"

"Gresham." I snap a card out of my wallet and pass it to him. "Can you describe the police? What they looked like?"

"Two guys in cheap suits. One was a beanpole Watusi chief maybe seven feet tall. I ain't exaggerating. The other was a spic. Can't CPD hire white guys anymore?"

"Those sound like the men we saw at the crime scene."

"Where was that?"

"At the school. Wendover Field. This morning."

"Well, Jana wasn't at the game."

"Tell us where he was."

"He was upstairs in his room with the door shut, probably looking at girls on his computer. He's that age, you know. Can't leave his tally-whacker alone."

Father Bjorn's eyes drop to the thin tan carpet. He rubs his hands together.

"Is there any way he could have left his room without you knowing?"

"Only if he could've flown a full story down to the ground. No, he never left. Plus, he came down for a sandwich about nine. He was here all night."

"You can testify to that?"

"I was here with him. So was Ruby."

"That's your wife?"

"Not exactly. Just someone I work with. One of our dispatchers down at the yard."

"You're a driver?"

"Local hauls. Indianapolis and back. I can do it in my sleep."

"One of the men I spoke with at the scene gave me a tip about a red muffler," says Father Bjorn. "Does my son own a red muffler?"

"No. But I do. It's always in the collar of my work coat."

"Would you mind letting us see it?" I ask.

"Sure. One second."

Tim disappears, and we hear him rummaging in the hall closet. Then he returns empty-handed.

"Damnedest thing. My muffler's missing. It ain't on my coat."

I nod. Father Bjorn has no words.

"I will send out my investigator to take your statements, yours and Ruby's. Is that okay?"

"Sure. Why not? I just want my sister's kid back. No offense, Father, but he belongs here with me until my sister comes for him."

"Well, that's all for now," I say. He knows very little, but he is an alibi witness. Not a compelling one, but you don't always get Oprah.

We stand and shake hands. We say goodbye. Father Bjorn and I walk out to the car.

Once inside and buckled, he looks across at me, his eyes wide. "I need your help, Michael."

"How can I help?"

"I'm hoping you can help me with Jana. Tell the judge you'll take him if they allow bail."

"I suppose I could." Maybe. Dania would object. We have a toddler, only eighteen months old, and we don't need a possible murderer in the guest bedroom. No way will she go along with Father Bjorn's idea.

"Danny will not buy it," I tell him. "Not that I can see. I'm troubled by it, too."

"Well, I know it's asking an awful lot." He looks out of the passenger window, and I can see the frown on his face reflected in the glass.

"I can try. You never know with Danny. I mean, the kid was home. He's obviously innocent."

"Obviously."

But I wonder about that. With criminals, there's always a way.

Always.

8

"Morning, Mrs. Lingscheit!" I sing out to my secretary/receptionist as I come through the doors.

"You're due in Cook County in twenty minutes," she says, the telephone jammed to her ear and her hand over the mouthpiece. "Better move it, bub."

Inside my office I find Danny waiting. We've been married awhile now, and my life is better than it has ever been. Our daughter makes our lives beautiful, and our family is what I live and breathe for.

"Where were you last night?" she asks with feigned wifely concern. She knows where I've been; my hours are crazy and I often sleep at the office. Last night I was preparing for Jana's initial court appearance until almost two in the morning, but I still got up early enough for a brisk walk to grab the *Tribune*.

Danny is tall and lean, the pregnancy weight-gain all but worked away, and she is my brilliant law partner. She started out in my office as a newbie and proved her value to my

practice ten times over. She is in her early forties, shorter
dark blond hair just above her ears with longer bangs, what
some women call a pixie cut, and there is always a natural
blush of color in her cheeks. She is quick to laugh and slow
to anger though I've seen her unload on one unfortunate
who came into our office and offended her with excuses for
domestic violence. He did not understand what kind of fuse
he was lighting off. He hasn't been back.

She hands me a coffee, and we head for the parking garage.
On the way out to California Avenue and the Cook County
Court, we talk about Jana's upcoming appearance.

Here's the deal. Seventeen-year-olds in Illinois charged with
first-degree murder are transferred from juvenile court to
adult court. Because Jana is seventeen, he qualifies. Meaning, the fact he hasn't reached adulthood doesn't stand in
the way of the State trying him as an adult.

We had talked about the case over pot roast last night before
I came to the office. She insisted on going with me to court
when she heard about Father Bjorn and his son. She loves
Father Bjorn like I do and would do just about anything to
help him. So I bring her with me. We walk up the sidewalk
and climb the outside staircase.

When we arrive inside, the Leighton Criminal Court is
crammed with media; someone has murdered the mayor's
daughter, and everyone wants the story. WGN is there, and
CNN. I haven't yet entered my appearance in Jana's case, so
no one is interested in me.

Two fortyish white women drinking from 30-ounce Styro-
foam cups call to Danny and make room in the pew. I
squeeze her shoulder before she settles in, and then I make

my way to the front of the courtroom and take a seat in the jury box with twenty other lawyers. We'll wait here for our cases to be called, which could happen right at the start of the calendar call or might not happen until noon. You never know just what kind of free-for-all you're in for. But one thing's for sure: it's never dull. Decked out in signal-orange jumpsuits, the prisoner dock is crawling with humanity in its basest form for everyone to see. Court is like turning over rocks; you never know what's going to turn up. Jana isn't among them, which tells me the first-call calendar doesn't include him, and I'll be here for a while this morning.

I hear a familiar voice stage-whisper my name and turn around. Father Bjorn has seen me and is making his way through the bar toward the jury box. I stand and shake his hand and pull him off to the side.

"Jana called me this morning," he says.

"There's a breakthrough. Good for you!"

"He wanted to know if I will get him out on bail today. I didn't know but said you'd be there and you'd do everything you could."

"There won't be bail, Father. This is the mayor's daughter we're talking about here. Too much pressure."

"What if you agree to take him in, Michael? You're an officer of the court. Wouldn't that carry some weight?"

"Unknown. Maybe, maybe not." I add, "If you want, I can try."

"Please. He says he's dying in there. Plus, he says the Aryan Brotherhood is going to move against him. Jana evidently told them he's not interested. I guess that didn't go over so well."

"Not good. I hate hearing that," I say. The kid's got big problems if those guys are upset with him. I take a deep breath and consider. Will Dania go off the deep end if I bring him into our house? Or will her feelings for Father Bjorn make her want to help out by taking in his kid? I decide I'll go for it.

"All right, I'll do it. I'll ask that he be released into my custody."

"What are his chances?"

"Unknown. At this stage we don't know what the cops think his connection to the girl's death is. But the law says where the proof is evident and the presumption is great bail should be denied. All else being equal, we might luck out and get bail set even though it's the mayor's kid who died. It's a judgment call, Father. It depends on the size of the judge's cojones."

Father Bjorn nods solemnly. "Tell the judge I'm the boy's father. That I will be intimately involved."

"Seriously? You want that on the record that the head of All Saints has a son?"

"It's time for me to step up, Michael. Put it out there."

"Well, that changes the picture. I'm sure the judge will know who you are."

"Just do it, Michael. It's my kid, and that's the bottom line for me."

"Whatever you say. That will go a long way, Father."

"Here's hoping."

I can already hear the newscasts and see the headlines.

All Saints will be the scene of a tremendous outpouring of prayer after we're done here today.

For the sake of all involved, I can only hope that God is feeling merciful.

J udge Winifred Lancer-Burgess takes the bench at five minutes past nine. She shakes out the billowy sleeves of her black robe and sweeps her reading glasses onto her face. Without looking over, she asks the clerk to call the first case of the day.

And we're off.

Seventy minutes later, after the mid-morning break, the clerk calls *State of Illinois vs. Jana S. Emerich.* The spate of prisoners has been replenished with new blood. Among them sits Jana, looking pale, his eyes on the floor of the prisoner dock. Almost by reflex, I am on my feet and taking my place at the lectern. Jana is unclipped from the long chain binding him to twelve other unfortunates, and a burly deputy sheriff seizes his elbow and walks him to the lectern. He takes his place beside me, stands up straight, and draws a deep breath. His hands are shaking, and it is with great difficulty that he keeps eye contact with the judge as I have asked him to do.

Judge Lancer-Burgess launches into the litany of rights, the purpose of the initial hearing, and basic data-gathering as required at the initial hearing. She speaks quickly, a communicating machine.

Then she turns her attention to me, the attorney for the defendant who, until now, has had little to say beyond yes and no.

Again, without looking at the person she's speaking to, the judge asks, "Mr. State's Attorney, is there a position on bail?"

"No bail," the State's Attorney replies by rote.

"Mr. Gresham, what say you? I'm sure you're seeking bail on his own recognizance on this first-degree murder charge."

I look toward the spectators. Danny sits in the front row. I make the you-and-me hand sign, and she nods. She's in.

I turn back to the judge. "No, Your Honor. I'm seeking bail that you are satisfied will guarantee the defendant's appearance at trial. As the court is aware, the key detail the court must consider when setting bail is the defendant's ties to the community. Here, Your Honor, the defendant's father is Frederic Bjorn, the head of the All-Saints-St. Thomas church, five miles from here. Father Bjorn has requested that his son be released into my custody, Your Honor. I'm willing to accept that responsibility, as is my wife, who is also in court here today, if the Court sees fit to set bail on those terms."

"How much bail, Mr. Gresham?"

"I don't know what Father Bjorn has in the way of assets. I guess he knows people who will step up for him and help him make bail for his son."

"Are you one of those people?"

"Your Honor, it would be against the law for me to make bail for a client so I won't be doing that. However, it is quite within my rights to request that the defendant be released into my custody when he makes his bail. I request that be done."

"Mr. State's Attorney, the Court will set bail unless the proof is evident and the presumption great, and in those cases, the bad guys don't get bail. What are you prepared to tell us about the proof and the presumptions at play here?"

The State's Attorney comes to his feet and launches into what he's been cleared by the police officers to reveal today in court. This is a ticklish proposition for the prosecution because, one, they need to tell enough to stop the setting of bail while, two, they don't want to give away the whole case against the defendant.

"Judge," says the SA, "the victim, in this case, is the daughter of our Mayor, Abraham Tanenbaum. The girl's name is Amy, and she was fourteen. Amy was last seen in the defendant's company at Wendover High School. She left him in the bleachers to use the restrooms. Our witness will say Jana Emerich remained behind. Our witness then turned away to watch the game, and when she again looked, she no longer saw the defendant. She has no idea where he went, but she didn't see him again that night. The next morning, someone found the dead girl's body underneath the bleachers where the night before she had sat beside the defendant, laughing and cheering as the game progressed. It's the State's position that bail should be denied as the proof is evident and the presumption is great that Jana Emerich was responsible for the death of Amy Tanenbaum. Thank you."

The judge swings her gaze back to me. "Mr. Gresham?"

"Whatever the circumstances looked like to the witness, the fact remains that nobody can tell this court that Jana Emerich committed this terrible crime. It's no different from saying we should arrest the police officer who takes a defendant to jail who later hangs himself in his cell. There's just no continuity, no evidence linking the original act—Jana sitting with Amy in the bleachers—with the fact of the murder, which occurred who knows where and when? The presumption here is not only not great, but there is also no presumption at all. My client should be admitted to the benefits of bail, and we implore the court to do the right thing. Particularly in light that his father is a well-known member of our community, and I again tell Your Honor that I will take on the responsibility of supervising the defendant while he's out on bail."

"Gentlemen, I've heard nothing regarding the defendant's ability to pay bail. The court, after taking into consideration the arguments of counsel and the factual representations, will set bail at one million dollars with the standard conditions of release. Is there anything else, gentlemen?"

We both agree there are no further issues between us, and the court moves on to the next case. Jana Emerich is fetched by the same deputy and reattached to the chain with the other prisoners. I step into the hallway, and Father Bjorn follows me there. Danny emerges and stands apart from us, waiting.

He raises a hand before I can say anything. "Thank you, Michael. I have a parishioner or two who I can call on for the cash bail. They require ten percent?"

"That's right. They can come here to the clerk's office and make bail, and your son will be released about two or three hours later. You should be here when that happens so you can meet with him and tell him where you're at with all this. He needs to hear it from you, Father."

"Agreed. We'll have him out before the sun goes down."

"After you're done having your talk, please bring him to my house."

"The church registry has your address."

"Yes. We'll be looking for you."

He extends his hand. We shake.

"Thank you, Michael. I don't know how I can ever repay you."

"You've already repaid me. You all but raised me as a kid."

He smiles. "Well, I did a top job, I would have to say."

"I'm glad you think so. I hope it's true."

"See you tonight, Michael. Leave a light on."

"We'll be ready, Danny and I. For whatever is coming down the road."

"It will be good. I've got good feelings about this."

I say no more.

The good feelings are his alone. I'm astonished it even happened. We're about to take in a seventeen-year-old boy accused of murdering a classmate. And all we know about him is that we know nothing about him.

I have to pinch myself and make sure I'm not dreaming all this up. Did I really just agree to this?

Danny and I walk toward the elevators away from the court-room where more and more rocks are being turned over.

10

The owner of three Chicagoland GM dealerships accompanies Father Bjorn to the Clerk's office at the Cook County Courthouse. The auto dealer will put up the bail money for Jana's release. They wait in line, talking. Father Bjorn is still dressed in his black suit and the cashmere overcoat. He looks wilted and pressured, but hopeful.

The GM dealer's name is Anwar T. Bledsoe, a jocular, smiling man wearing an open-neck shirt, blue blazer, and gray slacks and whose wrists and fingers are adorned with the mandatory Rolex, an ID bracelet made of 14k gold, a cat's eye pinky ring, an enormous diamond-studded wedding ring, and a Super Bowl ring that once belonged to J.D. Dimant. Bledsoe purchased the NFL championship ring on eBay for seventy-five thousand dollars. A gold Cross pen is clipped to the front of his shirt, and in his shirt pocket is a blank check from his dealership's general checking account.

While they stand at the counter, Bledsoe reads the notice posted on the wall, explaining how to make out bail checks to the Clerk, and he writes on the check with the Cross pen.

He leaves the amount blank, thinking there may be hidden costs such as those that pay the overhead at his dealerships. Their turn in line comes and, to Bledsoe's surprise, there are no hidden add-ons. He makes the check payable to the Clerk of the Cook County Superior Court for one-hundred-thousand dollars and hands it across the counter.

The clerk then disappears for a good ten minutes while forms are filled in and printed out. While he is gone, he calls the issuing bank. The check will be funded, the bank tells him. He finishes up with the forms and returns to the counter. Then the priest and the car dealer are presented with a bail receipt in the case of *State v. Jana S. Emerich, Defendant.* They are told to proceed down the street to the jail where they will present their receipt, and the Sheriff will check his online records to confirm the receipt. After that, they will process the young prisoner out.

At seven-thirty Monday night, a black Cadillac pulls into my driveway, and three men step out. Danny answers the door since I am busy at the Jenn-Air, grilling pork chops. On the nearest burner, the water is boiling in a half-full pot ready for the rice.

Danny calls me into the living room where she has settled the trio and is taking drink orders. The car dealer puts in his order for the Glenlivet 12 single malt we keep around, Father Bjorn chooses coffee, and Jana Emerich says he would like a bottle of water. I sense discomfort, and I sit down across from Jana, hoping to join in and break some ice.

"So..." I say to Jana, "you're out. That's a good thing."

"Yeah," he says and sniffs. "I stink. Can I take a shower?"

"Sure," I say, "but let's talk here a few minutes first with your dad. He's got some ground rules for how this will work, and I know I do, too."

"Like what kind of rules?"

"Well, general living rules," Father Bjorn says. "And like the bail conditions have stated—no illegal drugs, no alcohol, no firearms, no—"

"Yeah, I get all the nos. But what are some of the yeses? Do I just get to go to school and study? Can I still go to football games?"

Father Bjorn looks at me. He has no right answer. I say, "Well, as long as we have you home before curfew, I don't see why you shouldn't go to a game. Father?"

"That sounds fine. I know Jana loves football and wants to get out with his friends. It all looks pretty wholesome."

"I agree," I say, "but there needs to be some guidelines. This is your lawyer speaking. I will send Marcel, my investigator, with you to the games. He'll keep out of sight; you won't even know he's around. But he will keep an eye on you so nobody can claim you've done something wrong again. Especially so no one can claim you violated the conditions of your release. Fair enough?"

"I'm cool with that," says Jana. "I don't have any good friends except Bobby. Nobody's gonna even notice anything."

"Another guideline. You are never to break off from the group. Always stay with the crowd. We don't need someone saying you did something wrong. When you're with the group, you've got a bunch of witnesses around you. Especially this—never go off alone with a girl. They will—"

"Think I might choke out another one, Mr. Gresham?" the teen asks.

I smile. "No. That's not my fear at all. My fear is what someone might say you did. That's why no alone time with anyone, boy or girl. It all gets back to staying with the crowd."

"What about at school, Michael?" asks Father Bjorn.

"That's a good question." I ask Jana, "Are there ever times where you're alone at school?"

Jana shakes his head. "Only to hit the john during class. Sometimes you're alone in there."

"Do you need a hall pass to do that?"

"Nope. Just the teacher's okay."

"But you do have hall monitors?"

"Man, where have you been? We have armed security and cops in high school now. Hall monitors were like fifty years ago."

"That sounds even better where you're concerned. The more eyes on you, the better. Eyes equal witnesses, and as long you're a good boy and don't do dumb stuff, you'll comply with your conditions of release. Now. I have heard that in California you were smoking pot. You need to know Illinois looks very dimly on pot use. Pot is a crime here. If you get caught here with even one joint, even just a roach, you will find yourself back in jail faster than you can blink. This judge won't put up with even a single, tiny violation. So the rule is no pot. Same for alcohol. You must be twenty-one to drink in Illinois. You're not only underage, but you've also been told by your judge that one condition of your release is no alcohol."

At that moment, Danny returns with everyone's order. As she passes the bottled water to Jana, he makes eye contact with my wife and flashes her a faint smile. I think this is a good sign. It never occurs to me that it might mean anything else.

"You also have a curfew," I remind Jana as I read down through the court document that released him. "That's nine on school nights, eleven on weekends. They also require you to remain in school or, if you drop out, to get employment. As your lawyer, I'm telling you that you will not drop out and you will make excellent grades. How were your grades in California?"

He sits back in his chair and pushes his long brown bangs from his face. He shakes his head. "Tell you what, I never missed the honor roll in over three years. I'm right at the top."

"That's terrific," says Father Bjorn. "I was always on the honor roll, too."

The son ignores the father, taking several long swallows of the water in his bottle.

"Final thing to note—you cannot commit a crime. If you do, just like all the rest of the rules, straight back to jail. This means a crime as minor as shoplifting. Or vandalism. If they catch you with a can of spray paint beside a graffiti wall, you're headed back to jail. Or if you swipe an apple from a farmer's market, back to jail."

"Can I have people over to my room?" he asks from left field.

Danny shoots me a look and shakes her head.

"For right now, we would prefer you wait on that. Let us see how it goes with our new family unit as we get used to each other. Then we can talk about bringing in other people. Fair enough?"

He nods and wipes his mouth. "Guess so. You sound like you know what you're doing, Mr. Gresham. I'm just lucky as all hell you're giving me a place to stay. I want to finish school and start college next September. So I'll do everything by the book. You can count on it from me."

The words are the right words, but the feeling behind them is incongruent. He is more in a surrender mode than a compliance mode. More like he is being forced at gunpoint to conform rather than jumping at the chance to comply and stay out of jail. It worries me. I look for Danny's check-in with me, but she has broken off into a whispered conversation with our new houseguest and doesn't meet my eyes.

I can tell Father Bjorn is increasingly uncomfortable chit-chatting with Bledsoe about the car business as he sneaks opportunities to stare at his newfound son. I can see that he is amazed at the turn his life has taken, and he is eating up the chance to be with his son and to have an impact in his life. Even under such perverse circumstances, Father Bjorn gets to be involved in the real world.

Finally, I say, "Well, everyone, I guess we can open it up to questions now. Jana, this is a good time for you to ask away. We're all here to help you, and we need to know what you don't know."

The young man looks across the room and focuses on the far wall. "I can't think of anything. But if I remember, I'll just whistle," he says and emits a short, sharp whistle. It is a wolf whistle, actually, and he follows it up with a huge smile at Danny.

She blushes and looks down at the floor. Distractedly, she brushes her hair away from her forehead and then adjusts the silver barrette she's wearing. She wets her lips with her tongue and turns to smile at me. I return her smile and notice that Jana hasn't taken his eyes off her since the whistle. I imagine it's new to him to have a woman around who isn't needy like his mother. He's probably thinking hard about that, and I know it will take some getting used to.

So I ignore his interest in my wife.

"Can I bring my snake from Uncle Tim's?"

"Snake?" says Danny in a strangled cry. "Please tell me you're joking!"

"No. It's a small python. It eats mice. It won't hurt your baby."

"Oh, my God," says Danny, "just the image of that—"

"Let's give the snake thing a few days," says Father Bjorn. "These kind people are dealing with enough without that."

"Thank you," Danny says.

She shivers and rubs her hands on the sleeves of her sweater.

Jana watches her. He's open with his eyes as he takes her in and doesn't give a damn who sees.

11

Tuesday morning and Tom Meekins has drawn Renz Jannings as his judge, which is a good thing and a bad thing. The good thing is that Judge Jannings is known to be amenable to reasonable bail. The bad thing is that Judge Jannings is very slow to accept plea agreements he considers lightweight, less than the severity of punishment he might have wanted when he was a prosecutor. Yes, the Honorable Renz Jannings was at one time the U.S. Attorney for the Northern District of Illinois, a Bush appointee, and then was elevated to the federal bench in 2007 as George W. Bush was packing his suitcases. A so-called court-stuffing appointment by a lame duck president. He is what he is.

Today we wait in District Court for the judge to appear. Tom is in the custody of two U.S. Marshals, no-nonsense-looking guys wearing flak jackets and big guns on their hips, the kind with double-stack magazines, enough to shoot up several rogue sheriffs if gunplay is called for. I cannot imagine the sheriff's constituency attempting to break him out of jail, but one never knows.

Thirty minutes later, Tom's case is called. Formerly the marathon man, but not today, Tom is looking peaked and subdued. I guess the jail shrink has medicated him, which doesn't trouble me. He is cuffed and waist-chained and hobbles. A demeaning come-down for a man who, last week, was escorting prisoners into courtrooms for their appearances. Probably it was his deputies who were doing the actual escorting, but my point is valid. He steps up beside me at the lectern, and I identify myself for the court record.

"Mr. Meekins," says Judge Jannings with a severe look on his face, "you appear today on a criminal complaint charging you with a single count of embezzlement and a single count of kidnapping. The factual basis for your alleged offense is no mystery to the court since I was in session in this room, two floors above where the alleged kidnapping incident took place. Armed marshals interrupted my session to take my staff and me into seclusion while you were allegedly doing your misdeed down below and, sir, I did not appreciate that one damn bit. To say I am disgruntled with you is a gross understatement. Moreover, I'm astonished the U.S. Attorney has seen fit to go in with a single count on a series of alleged offenses which would have, if you were convicted, put you behind bars for more lifetimes than you have. So, for the record, I am dismayed with the charging document, and I will take this matter up with counsel. Counsel," he continues, pointing both to the Assistant U.S. Attorney and me, "you are on notice. The court is very displeased with what appears to be a lightweight plea bargain going in. Very displeased."

The Assistant United States Attorney and I both nod. She is a diminutive woman dressed in a light gray suit with a white shirt and striped club necktie. I have worked with Assistant United States Attorney San-Jish before. She is a mid-fortyish woman of Indian descent and has no ax to grind. She rises to her feet and addresses the court. Her voice is small, courteous, and straight to the point.

"Your Honor, the government appreciates your position. However, the charges were guaranteed to save lives. Perhaps we can address the court's concerns at the status conference?"

"Very well, Ms. San-Jish. The court will accept that. Now, we're here today to determine whether the defendant has counsel, and he does, Mr. Gresham appearing with him. Mr. Gresham is a member of the federal trial bar of the Northern District and, I am sure, will do an excellent job representing his client."

I am flattered, and my neck reddens. No need for the compliment, but Judge Jannings is known for his friendliness to the defense bar. Probably at one time a U.S. Attorney who also bore no ax to grind.

"Thank you, Judge," I say. Tom keeps his eyes fastened on the judge just like I've asked.

"So our next chore is to consider the question of bail. Mr. Gresham, please give the court your position."

"Your Honor," I begin, "the proof is evident and the presumption great. No doubt the defendant has committed the acts alleged in the complaint, or at least similar acts. I say this with the reservation that if an indictment does come down that is substantially dissimilar to the complaint in the number of counts, then my comment does not apply. But for now, I am comfortable with the complaint."

"That's nice of you, Mr. Gresham, to pass on the complaint. Good sport," he says with a smile.

Comeuppance received. Poor word choice.

"At any rate, the question of bail comes down to the safety of the defendant and the safety of the public. My client is charged with pointing a loaded firearm at federal law enforcement officers and citizens as well as members of the grand jury. I do not take this lightly, and I'm sure the court doesn't either. However, if the court is amenable to bail—"

"Not without the results of thorough psychiatric testing, Mr. Gresham, so I'll just stop you right there. There will be no bail without a psychiatric evaluation and report to the court. I'm sure you'll quite agree that this is called for. We'll be continuing the question of bail until I receive the report. Whether the defendant has received a copy of the complaint, counsel has indicated the defendant has. Unless there is anything further, this matter is continued until..."

Judge Jannings looks to the clerk who provides a day to the court. Three weeks down the road. I am powerless to argue otherwise given the nature of Tom's actions. Tom slumps beside me, and I can sense the wind has gone out of his sails. But I had warned him last night he shouldn't expect to be going home today, not after his cowboy rodeo time in the courthouse. In fact, I told him it could be a long time before he walks the streets of this or any other city again. Tom is contrite and receptive to my words as he knows how any judge and any prosecutor will respond to what he did. So I place my hand on his shoulder and squeeze. He doesn't move, but I know he's disappointed.

"I will set the preliminary hearing in this case for one week. Will there be an indictment before then?" Judge Jannings asks the prosecutor.

"Yes. Next day or two."

"Then the preliminary hearing will be scrubbed at that time. Anything else, counsel?"

We both indicate nothing further.

We are done here. The marshals step up and take Tom away, so I hurry out to the elevator and press the up button. I have another appearance yet today, an appearance on a drug case so oddball I'm eager to see what happens with it.

12

Guy Lafitte is my newest client. A narcotics distributor, his story is something you will have to judge for yourself. It all began with a call to me from his father.

"Michael!" exclaimed Kenneth Lafitte, a lawyer whom I know to be a civil litigator from one of the silk stocking firms downtown.

"Ken," I reply. "Is one of my clients pissed and hired you to sue me?"

Ken laughs, one of those loud, rich-guy laughs that attracts attention across restaurants. "Not hardly! My kid. Got himself arrested. Drug beef."

"How old?"

"Thirty-six."

"What's the charge?"

"I don't know. But it's federal court. I refused to bail him out. Thought I'd let him cool his jets in jail for a day or two."

"That's probably a bad idea, Ken. The jail is a zoo. He could get seriously hurt in there."

"I know it isn't a fun place, but I'm hoping it will teach him a lesson."

"If he were my kid, I'd bust him out on bail first thing today. Word to the wise."

"If you say so. Look, could I retain you on his case? I'm looking for a plea, probation, and dismissal of the charges on successful completion."

"I could help with it, sure. Be glad to defend your son."

"I'll send over a retainer. Whatever you need."

"Mrs. Lingscheit will call your office. She's my secretary, and she'll make the arrangements with your secretary."

So I'm in federal court and waiting for Ken's son's first appearance. I talked to him last night and got the lowdown. To begin, Guy is a Yale law grad and should have known better. But he didn't. He was running out of cash. He needed to make a score. A disbarred lawyer (failed to file tax returns for ten years), he had no other skills by which he was capable of supporting himself even in the sparsest of conditions. So he took $30,000 from a $150,000 accident settlement for the loss of a kneecap in a car wreck and bought a used sailboat. It was teak, exquisite, and had been seized by the feds during a cocaine bust south of Miami and then resold at a government auction. Guy made the winning bid and became the lucky new owner.

Guy sailed his teak sailboat to Columbia where he put into port and toured the country for six months. During that time, he trekked into the jungle and became acquainted with cocaine producers. Would he like to take some cocaine back to the States and make his fortune? Guy was game, so they sold him twenty kilos of pure powder. Now, according to the Medellin Drug Cartel's chief bookkeeper, a kilo of cocaine costs $1500 in Bogota, $16,000 in Mexico, and $77,000 in Britain. That same kilo will sell for about $30,000 right here in Chicago. So there's a tremendous amount of profit in a kilo of coke if you can get it here. Guy paid $30,000 for twenty kilos in Havana. The money he invested was what remained from the accident case where he had been T-boned at a stop sign. The wreck left him with a permanent limp and just enough cash to buy a sailboat and fund his adventure in the drug trade.

For some reason known only to the angels, Guy with his twenty kilos could sail into New York and up the St. Lawrence into the Great Lakes, eventually dropping anchor at the Chicago Yacht and Sailing Club on Lake Michigan's western shore. Why did he come all the way to Chicago? Guy has no plausible rationale for the trip, at least not that I have been able to discern. His family is here, his dad being a lawyer and all, and he was married to an airline pilot at one time and her home base was O'Hare, but it would have been much easier to unload at hundreds of closer ports along the East Coast. At any rate, it was in Chicago that he set up the cocaine deal that would bring him to the Law Offices of Michael Gresham.

He was a pure novice at the drug trade. He wouldn't have known an undercover agent from a Hollywood agent if they wore name tags. As a lawyer, Guy had worked for the Internal Revenue Service on bankruptcy cases where there was a tax debt owed the government that some slippery soul was attempting to discharge in bankruptcy. In would rush

Guy for the IRS, they would except the government debt from the debtor's discharge, and off he would ride into the sunset, another day closer to the federal retirement gold ring. Except, as I mentioned, Guy neglected to file tax returns from 2003 to 2013, and when his employer found out, they bounced Guy out into the street. The IRS has no patience with non-filers, even if they happen to be one of their own. When he left behind the only job he'd ever held in law, he still had never dealt with any form of a criminal element, and he was as naïve about the drug trade as any first grader.

So, coming ashore in late October 2014, Guy knew only that he wanted to dispose of his coke and make it back down to Florida in his sailboat before winter sealed off the Midwest and the St. Lawrence and he was forced to store his boat for the winter. He had zero desire of spending one more day in Chicago than was required.

His first day ashore, he tried to locate his ex-wife. Failing that, he turned his efforts to unloading his Columbian booty. He decided a dance club would be the place to look for drug dealers. It didn't take him long to locate the Cheshire Club downtown where the DJ's rocked the crowd. The nose candy for sale right on the dance floor kept the patrons happy and hopping.

On Saturday night at ten o'clock, Guy paid his way into the Cheshire and went to the bar, bought himself a scotch, and placed his back against the bar top so he could look out over the frenzied, dancing sea of faces years younger than himself.

He watched the drug buys going down as dancers swirled into and out of the penumbra of a tall, Latin-looking man with a pencil mustache and yellow-lensed glasses. The man seemed to be under the care of three other men, who examined all comers, searching with their eyes, most likely for weapons that might hurt the dealer. Two more scotches, and Guy himself sauntered up to the dealer. They talked.

Four hours later, the three torpedoes and the dealer, Monte, were guests aboard Guy's sailboat at the yacht club. It was freezing on the boat that night, so they rushed the deal since there was no heat on the boat.

Guy and Monte bartered for a good ten minutes before agreeing on twelve thousand per kilo. It was far less than Guy could have gotten if he had more time to look around ashore, but the lake effect snow was blowing across the moored deck of *Guy's Folly*, a reminder he needed to be on his way before it iced him in.

Once the price was agreed, only the terms of payment and delivery remained.

"Do you take checks?" Monte asked Guy.

Like I said, Guy knew next to nothing about drug deals.

"Is the check any good?" he asked.

"The money's all right there. Fifth Third Bank on Wacker. There will be no problem for you."

"What if the check's no good?" Guy thought to ask.

Monte and his entourage looked at each other and burst out laughing.

"El Capitan," said one man, "you don't know who you're dealing with here! His check is his word! Good as gold!"

Monte gave his man a sideways look. "Thanks for the voucher, Eduardo," he said and smiled.

"No, no, what if it's no good?" Guy persisted.

"Sue me," said Monte. "Take me to court and sue me. You're a lawyer. Here, let me test some."

Monte inserted his pinky finger inside one kilo and removed half a gram. He held it under his nose and snorted. It performed, and he was happy. Once he had seen how it was done, Guy snorted a gram-and-a-half. Within seconds, he was all but delirious.

"Yes, I am a lawyer," Guy said, marveling at his great fortune. But it made Guy think. He narrowed his eyes and wondered if it was possible to sue Monte in court over a bad check offered for the purchase of cocaine. It seemed wrong in so many ways, but Guy didn't want to come across as naïve, and the coke was fantastic. He nodded at Monte.

The check appeared, and Monte wrote it out. He blew on it and handed it across the small galley table to Guy. Guy took it, studied it, and folded it before placing it in his shirt pocket. Two-hundred-and-forty thousand dollars. He could retire on the money, but it also occurred to him he could repeat this exercise in drug sales.

Then he asked Monte, as if a new business enterprise was in the offing, "If I come back with more, will you buy it?"

Monte looked at his bodyguards and smiles appeared. "I will buy as much as you can bring."

"Then I'll be back in the spring. I'll bring fifty kilos next time."

Monte snapped his fingers. "Done!" he said. "I don't have a card, but you know where to find me."

When Guy held out his hand, Monte took it and shook. To show his complete dedication to future transactions, Guy then went from bodyguard to bodyguard and shook their hands, too. The bodyguards wouldn't meet his eyes, but Guy didn't notice or, if he did, he didn't care.

The men went on deck then climbed back onto the boat ramp. As they made their way off into the night with Guy's twenty kilos of pure Colombian coke, Guy heard laughter that, at first, he wasn't sure was human. It sounded very much like the monkeys he had heard in the jungle. Then there it was again, and this time a sudden bolt of fear in his abdomen caused him to lie down on his bed and stare at the ceiling. He patted his pocket. The check was still there, so it was all good.

The next day he took a cab to Fifth Third Bank on Wacker Drive in the Chicago Lower Loop.

The teller explained once, twice, then three times that the check wasn't good. So Guy had her produce her manager. The manager bent to the terminal, brought up Monte's account, and for the fourth time delivered the bad news: the check was NSF. Guy went back that afternoon and tried again. He went back the next day and the next and presented the check four more times and was rejected four more times for non-sufficient funds.

Thinking he would broach the problem head-on, Guy returned to the Cheshire Club three nights running. But Monte was gone. True, drug deals were still going down on the dance floor while Guy watched, but none of the dealers looked anything like Monte or any of his henchmen from the night they consummated the sale.

So Guy did the next indicated thing. He took the check and showed up at the office of the Cook County District Attorney. That's right; he pressed charges against this Monte character. He made up a song and dance about the check, telling the warrants attorney it was payment for a load of industrial solvent. They issued the warrant and, much to Guy's great surprise, an arrest of Monte followed. Guy received a phone call to that effect on the Monday of the second week he had dropped anchor in Chicago. That was fast, Guy thought, but he was pleased with the DA's efficiency.

But there was one hitch. The DA wanted to meet with Guy again. There were questions. Guy appeared at the DA's office as directed.

The prosecutor who had drawn the assignment was a young woman working out of the DA's office I had encountered before. Her name was Linda Lyons, and she was a top-ten-percenter of the University of Chicago Law School. I knew her to be quick-witted and fair; she was also ruthless in the prosecution of the cases assigned to her. Ruthless would even be an understatement. She was death on drug dealers, her area of practice.

Linda showed Guy into her office. A second man was waiting there. They introduced him as the narcotics officer who had worked up the case they were about to discuss.

"Narcotics officer?" asked Guy. "Why a narcotics officer?"

Ms. Lyons cut right to the chase. "The man who gave you the check? You know him as Monte? He's an undercover narcotics officer with the Chicago Area Drug Task Force. He came to the Task Force from the DEA and runs his own squad. Now you know why we wanted to see you."

"Oh, my God," Guy squeaked out. "A narcotics officer? But I saw him selling drugs."

"No, you thought you saw him selling drugs. They stage the whole show at the Cheshire Club for the benefit of players like you, Mr. Lafitte. Now, if you'll stand up, Officer Jericho here will apply a set of handcuffs to your wrists. I'm sure you understand."

Guy staggered to his feet, and they made the arrest official.

Guy's dad called me, I was retained, and it's all uphill from here.

The jailers produce Guy in court, chained to a dozen others who are also appearing. He looks forlornly at me, and I nod at him. We met last night, put our heads together, and decided that we would have to ask for an unsecured bail bond. Unsecured, because Guy has no money and no assets to put as surety on the bail. His boat, *Guy's Folly*, was seized under the state's RICO laws and will be auctioned off so they can purchase more toys for the Drug Task Force. Or maybe they'll keep the boat and use it in future stings. The point being, it no longer belongs to my client and so he has no property to bail him out of this mess.

The judge, after a perfunctory hearing, sets the bail at two million dollars. The amount is high because of the massive lode of narcotics in Guy's possession. Plus, Guy has little tie to the community and thus poses a flight risk. That, too, helps enhance the need for a higher bail.

After our appearance, the deputies take Guy away. Back to jail he goes, and I am left with a sale-of-narcotics case that is easily proven with a signed check made out by the starring member of the task force and endorsed for deposit by my client. Open and shut.

Except for one tiny thing. I have asked that a sample of the cocaine be produced so I can have it tested. I take nothing for granted, including the DA's claim it was cocaine. Why? Because my client was so naïve, I'm not convinced it was even cocaine he was peddling. It might have been baby powder for all I know.

And guess what? The DA is dragging her feet in making a sample available to my laboratory.

I'm wondering whether they might have misplaced the largesse from the midnight drug transaction. Now that would be a great help to Guy's defense. It would mean they would dismiss the charges, the boat would be returned, and Guy would sail away.

He should be so lucky.

Still, I am waiting.

13

Jana and I collect up his belongings from Uncle Tim's house. There isn't much, but there is a snake.

On the trip back from Uncle Tim's, even though I'm driving, I can hardly keep my eyes off Jana who's riding in the passenger seat, his pet python wrapped completely around his lower right arm. I gave in and brought the snake along when I saw the look of disappointment on Jana's face as we were leaving without his pet.

"His name's Leonard," says my houseguest. "He's a Ball Python. That's just about the most popular snake there is."

"Why ball?"

"I don't know."

He is petting the snake and scratching its head. I can just see this thing wrapped around my daughter's neck. It's a horrible image, and I change the topic. "Are you up to going out on my boat with me?"

"Are you kidding? Hell, yes!"

"Let's drop off Leonard and his cage and get him locked in, and then we'll drive down to the yacht club."

"Yacht club? You seriously belong to a yacht club?"

"Of course. It's where I keep my boat. It's no different than belonging to a golf country club. You get the idea."

"Lots of drinking and grab-ass and card games. Am I right?"

"Pretty much. Throw in a few regattas, a New Year's Eve blowout, costume parties, and you've got the full picture."

"What kind of boat you got?"

"Sundancer. It's a three-fifty model," I add, guessing that he knows nothing about Sea Ray boat models.

"Thirty-seven foot. I know your boat exactly."

"How's that?"

"When we lived in Santa Monica, I worked on a boat cleaning crew. We saw lots of Sundancers, Mr. Gresham."

"Why don't you call me Michael? That okay with you?"

"Okay. So Michael, what are we fishing for?"

"I like trout and salmon. We have King and Coho in the lake."

"You eat your catch?"

"Pretty much."

"I wonder if Leonard would like fish. Probably not. He prefers pinkies."

"Pinkies being what?"

"Baby mice. He loves them."

Again, the image. Some lock will have to be a must.

"I doubt that he'd like fish. Besides, I eat the fish. He can stick to the mice."

"Fair enough, Michael. Damn, I can't believe you have a 'Dancer!'"

"You like being on the water?"

"I do. I even crewed a little back in California. I loved going out on day trips."

"What was your job?

"Jack-of-all-trades. Mostly baiting hooks for rich people. Tossing chum into the water to get things going. That kind of stuff."

We ride along in silence then. Several miles later as we're passing a Starbucks, I suddenly cross two lanes and fall in line at the familiar green sign. I'm up for a sweet Starbucks drink, something like a mocha.

"You like coffee, Jana?"

"I do. I pretty much stick to the basics. French Roast, Sumatra."

"I'm in the mood for a mocha. Care to join me?"

"Hell, yes. Let's both have one."

I order in the speaker, and then we pull up. As we wait at the window, Jana allows the snake to move up his arm and encircle his neck. I remember that the Tanenbaum girl was garroted. And in the same moment, I am wondering whether I'm sitting beside her killer. An involuntary shiver shakes my body.

Jana looks over at me. "What?"

"Nothing. Just a chill."

He reaches out and adjusts the dash control for the fan speed. He creeps the temperature a bit more into the red. Quickly, it's unbearably hot in the SUV, but I won't admit it.

TWO HOURS LATER, we have the snake set up, and we're out on the lake on *Condition of Release*, my Sundancer. I am at the helm while Jana sits in the back of the boat watching the wake as we make our way parallel to the shoreline. Even though the sun is out, I'm wearing my wet gear. Just the jacket and boots since there is a sting in the offshore wind this time of year. While I keep my chin tucked into the high collar of my slicker, Jana isn't even wearing his jacket and has on a short-sleeve shirt.

By four o'clock, we are tired. We both caught and released several fish, and we each selected a salmon for keepers. I add a third for Danny, and we head back to my slip. The crew on the boat dock relieve us of our catch and head down to the fish cleaning table and sink.

The damn python is still on my mind so I decide to talk as we pull out of the yacht club parking lot. Our daughter, Dania, is named after my wife. We call the mother Danny and our little girl Dania, and I'm worried immensely about this snake and our baby girl. "Okay, here's the deal with Leonard..." I begin.

"What's that?"

"One, Leonard never leaves your bedroom. If I catch him outside your room, he's going to the animal shelter. Understood?"

"Dude, why so rigid? Leonard isn't going to hurt your baby."

"I know. But I can't take that chance. If I catch Leonard outside your room, I'm taking him away. I'm not telling you first. I'm just going to disappear with him. Understand?"

"Yes."

"And if he's ever within ten feet of Dania, he's a goner, too. Deal?"

"Deal."

"The idea of your snake around my little girl is more than I can handle, Jana. It makes me crazy, and I'm not having it."

"Okay."

"While we're on the topic of my women, here's another thing. You have a habit of never taking your eyes off Danny whenever you're around her. You're staring at her even when she's not talking to you. I was seventeen once, Jana. I know what it's like. But I'm asking you to be a little more respectful of my wife. And of me. Can you do that?"

"I like Danny. But that's all it is. She's thirty years too old for me."

"You did the math?"

"Oh, man, come off it. You're making me very sad here, Michael. I don't think I can stay around like this."

I decide to see where this goes. "Where are you thinking of going?"

"I don't know. Maybe I'll go to my father's place. Wherever he lives."

"He lives in a dorm with other men. They each have an apartment. I doubt he would have room for you there. No, you need to consider our feelings. That's all I'm asking. It's called self-control, Jana. It's straightforward."

"You've got my promise, Michael. I don't want to make anyone uncomfortable."

"That's the spirit."

We're a mile from home when it occurs to me. I haven't asked. "Jana, did you hurt the Tanenbaum girl?"

"Dude, seriously? Is that what all this is about? You think I killed that girl?"

"I'm asking and waiting for you to answer me."

"I didn't hurt anyone. I'm not like that. Honest, Michael."

"Good enough. Now, let's go home. I'm beat, and I need a shower."

"Sounds good. Sounds great, in fact."

I don't know any more than I did when we left home this morning.

14

"Morning, Mrs. Lingscheit," I call out as I come into my reception room. It is raining outside. I remove my trench coat and shake off the water, stamp my feet, then hang up the coat and proceed to my office. Mrs. L hasn't responded because she's tied up on the phone. It's eight-thirty, and she's been at the office a good hour already. Which always leaves me feeling guilty. I try to hit the front doors between eight and eight-thirty, earlier if I've got a nine o'clock court call or trial, and then Danny comes in with Marcel an hour after me and stays an hour or two later than me. Why? Because Chicago is a dangerous place to drive and we don't want to make an orphan out of our daughter in one colossal accident. I don't know of any other commuting couple who doesn't ride together, but Danny and I don't believe in tempting fate. So we travel separately. Always.

On top of the small stack of files on my desk, I find the new indictment in *USA v. Thomas Meekins, Defendant*. While I make coffee with one hand, I hold the indictment with the

other and scan through it. There are sixteen counts of theft
by embezzlement, twenty-two counts of kidnapping, and
several lesser, though just as serious, counts having to do
with bringing a firearm into a U.S. courthouse for improper
reasons and discharging a firearm in a U.S. courthouse,
enough of the little stuff to draw a good ten years in Leaven-
worth alone.

The indictment stuns me. Last I heard, we were talking one
count of theft and one count of kidnapping. No other
charges were to be brought. I sit down and dial-up Rene
San-Jish, the Assistant United States Attorney. The recep-
tionist tells me she's in court but gives me her voicemail.

"Mrs. San-Jish, this is Michael Gresham. To say the new
Meekins indictment shocked me is a gross understatement.
Our agreement was one count of theft and one count of
kidnapping. Today you've given me an indictment with over
forty counts. What in the world were you thinking? Or did
you forget? Please call me, or I'll be forced to move to
dismiss based on your failure to honor our agreement."

I have just had my first sip of coffee when Mrs. Lingscheit
buzzes and tells me that Ms. San-Jish is on the line.

"Mr. Gresham, this is Rene San-Jish. I apologize for the
indictment as we usually limit ourselves to fifteen or fewer
counts. The Assistant United States Attorney who prepared
the indictment got enthusiastic, so we ended up with forty-
four. I can amend if you'd prefer."

"What I'm calling about was the plea we had going in. One
count of theft and one count of kidnapping. What
happened to that?"

"We've discovered additional acts of theft from the state employees' retirement fund. You probably haven't digested the indictment yet or you might've read right over those. As to the kidnapping, the U.S. Attorney himself insisted on including all grand jurors because of the seriousness of the crime."

"But we had an agreement!"

"Not in writing, we didn't."

I slowly inhale, trying not to break into four letter words aimed at my adversary. *Calm down, steady*, I tell myself. I can still do this.

"Well, I will file to dismiss the indictment if you're unwilling to amend to reflect our agreement at the shooting scene."

"Mr. Gresham, you're more than welcome to file your dismissal motion. We shall oppose it. Things have changed since then."

"But we agreed.

"Not in writing, we didn't."

"I've been had."

"No, you saved your client's life. A SWAT team was about to burst into the room and open fire on him. He's alive because of you, Mr. Gresham. Please try to impress the reality of his situation on him."

"Hell, Ms. San-Jish, I'm trying to impress a reality of *any* kind on him."

"Really? Is the evaluation underway?"

"He's done paper testing. Now they're doing verbal. We'll know by Monday which way they're leaning."

"Let's talk then. I'm hanging up now, Mr. Gresham."

"Thanks for calling right back."

I hang up and sit there in silence for several minutes.

She's right. Our quick, on-the-spot plea agreement saved Tom's life. And maybe the lives of all the others in the room. Including me. But on the whole, she lied to Tom and me. She agreed to a two-count indictment, pure and simple. Not forty-four counts. She flat-out lied, and I will not put up with it. I draft a motion to dismiss the entire indictment. Three hours later, I have signed the motion and filed it with the court. Ms. San-Jish will see it today, or tomorrow morning at the latest, and I hope she'll call me and agree to amend. While the law isn't wholly on my side, neither is it wholly on her side. There's room for argument either way. But the fact remains, we had an agreement, and she won't, I am positive, deny that. Father Bjorn heard her state what plea she would agree to, and he related it to us in front of a roomful of other witnesses. The deal was struck and does not differ from any other pre-indictment plea agreement.

Then I drive out to California Avenue to pay a visit to Tom. I want to make sure I talk with him before he sees the indict-ment and goes off the deep end in shock. Fifteen minutes later, I am waiting in attorney conference room 202, and the deputies are fetching Tom for our one-on-one.

A single deputy comes in five minutes later without Tom.

"You're Michael Gresham?" she asks.

"I am."

"Mr. Gresham, I have some alarming news for you."

The hair along the back of my neck prickles. Instantly, I know he saw the indictment.

"Please tell me."

"Your client, Thomas Meekins, was just now found dead in his cell. He hung himself with the trouser leg of his jumpsuit."

"I thought the jail took precautions against that! What are you telling me?"

"Someone found him with his papers stuffed in his shorts."

"Papers? What papers?"

"The indictment that came to him this afternoon. The log says he was crying when he read it."

"Oh, my God! Did anyone send for help for him?"

"He was on a mental watch. A nurse was paged but hadn't seen him before he took his life."

"No! Is his family aware?"

"Family Services is taking care of that as we speak. I am very sorry, Mr. Gresham. I will escort you to the jail exit now. Please come with me."

I'm in a fog, but I follow her. This all feels surreal. They knew he was unstable, knew he was being tested, yet they somehow made it possible for Tom to take his life? Over a trumped-up indictment?

A lawsuit was begging to be filed.

But first was the matter of a funeral and time for his family to mourn.

After that, I would offer to help. I had promised Tom I wouldn't let him down.

And I won't.

15

Franny Arlington rode with her father in silence to the Friday night game against the Owls. There was a bitter standoff between the girl and her parents over yoga tights and football. The girl thought the tights were perfect under a short skirt for the game, especially now that the nights were cold. But her mother, who enlisted her father's help, was dead set against it, claiming yoga tights shouldn't be worn in public. She could wear regular tights, her mother had proclaimed, but not yoga tights. Franny's mom held the position that yoga tights were too revealing, and she would not budge. Finally, in total frustration and feeling beaten, Franny had changed into jeans and a pink shirt beneath a hoodie. The hoodie was black and so were the jeans. Franny wasn't Goth—that was so yesterday and, besides, her parents would never allow it—but she loved her black outfits. So, mother and daughter had tussled once again in the age-old struggle that has existed between teens and their mothers for a million years.

Franny's father, Henry Arlington, "Hank" at the Ford plant, was a third generation auto worker who had worked his way up from transmission service to quality control in twenty years. Hank's specialty vehicle was the Ford Police Interceptor at the Torrence Avenue plant. He was well-liked by the men who worked around him and could always be counted on for a great dirty joke on Friday evenings after the week was over and the workers had gathered for beer call at Waldo's. So, as he drove Franny to her football game, he was calculating he'd had his last beer two hours earlier, but had downed four altogether, and he was sure he was under the legal limit as they made their way toward Wendover Field. Plus, he'd come home and shit, showered, and shaved, so that detour had helped burn off any residual alcohol since his last mug of beer.

"You reek of alcohol," said Franny as they drove south on 87th Street. "Why do you always do this?"

She had a loving relationship with her father, and she could say anything to him without bringing down the parental ire she tried to dodge from her mother.

"I gargled with mouthwash, and I've eaten your mother's supper so I know my breath doesn't reek of alcohol, as you so delicately put it," said Hank.

"And I suppose you'll hover around me all night?"

Hank smiled. "That's the general idea. Since the Tanenbaum girl got killed, I won't be the only worried father hovering around his kid."

"Well, I hope my friends don't see you loitering around us. It would mortify me if they did, Hank."

"Well, they won't. I'm very good at becoming anonymous in the stands at football games."

"I hope so. Don't think I'm embarrassed about you, either. It's not that."

He reached across the car and gently cuffed his daughter on the back of her neck. "I know that. You'd feel the same way if I was a bank president."

"That's right, Hank."

"And please stop calling me that. I'm your dad."

"All my friends call their parents by their names. It's inevitable."

"What the hell does that mean, 'it's inevitable'? Where do you hear such baloney?"

"I don't know," she said and looked vacantly out the passenger window as they pulled into the parking lot of Wendover Field. The place was packed, she observed, so Amy's murder hadn't deterred the crowd one bit. In a way she was glad; she loved going to the games with her friends. But in a way the enthusiasm of the fans also depressed her. Shouldn't there be some respect for Amy? Something to remember her by? Like black armbands? Maybe she would bring it up with her friends. Maybe they needed to do some assembly at school in memory of Amy Tanenbaum.

* * *

Jana Emerich was escorted to the game by Marcel Rainford, who served as key investigator, bodyguard, and chauffeur for Michael Gresham. He was a big man with short dark hair, much taller and broader than Jana. He wore a leather bomber jacket and jeans with some serious kick-ass black motorcycle boots. The whole getup plus reflective sunglasses equaled a man on a par with The Rock, but as much as Jana respected that about the man, he still didn't want him around.

Marcel drove a Ram 2500 and, Jana had to admit, as they moved along South State Street, he enjoyed riding perched on the passenger's seat of such a popular ride. Everyone wanted a Ram truck whether you were living in Santa Monica or Chicago. And it was way better arriving in style versus the shitty 10-speed bike his uncle got Jana to get him to school and back. No one rode those bikes anymore, but his uncle had picked it up at a garage sale for cheap. Jana was so embarrassed he left it in the bushes at the far end of the school parking lot instead of in the bike racks at the front of the school.

"Look, Mr. Rainford," said Jana.

"Call me Marcel, Jana. That's my name."

"All right. Look, Marcel. I'm impressed you're bringing me to the game and everything, but could you let me out a block away?"

"Why's that? You embarrassed to be seen with me?"

Jana twisted his hands together. "No, man, it's not that. It's just that I'm a senior, and I should drive my own ride to the game, not be driven in by someone. It's just uncool."

"Uncool or not, I'm sticking to you like an ex-wife after late alimony. You and I are joined at the hip tonight, little brother," Marcel said. "But don't worry. None of your buds will notice a thing. I make my living around the edges. Tonight won't be any different. No one will know."

"I hope so. Nothing personal, Marcel. It's just hard to come into a school senior year and expect to have any friends. These kids have been buds since first grade. They don't give a damn about somebody like me. Much less someone with a babysitter attached to them."

"Not to worry. No one will notice a thing. And as for you and having friends, my old man bought me a crotch rocket when I was your age. The only thing he ever bought me. And you know why? Because he was tired of hauling my dumb ass around town. It burned him out. So I'm suggesting you raise the subject with Michael or your dad."

"What are you saying?"

"I'm saying you need to lobby for a motorcycle. There's nothing cooler than a guy showing up on a bike."

Jana was nodding and scrunching down in the seat as they pulled into the parking lot at Wendover Field. "Maybe I'll just do that. Maybe I'll shoot for a goddam bike."

They parked, and Marcel told Jana he would give him a five-minute head start. He told Jana not to look for him that it wasn't necessary for Jana to see him. But he would have Jana in sight. At all times. So just act normal and try to have fun.

Jana climbed up into the stands. He was keeping an eye out for Franny Arlington. There was just something about that girl.

She might have even smiled at him during their life drawing class.

It was worth finding out.

* * *

Rudy Gomez rode his bike down to the game where he nosed it into the metal bike stand and passed the locking chain through the front tire and around the frame. Bike theft was raging in this part of town since the kids who lived around here all had expensive bikes, including Rudy. His dad was an oral surgeon who advertised on TV and employed four associate dentists in his practice to handle all the patients scared up by the TV spots. Dr. Gomez, who was seldom at home by suppertime because of the long hours he kept at the clinic, had spared no expense on Rudy's bike. It was titanium and had cost over two grand. But Rudy had picked it out and seemed to know what he liked without question, so the dentist stayed out of the process, coming up with his professional practice's Visa card to clinch the deal. Besides, it was the least the dentist could do.

Dr. Gomez staggered under enormous guilt when reflecting on how well he did or didn't know his son. He hadn't been there for Rudy at all. Once the practice bloomed, Dr. Gomez just dove in that much deeper, keeping as many patients for himself as possible, no matter the twelve-hour days, until he was forced to hire his first associate. By then, Rudy was in tenth grade, and the damage was done. The father looked at his relationship with his son in the same way as he would tooth decay: below the surface, lurking. He intended to dig in one day and repair the damage, but it hadn't happened yet.

Rudy's mother was also an absent parent since her time was spent trying to keep her youth and help others. When would it occur to parents that helping others needed to start with their own children?

* * *

Franny Arlington spotted Jana as he climbed the bleachers toward their clutch of seniors at the far end of the crowd. Her group was seven senior girls and six senior boys. Jana would make boy number seven. Franny had had her eye on him, hardly acknowledging it to herself, since he had transferred to Wendover. He was a cool California kid in his baggies and surf shop shirts. His long brown hair, cut in a tousled shag, made her want to run her fingers across his face and into his hair. He was cute, dammit, and she planned to make him her own. As she watched him climb the steps, their eyes met, and she couldn't help herself—she smiled. And then immediately looked away. For Jana, he felt his heart leap when Franny smiled at him; she was the only one of all the senior class willing to give him a break on the murder case. Evidently, she didn't think he had done it and was willing to cut him some slack.

She wondered if Hank had seen the smile. Even if he had, she doubted Hank would know who Jana was. He only knew they had arrested a senior boy for the freshman girl's murder; he didn't have a clear mental picture of who that was.

Hank didn't realize it was Jana who was the accused, but he saw Jana smile at his daughter. *Kids*, thought the father. Always with the flirting eyes and eager smiles. Still, it was good to see his daughter was attractive to her peers. Any father would be proud, and Hank was no exception.

* * *

Rudy Gomez needed a vantage point from which to pick a victim. The knot of senior classmates were at the south end of the bleachers so he went up the north end. He climbed to the top row of the stands and edged his way to their side. He was a good twenty rows above them when he took his seat. Within five seats of him in one direction sat Jana's angel, Marcel. Within six seats of him the other way sat Hank, Franny's father. Of course, he didn't know these men or he wouldn't have selected the seat he did. But it was done, and the two men were paying him no attention, anyway.

From where he sat, Rudy could focus on the backs of his classmates below. He watched Sue Ellen Baumgartner in her cutesy little cheerleaders' outfit come bouncing up the steps to check on her man, Fuzzy Oberlich, who ordinarily dressed out with the football team but was nursing a fractured foot and getting lots of attention for the plastic cast he was wearing. Rudy hated Fuzzy and wished he had the strength to take down another male, but he didn't. A female would just have to do. Besides, there was the sex thing, and tonight was the night. His gaze shifted to the twins, Wanda and Wendy Ketcham, who still dressed alike even though they were seventeen years old and should have known better. He crossed them off his list because those two were inseparable and would never go to the bathroom or anyplace else without the other along. That would not happen. Then there was Olivine Washington, the daughter of their chemistry teacher, who was black and ran the hundred-meter dash during track season. Rudy didn't like admitting it, but Olivine frightened him. She had twice his musculature and wasn't hesitant about speaking out and stepping up when she saw injustice in the world. Not only that, Olivine was smarter than the entire class put together and that was off-putting. If he were successful in trapping her alone somewhere, she might likely out-think him and dump his dumb ass before he did the deed. So she was out.

Which only left Franny Arlington as the girl he would like to do tonight. She was playing pull and shove with Jana, the kid they arrested for Amy's murder. So what the hell was she doing with him anyhow? Didn't she know he was accused of murder by the Chicago Police Department? He hated her for ignoring the heinous nature of Jana's attack on Amy. He wished she wasn't flirting with the new kid from California. He had loved her from afar for a long time. There, he admitted it. Now he had to make her notice him, and there was but one way to do that. He would observe for his opening, and he would be bold.

At the end of the first quarter of the game, the score was Wendover 11 and Niles 3. Everyone stood to stretch, including Rudy. As he was stretching, he stepped up on the bench just below him and got a good look at Franny and Jana. But Jana wasn't around. Franny was alone. He kept his eyes on her for what she might do next. Someone passed her a program, and she flipped through it. Someone else passed her a lighted cigarette, but she shook her head. Hank was watching all of this, and she knew better than to smoke in front of Hank. Then, Jana returned with two Pepsi cups and handed one to Franny. She accepted and smiled and leaned into him with her shoulder. He feigned pulling away but then moved right back up against her. Rudy was put off by this, and he hated Jana for sitting where he, Rudy, should have been sitting. Right beside Franny Arlington, the coolest and prettiest girl in the senior class.

She stood up and came up the steps in double-time straight at Rudy. He was about to say something to her when she stepped off to the side and talked to a slight man wearing khakis and a denim work shirt. "Hank," he heard her say, "all of us are going to the restrooms, boys and girls. We'll be okay, so please just wait."

"No," said the man, Hank, "I'll tag along."

"Please! You're embarrassing me!"

"I am? Why?"

"You just are. Now stay put, please, or I'll never speak to you again."

She turned and two-stepped down to her friends. They said something, and they rose as a group and filed down the stairs to the bottom of the bleachers where they turned left toward the restrooms. Then Rudy saw that Jana had remained behind. Jana turned and scowled at Rudy—Rudy thought it was meant for him, not realizing Marcel was close by—but Rudy ignored the look. By the time Jana had turned back around to face the field, Rudy was up and gone.

Before the other seniors had reached the bottom bench, Rudy was down and running in the shadows for the restroom. He cut inside the girls' restroom and decided he would wait inside the farthest stall. Why? He reasoned that Franny was a leader. Which meant she would come through the door first and would seek the farthest stall. It seemed to make sense. Besides, if it was anyone else, he would just have to settle for whoever. Either way it happened, it was all good.

He was back against the wall of the stall when the door creaked open. In one move he was on Franny, pressing the knife blade against her throat, demanding her absolute silence. He whispered for her to sit on the toilet and urinate. He stood behind her with the knife drawn against her throat while she complied. One by one, they heard the other stalls flush and the occupants wash and leave. Soon the restroom was quiet. He dragged his prey to the light switch and darkened the restroom. Then he shut off the exterior light. In the darkness, he walked his hostage out of the restroom and back along the fence, out of view of anyone in the bleachers.

He pushed her under the stands. She struggled, trying to run past him, but he seized her arm and flung her farther under the seats. She fell backward, and as she fell, she bashed her head against a lower portion of the bleachers. Then she didn't move. Her eyes were half-shut.

"What the hell happened to you?" he said in disbelief. He was frightened, and terror swept through his body.

He decorated his prey before standing straight and casting around for prying eyes. He saw none.

He was gone in four minutes. Three minutes and fifty-eight seconds, actually, according to the digits on his watch.

After he unlocked his bike, it slipped backward from the rack, and he was riding along the dark street moments later.

A hue and cry went up from Hank, who returned from purchasing a large black coffee and realized Franny wasn't among her friends. He didn't see that Jana had already gone to the security officer at the far end of the stands and was speaking animatedly with him. Had he been watching, he would have spotted the security officer throw Jana to the ground and cuff his hands behind him with plastic handcuffs.

But Hank was already headed for the opening under the bleachers. So he saw nothing of the arrest of Jana and nothing of the police officers who arrived moments later and replaced the plastic cuffs with stainless steel ones.

Then Hank was screaming and men were rushing toward his cry.

16

E dward Ngo invented what he called the 12:1 Rule of Detective Work. His rule said twelve minutes inside the police station at his desk in the homicide bureau was the equivalent of one minute at a crime scene. Sixty minutes in the office went by in five minutes at a homicide. So when the shift changed at six p.m., the robbery-homicide dicks who'd been stuck in the office headed for Stuyvesant's Tavern on Clark Street, which they also called the 12:1. By midnight, the murders had all been compared; they had exhausted theories in long, heated exchanges, and all the bad guys were under arrest. It was time to go home for six hours of sack time until the day shift started again the next morning.

The days were an endless stream on Robbery-Homicide; there was never a day off. Another of Ngo's sayings, oft-repeated around Chicago's Loop Precinct, "Homicide is a killer." Meaning RH was a meat grinder. A dick was allowed three years in RH before being rotated out for a breather in vice or burglary. Too many dead guy pictures, and a detective would show up at the head shrink's office, scoring depression meds or getting dried out in rehab. The lieutenants knew productivity fell off after thirty-six months in RH. On the day they found Franny Arlington under the bleachers at Wendover Field, the back of her head bloodied, Edward Ngo had just eighty-eight days left of his three years. And more than anything, he wanted the bleacher homicides solved before he rotated out.

He ate, slept, and talked nothing else during the twelve hours shifts he shared with Andy Valencia, his partner of five years. At lunch break, over fish tacos or beef teriyaki, they talked the bleachers. At night at Stuyvesant's, he talked the bleachers with anyone still willing to listen. At home on weekends with his wife, who was divorcing him but didn't have first and last month's rent saved up yet, he talked bleachers even though Charlotte had quit listening long ago. And at night he dreamed the dreams of a homicide investigator who had seen one too many high school girls with their throat slashed ear-to-ear and or a child with a closed head injury. They were awful dreams, full of wails and cries for help and dark faces without features that grinned at him out of the shadows.

And Edward Ngo was on a full-blown course of Zoloft for clinical depression. You weren't supposed to ingest alcohol when taking the drug, his shrink had cautioned him, but the nightly 12:1's at the tavern were an exception that Ngo had carved out for himself. A dick couldn't be expected to just drop out of 12:1's. It just wasn't done. You were expected to be there, you were expected to take part, and they expected you to keep sane with the help of your brothers' sharing and your own. Ngo saw it as no different from group therapy, and so he declined his shrink's invitation to engage in an official non-alcohol group. Cops just didn't do such things. They couldn't. If they did, the word might get out just how insane homicide detail had left them. So it was 12:1 and done, home by twelve-thirty and dreaming the bad dreams alone in a bed vacated by a spouse counting dollars and days until she could escape from you. Which left only your buddies at the station.

Edward Ngo had been flown to America by Catholic Social Services at the age of thirteen. He had grown up as a member of Father Bjorn's All-Saints Church, although he attended so rarely the priest hadn't recognized him under the bleachers when he and Michael Gresham had approached the tall African-born detective. But Ngo recognized Father Bjorn. Knew who he was and knew why he was there: Jana Emerich was Bjorn's natural child, and Bjorn's guilt was as deep as a mountain of bullshit in a feedlot.

While Ngo couldn't say so, he knew all about guilt. Boko Haram had recruited him into its jihadist militant corps for a kidnapping at age eight. Ngo had killed mothers and fathers and children all over northeast Nigeria under the orders of other killers who kidnapped and ruled the pre-teen murderers. The motivation had been simple: either you do what who we tell you to or we kill you. Ngo had learned at eight he was without principles. He opted to kill rather than be killed. So he understood Father Bjorn's guilt; he understood what it meant to feel like your own flesh and blood had murdered an innocent. They were brothers in arms. Killing was killing and guilt was guilt. The son's guilt became the father's as easily as the trigger-finger's guilt became the heart's. Ngo knew this and Father Bjorn knew it, too. At least he did now that his son had murdered the

Tanenbaum girl and, according to the police, the Arlington girl.

Late Friday night, after Jana had been thrown to the ground and handcuffed by the uniforms, he had been driven to Loop Precinct and delivered into the interrogation room to await Ngo and Valencia. The two detectives were nursing their second whiskey at the 12:1 when Ngo's cell phone vibrated. He fished it out of his coat pocket and read, "Another dead girl Wendover Field. Jana Emerich in custody. Come now."

Twenty minutes later, Ngo and Valencia were pulling their unmarked car into the reserved parking behind the precinct.

The son had remembered the lawyer's words, spoken that first night at Michael Gresham's house when he went to live there. *If the cops want to talk, call me first.*

So when they offered him a soft drink in the interrogation room, he declined. When they offered him a cigarette (even though he was hooked), he said no. When they told him if he cooperated they would take him home, he said no. He remembered the look on Michael Gresham's face when he said the words *call me first*, and he meant to do just that.

"Why did you kill her?" Ngo asked Jana.

Jana leaned away from the table. He placed his elbows on the hardwood chair arms and slipped his thumbnail under his front teeth. Then he said, "I want my lawyer."

"Your lawyer can't save you. But you can by talking to us."

"I want my lawyer."

Then the bombardment and the bullying started by both dicks.

"Do you have a girlfriend?"

"Do you like girls?"

"Do you like sex with dead bodies?"

"What does it feel like when you kill someone?"

"We can tell the District Attorney you cooperated."

"We can make them go easy on you."

"You need medical help. A year in a hospital and you walk out a free man."

"Do you want coffee? A Coke?"

"Do you smoke?"

Through the barrage, Jana's answer remained the same.

"I want my lawyer."

Ngo and Valencia left the room and stood in the hallway to regroup.

"He wants his lawyer," Valencia reminded his partner.

"He wants his freedom," Ngo said. He remembered what restraint against one's will in a strange place felt like. "Let's try that angle."

The two men re-entered the room and took seats across from Jana.

"Jana, we are ready to release you to go home," said Ngo.

The boy's eyes opened wide, and he looked between Ngo and Valencia. "Really?"

"Really." Ngo answered. "We need your statement first. Just tell us what happened, and we'll take you home."

"My lawyer said I shouldn't speak to you."

"Well, your lawyer doesn't know us. We want the real killer. If you didn't do it—and we don't think you did—we'd like you to help us catch whoever did do it. Can you do that? Just a good citizen statement?"

"Just tell what I saw? I already tried that with the security cop, and he threw me on the ground."

"Well, we're not here to throw you on the ground. In fact, we're sorry that even happened. It wouldn't have happened if we had been there."

"If you say so."

Ngo leaned back and folded his arms. "Now, were you talking with Franny at the game?"

"Yes."

"And someone said you were sitting next to her. Is that correct?"

"Yes. She came up the stairs and came over. I didn't ask her or anything. She just did it."

"Which made you happy, I'm sure."

"Yes."

"And you would have been the last person who wanted to see her harmed, correct?"

"Of course I didn't want her harmed. I didn't want Amy Tanenbaum harmed either."

"Did you follow Franny to the bathroom?"

"No. I started to, but then I thought I better wait in the stands."

"Was anyone else with you?"

"My lawyer's investigator was watching me. He was behind us."

"What's his name?"

"Marcel something. I don't know his last name."

"Why was Marcel there?"

"He was sent with me by my lawyer."

"Were they afraid you would do something wrong?"

"No."

"Then why?"

Jana smiled. He looked up at the camera and said, "They weren't afraid of what I might do. They were afraid of what you might do. Like, try to say I hurt someone else."

"They told you that?"

"They said you would stop at nothing to convict me. They didn't want me to go to the game. But I raised hell with them and got to go. But Marcel had to tag along."

"Was Marcel with you all night?"

"Except for when I went into the restroom. He waited outside."

"Then you came back out?"

"No, there was a back door. He didn't know it. I walked out and circled him in the shadows."

"Where did you go?"

"Franny and I agreed to meet in the parking lot. We were going to walk and talk."

"You weren't going back to the game?"

"No. She wanted to hear about California. My old state."

"So did you meet her?"

"That's just it. I went out to the ticket booth where we would meet. Except she never showed up."

Ngo shot a look at Valencia, who was frowning. There was a follow-up needed.

"While you were at the ticket booth, were you watching for Franny?"

"Uh-huh."

"Jana, think carefully about this next question. Did you see anyone else come out of the field?"

"Yes. That's why I went to the security guard. I saw a kid come out in a huge hurry. He jumped on his bike and tore off. When Franny didn't show, I asked the security guard if he saw a group of girls walk by. He asked my name, and I told him. That's when he threw me on the ground. Then the cops brought me here."

"Okay, okay, back up now. Who was the kid you saw leaving when you were at the ticket booth?"

"Rudy Gomez. He's in my College English class."

"Could you identify the boy you saw?"

"Rudy? Hell yes. What is all this about? Is Franny okay?"

"Franny is not okay. Franny was found dead."

A look of shock, then dismay, crossed Jana's face. The video camera recorded the sequence.

"What happened?"

"Under the bleachers. Same as Amy Tanenbaum."

"Oh, Jesus Christ!"

"Yes."

"Oh, hell no! And now you think I—"

"We're only asking questions. We don't think anything."

"Well, you've got the wrong guy. I was never with her except in the stands."

"We believe you."

Jana looked from face to face. "No, you don't. If you can pin this on me, you will. I want my lawyer. That's the last time I'm going to say it."

"All right, we'll call your lawyer."

The two detectives left Jana alone in the room. Again, they held a hallway conference.

"So," said Valencia, "do we charge him?"

"Uh-uh," said Ngo. "No case."

"That's what I'm thinking."

"We take him home. Then we go round up Rudy Gomez. Get his address."

"Load up the kid. I'll be right there."

"Here we go."

17

"Where are we going?" Jana asked the officer driving the car.

"We're going to pay a visit to this Rudy kid. We need you to ID him as the guy you saw."

"I just want to go home. I don't want to ID Rudy."

"You're saying you won't help us? What about Franny? Wouldn't she want you to help catch whoever hurt her?"

"Maybe," said Jana. He was riding alone in the backseat. He looked out the side window and thought about Franny. Just two hours ago, they were together, and he had loved every minute. He hadn't expected she would like him. Now, she was gone. Just like that. "I want to help," Jana said. "At least I can put the finger on the guy."

"Great. We're only two miles from his house. Sit back and relax."

The cops up front talked together. The radio squawked, and Jana tried to make out what it was saying. The detectives didn't answer whoever was talking. He'd seen enough cop shows to know his two cops were already on their way to an urgent call and they wouldn't get sidetracked by something else. He wondered if he could be a cop someday. He thought he might actually like that. Except for the fact he now faced a charge of murdering Amy Tanenbaum. He didn't know what that would do to his chances even if a jury found him not guilty.

Detective Valencia, who was driving, caught Jana's eye in the rearview. "Did you ever have a date, you and Franny?" he asked Jana.

"No. We never even talked before."

"Did you have any classes together?"

"Just one. We were taking life drawing class. She sat somewhere behind me."

"Life drawing? What's that?"

"Nude models. Except ours were only partly nude. They were always wearing underwear or shorts."

"Did you like the nude girls?" Valencia continued.

"As much as any other guy in the class did, I guess. Yes, I liked the nude girls."

"Did it make you want to have sex?"

"Hey," said Jana. "I thought you were done asking me questions. If you want more answers, get my lawyer in here with me. I'm not saying anymore."

"Good for you, Jana," said Edward Ngo. "Don't let him trick you." He turned in his seat and smiled at the young man. "We've moved on from you. You're not a suspect."

"That's good to hear. How about dropping the Amy Tanenbaum charges against me while you're at it? I didn't kill her, either."

"No, that's another case. We found your muffler near the body."

"It fell through the cracks. What do you want me to say? It dropped through."

"That's what your lawyer can argue. We think otherwise."

"I can prove I didn't hurt Amy."

The cops turned to look at their passenger.

"How?" they said.

"Give me a lie detector."

"Now, that might not be a bad idea. What does your lawyer say?"

"He'll do it if I tell him. He's working for me."

"Maybe not a bad idea. We'll take that up with the DA and get back to you. Okay, here we are."

They pulled into the driveway of a low, ranch-style house. It was set back from the road and appeared to be under siege by Halloween ghosts propped up in the yard.

"Wait here," Valencia told him.

Jana stayed put while the two detectives went up on the porch and rang the bell. They waited. Then Valencia pressed the doorbell a second time. The door opened, and a woman with gray hair stood there, swaying slightly in the backlight. They spoke together, and then the cops turned and returned to the car.

"He's babysitting," said Ngo once they were back inside. "She won't say where because she doesn't want them disturbed."

"I want to go home," Jana said. He was frightened and wanted nothing more to do with the cops. This detective work could go on forever, and who could say they wouldn't focus on him again? He wanted out.

18

Rudy Gomez rode his bike to Wendover Field and stopped, still straddling the bike. Other riders were milling around, and with them, he watched the long lines of spectators processing through the police checkpoints as they exited the playing field. He looked at his digital watch: 10:31. Babysitting had earned him ten bucks per hour for four hours. He should have gone home, but a momentary urge made him turn his bike around and return to the playing field. What he saw was magic, bigger than anything he'd ever seen.

Among the gawkers, there was a general buzz over all the police vans and vehicles. The students had never seen such a display of police effort in their near-northside neighborhood. Not even when banks were robbed or gang bangers shot and killed each other. Not even when Amy died. This was different. The scene tonight was something to write home about.

Rudy was enchanted. It turned him on to see all the cops and techs and plainclothes detectives coming and going, radios squawking, sirens blasting on and off, and the omnipresent coffee cups from Jungle Joe's coffee bar just up the street.

"Whatcha thinking about, Rude?"

Rudy turned to see who was speaking to him. It was Andy Voskuil, a senior boy wearing a letter jacket with a football logo over a baseball logo. Rudy wasn't accustomed to being included in casual talk with other students since Rudy was a loner and considered by his classmates as someone to avoid. Rudy could not answer. "I—I—"

"Yeah, me too," said Voskuil. "Some freak killed Fran Arlington."

"Who got killed?" Rudy said.

"Arlington. We were all in chemistry with her last year. She was gonna be a doctor."

"Oh, yeah," said Rudy. He went back over it in his mind. He had no desire to engage any further with Voskuil. He wouldn't even have come here at all except it was exciting to visit where it happened. Stupid fucking cops would have no clue where to look. And Rudy had made certain he was babysitting the Roth's nine-year-old twin boys all night. He'd gotten them involved in playing Warlord on the Play-Station and then let himself out the back door while no one was watching. The Roths only lived a block away from the football field, so the setup had been perfect.

He was just riding away from Voskuil when someone else came up behind his bike and kicked his back tire. The bike skidded sideways, and he could only keep it upright by using all his strength to push back against the slide. He turned, and there stood the meathead Joe Jamison and the girl who was giving it up to him, Connie Ebersoll. Jamison, or JJ everyone called him, was leering at Rudy, pleased with his rear assault on Rudy's bike.

"Hey, weirdo," said Jamison, "you're not the one who did this, are you?"

"Yeah, I did it," said Rudy. "Not."

Several younger kids standing nearby at the bike stand heard the exchange, and a look passed between them. Rudy Gomez had just confessed to killing Franny Arlington.

"Like shit," said Jamison. "My dad saw the cops come and take Jana away again. They threw his ass in a police car and tore out with the lights flashing. Now maybe we can all sleep, thanks to our local police force."

"Jana?"

"Yeah. Mr. Potato Head from California."

"Your dad saw it?" asked Rudy.

"Fuck, he's as fucking weird as you are, Rudy," Jamison swore at him.

"Hey," said Andy Voskuil as he approached again. "Leave the weirdo alone, JJ. You know how he gets."

"You mean how he runs to the principal? Yeah, I remember."

"I was a freshman," Rudy mumbled. "Besides, my arm was broken."

"Yes, but that was your fault for peeking in the girls' locker room."

"He's right, Rudy," Voskuil chimed in. "Asshat move, Rudy."

Rudy looked away. The cops were still swarming, and the coffee cups were still coming and going. He decided he wasn't going to see much more and wasn't enjoying talking to Andy and JJ, so he backed his bike out of the cluster of students. He had forgotten why he had even bothered to come here.

Then he remembered, and he felt that sweet ache swelling in his pants.

He wondered when the next home game would be played. He would babysit again. Rudy could work with that.

Just as he got his bike backed up and spun it around, JJ Jamison kicked him and knocked him sideways onto the asphalt. He lost his balance, fell with one leg over the bar, and received a blow to his groin from the force of the falling bike. Pain shot up his abdomen.

Andy Voskuil yelped at JJ, "That was stupid, JJ, and unnecessary."

Rudy laid on his side a minute more and then disengaged from the bicycle. He got out from under it and came to his knees. His balls were aching, and his boner was gone. It was all he could do not to throw up. Then he staggered to his feet and looked straight into the eyes of JJ's girlfriend, Connie Ebersoll. She was grinning.

She raised her right hand and pointed at him. "You aren't gonna be spanking that monkey for a few days," she said and tossed her head back and laughed.

JJ reached behind her and squeezed a handful of ass. So. That's how it's done when they belong to you. You grab them and feel them.

He memorized the look of hysterical joy on Connie's lovely cheerleader face. He would see her again.

Everyone loved the cheerleaders, and Rudy was no exception.

Rudy backed his bicycle around and stared into headlights on bright. He shaded his eyes.

Then his heart jumped into his throat.

They hit their red-and-blue lights, and Rudy froze. He heard the car shift into park, and he watched two large men get out.

One was enormous, black, and reaching inside his coat. "Rudy? We'd like to talk to you."

"Why me?"

"We've got someone in our car who says they saw you."

The cops showed their badges and introduced themselves as Detective Ngo and Valencia.

Rudy shaded his eyes and tried to see inside the police car. But he couldn't. The headlights, on bright, left him blinded and unable to look inside. So he stood, straddling his bike, remembering his story.

"Were you at the game tonight?" said the giant cop.

"No."

"Where were you tonight?"

"I was babysitting."

"Where was that?"

"With the Roth twins. Simon and Samuel."

"Where do they live?"

Rudy pointed. "About a block that way. I can take you there."

"How old are the twins?"

"Nine."

"You sure you weren't here earlier tonight? Even for just a few minutes?"

Rudy held up both hands. "Sorry, I don't know who you want, but I wasn't here. Swear to God."

"We have someone in the car says you were here. Says they saw you coming past the ticket booth. You deny that?"

"Hell, yes, I deny that. That's a flat-out lie!"

"Can you prove you weren't here?"

"Can you prove I was? I'm innocent until proven guilty."

The cops exchanged a look.

"Maybe. Maybe not," said Detective Ngo.

At just that moment, Marcel's truck pulled in behind the cop car. Marcel climbed out and walked up to the police car. Sure enough, there in the back seat sat Jana, looking to all the world like some orphan whose parents had disappeared. Small, withdrawn, and hunched down, he was peering over the front seats, watching the confrontation between the cops and Rudy. Marcel tapped on the window. Jana looked over, and his face lit up.

"Can you hear me?" Marcel shouted at the window.

"Yes!"

"I'm here to take you home!"

"I'm ready!"

"I'll talk to the officers!"

Marcel approached the detectives and cleared his throat. Valencia turned to him.

"I'm Marcel Rainford. I'm Michael Gresham's assistant and investigator. Jana rode with me to the game tonight, and I'm here to take him home."

"One second," said Valencia. "I need to ask him something."

Marcel returned with Valencia to the rear of the car, and Valencia unlocked the back door. Jana climbed out and stood there stretching.

"Oh," he said. "Free at last."

"Have you gotten a good look at the kid?" Valencia asked, indicating Rudy.

"Yes. That's the guy I saw."

"You're sure of that?"

"Positive. Same guy."

"Okay. You can leave with your lawyer's investigator. And thanks for helping us out tonight."

"Did I have a choice? You people arrested me."

Detective Valencia placated, "We are looking for a killer. It wouldn't be unusual to take in a suspect on a previous case for questioning. Please understand where we're coming from."

Marcel said, "Has it occurred to you yet that your Rudy guy just might also be the same guy who killed Amy Tanenbaum? Has it occurred to you that Jana just ain't your guy?"

"We'll talk about that, sir. Detective Ngo and I have a lot of questions to work through."

"What about the kid?" Marcel said, indicating Rudy. "Has he admitted anything yet?"

"Not yet. He's denying even being here."

"Well, he was here," Jana said. "I can prove it."

"How can you prove it?" the detective asked.

Jana pulled his cell phone from his pocket. He stabbed it on and held the screen up for Valencia. He was showing him a picture, a snap of Rudy Gomez exiting the football field on the same date at 8:34 p.m.

"You've got to be kidding me," said Valencia. "Why in the world would you have that?"

"It was one guy I saw headed for the restrooms when Franny was walking over there. I was suspicious when he left the field ten minutes later."

"Did he see you take his picture?"

"I doubt it. But I didn't care if he saw me or not. I'm twice his size."

"Email it, please," Valencia said, and he gave Jana his email. The transfer was made. Valencia took his smartphone with the picture and headed for Rudy and Detective Ngo. The dynamic was about to change.

Marcel loaded Jana into his truck, and they left without another word to the cops.

Valencia jammed the smartphone in the kid's face. "Well?" asked Valencia.

"I don't know," said Rudy. "Where did that come from?"

"It's today's date. At eight-thirty tonight. You tell me."

"I don't know."

Detective Ngo took a step forward. His face was inches from Rudy's. "You've been lying to us, son," said Ngo. "Now, don't get me mad. Just tell the truth here."

Rudy looked back and forth between the two cops. He thought, *I'd run, dammit, but I'll never get away from two of them. Especially with their car.* He looked back at Ngo.

"She fell," he mumbled.

"What's that mean?" Ngo said.

"We were under the stands to talk. She fell backward in the dark. Tripped and fell backward. She hit her head on the stands. I got scared and got out."

Ngo turned Rudy and moved him back to the police cruiser where he and Valencia bent him over the hood and frisked him.

Valencia came up from the lower part of Rudy's body holding a filet knife. The blade was serrated on one edge and razor sharp on the other. There was a one-inch crease of blood along the bulge in the blade. Ever so carefully, Valencia two-fingered the knife as he walked to the trunk of their car, popped it open, and shook open an evidence bag. He dropped the knife inside and sealed the bag, then pulled the cover off an evidence tag and wrote his initials on the seal. Then he placed the bag inside an evidence safe in the trunk and slammed the lid shut.

"Care to tell us about the knife?" Ngo asked him. "Or do you want to admit you killed the girl?"

"I carry the knife for self-protection, that's all."

"There's a skim of blood on the blade. Whose blood is that?"

"I dunno. Some animal, probably."

"What if it's human blood? What if it's Franny Arlington's blood? Did you have that knife against her throat?"

Rudy's eyes raised to the dark sky behind Ngo's head.

"It wasn't supposed to cut her. It was an accident because she struggled when I told her not to."

"Why don't we record all this," said Ngo, switching on the recorder in his smartphone. "Let's start at the beginning. You have the right to remain silent and have a lawyer present, but I would advise against that if you want our help."

Rudy took them through the entire evening—the babysitting, the twins' total attention to the video game, sneaking out of the Roth's house, cycling to the game five minutes away, climbing into the stands, watching the seniors, beating Franny into the restroom, capturing her, walking her back to the bleachers where he told her he would let her go. But he dragged her under the stands instead at the last second. Her surprise and dismay. His sudden anger when she resisted him, so he pushed her back into the metal seats where she struck her head and crumpled to the ground. He said he hadn't pushed her all that hard; it was more a tap to make sure she was listening to him. He had then turned and made his way to the parking lot. The bicycle took him back to the Roth's, and he found the twins as he had left them.

Ngo recorded the statement, the Miranda warning preceding the entire thing.

As they drove Rudy to the Loop Precinct jail, Valencia caught his eye in the rearview.

"I hear a songbird," said Valencia, "singing its little head off."

Rudy wept.

"Can I call my dad?" he asked.

"Tweet-tweet," Valencia said with a wicked smile.

"We will get your dad," Ngo told him. "You will need him big-time."

"He's gonna kill me."

"Your dad is the least of your worries."

"By the way," Ngo said, turning in the seat. "When I asked you about Amy Tanenbaum's death, you told me you knew nothing about it. If you want me to call your dad, I want you to think about that again. Did you kill the Tanenbaum girl, too?"

"Swear to God I didn't!"

"Not pretty enough?"

"Still wearing braces! Who could kiss that metal mouth?"

Ngo nodded. "You have your standards, Rudy. Good for you."

19

Wednesday afternoons are my time off, and this Wednesday I'm home before one o'clock. Our nanny, Priscilla, is still taking care of Dania. When I come in through the garage door, she asks if we can speak. Her face is tight, and she's unsmiling, which is unusual for Priscilla, who ordinarily is very bright and happy around here. I ask if I can change my clothes before we talk, and she says that works for her.

I change and come back into the family room where Dania is on the floor playing with an alphabet toy. Priscilla is sitting on the floor with her charge but stands up when I come in.

"So," I say, "what's going on with you today, Priss? Something about Dania?"

She shakes her head. I see her eyes brim with tears. "I wish that's what it is," she says. "But it's not. I wanted to ask you about Jana. How long is he going to be living here?"

"Well, probably until his trial is over. Maybe three months. Why, is that a problem?"

"It's just that he won't stay away from me. It's hard to explain. It's not like he follows me everywhere, but when I used the bathroom this morning, he was standing right outside the bathroom door when I came out. I don't know, but I had the definite feeling he'd been watching me through the keyhole."

"Did you see him watching you? Or hear him or something?"

"No. But I felt uncomfortable the whole time I was... sitting on the toilet. Am I just being stupid, Mr. Gresham?"

The tears run down her cheeks, and I am alarmed she is so upset by this. The last thing we want is for our nanny to be having any problem around the house. Her job is too important to me and Dania for her to be upset. The only problem: there's no definite proof that Jana was doing what Priscilla is thinking.

"Tell you what," I say, "I'll speak to Jana. Does that work for you?"

Now the tears flow. "I don't want to be a problem, Mr. Gresham. I feel so-so dumb! Like I'm making all this up."

"No, I don't think you're making anything up. Jana is new around here, and we don't know him all that well. But maybe we need to make rules for him. I'm happy you alerted me, Priss, because the last thing Danny and I ever want is for you to be upset or unhappy here. You come first, okay?"

"O-o-okay. But please don't tell him I said anything. I feel stupid now for saying it."

"No, no, no, I trust your senses. If you thought you were being spied on, possibly you were. People sense stuff like that. When he gets home, I'll take him for a drive and have a word with him."

My plan for the afternoon was to get out in the garage and sort through boxes of our Christmas decorations as Danny asked me to. She's the type who likes to get her tree up before Thanksgiving. Even though we have a month out until then, I take the time when I can to get stuff done. As a criminal lawyer, sometimes I don't know when my next day off will be.

But now I'm thinking about how I'll approach this with Jana. A thought occurs and I retreat into my office and shut the door.

I call Marcel. "This is stupid of me to be so late on this," I tell him, "but better late than never."

"What's that, boss?"

"I need you to run a criminal history on Jana. Start with his time in Santa Monica, California, and then let's talk."

"Fair enough. I'm on it right now."

"Good. Call me back, please."

A half hour later, as I'm still working on my first cup of coffee since arriving home, he calls back.

"Yes?"

"Okay, I ran it. It seems our little defendant has quite an extensive background."

"Any felonies?"

"No, just minor stuff."

"I'm listening."

"Well, three shoplifting convictions and a fourth that was dismissed when the store manager didn't show for trial. Two pot busts, one where the weed was seized from his locker at school, the other for smoking weed on the Santa Monica pier."

"Nothing like open and notorious, is there?"

"I know. Stupid kid. But here's one I don't like. He got caught hiding in the girls' locker room at his high school. It seems he was hiding in a restroom stall and watching the girls dress after showering. Dumb shit."

"What came of that?"

"He pled guilty to misdemeanor trespassing. They reduced it from a felony sex crime that would have had him registered as a sex offender. I also talked to the DA. I knew you'd want me to follow up, so I called her and spent about ten minutes getting my head wrapped around the case. She says she was going to nail him with a felony, but she couldn't find any girls who knew they were being watched. Evidently, he was good at doing whatever the hell he was doing, so nobody knew."

"How did you get her to open up about this sealed information, Marcel?"

"You know not to ask, Michael."

I did, but it never ceased to amaze me what Marcel could get accomplished. Sometimes I wondered if there was magic running through the man's veins. "So how did the school find out then?"

"Standard review of videotapes. The school's security staff reviews video from the hallway to the locker room during school hours. They saw Jana on the video on three different occasions sneaking in and out. They assumed he hid inside a stall and stood on the toilet seat to see over the top."

"Oh, my God. What the hell is this all about?"

"You've got yourself a sex nut there, boss. You want me to come out and eighty-six him the hell out of your house?"

"No, not yet. I'm going to talk with him this afternoon when he gets home from school."

"Wait, there's more on his rap sheet."

"Okay, give it to me."

Marcel clears his throat. "He's also got seven letters from the District Attorney over bad checks he passed, which his mom came in and paid, so there was no prosecution. Another arrest a week before he moved back here, this time for assaulting a police officer. That charge is still pending, and they have issued an arrest warrant for his failure to appear in court."

"His mother must not have known that when she moved him back here. Otherwise, she would've kept him in L.A. until the case was pled out."

"My thinking too, boss."

We hang up.

Danny and I have installed a video system in our house, which provides views of the living areas where Dania can be watched when we're home and when we're away. We can access it on our cell phones, our iPads, and our computer screens around the house. The screen is divided into six different views. But unfortunately, there are no views outside the bathrooms so I have no video of what went on outside the bathroom that Priscilla used when she felt eyes on her. I stop what I'm doing and put in a call to our security company. I request additional cameras in the hallways outside the four bathrooms. I make it clear that the installations need to be surreptitious while Jana is at school and the cameras need to be disguised. They understand exactly what I want, and I'm told it will be done tomorrow during school hours. Good enough.

Thirty minutes later, Jana walks past my office. I jump up and follow him down to his room where I knock. His door opens.

"Come with me, please, I want to show you something."

I lead him out to my car, and we climb in. The garage door undulates upward, and then we head east toward the lake. There's an overlook about a mile from my house, so I pull in there and climb out. The lake is slate gray today, reflecting the clouds. The water is choppy and the waves crash on the beach. Jana follows me down to the water's edge.

"Look," I say, turning to face him full-on. "I need to know something. Before you left for school today were you spying on Priscilla in the bathroom?"

He turns white. "No—no—I was—I came down the hallway, but I went straight into my room."

"You didn't stop outside her bathroom door and look inside through the keyhole?"

He shakes his head hard. "No, definitely not."

"Have you ever done anything like that?"

His brow furrows. "What do you mean?"

"I mean have you ever spied on women in a restroom before?"

"Hell, no! I'm not some pervert, Mr. Gresham."

I sigh a deep breath and stick my hands in my pockets. "Marcel did some checking around today. I told him to. It seems someone accused you of sexual stalking at your school in Santa Monica. They reduced the charge to trespassing, and you paid a fine and did six months of probation. That ring a bell?"

"Hell, that was a farce. They had me for it, but it wasn't me. I swear it."

"No? Then who was it?"

"This other kid at school. Dickie Sepman. He's a raging queen who likes to see what girls are wearing."

"And that's your story?"

"Ask the DA if you don't believe me." He throws his hands in the air. "That's why they reduced the charges from stalking to trespassing."

"All right. I'll give you that. But listen to what I'm saying. If I ever find out, there's anything like that going on inside my house, you're headed back to jail. There won't be a second discussion and there won't be any questions asked. I'll just call the sheriff and have you taken to jail. Are we clear on that?"

"Shit, Mr. Gresham. You don't believe me!"

"I believe Priscilla. She says she was being watched."

He kicks at a rock on the sand. "Did she see me in the bathroom?"

"No, but you were waiting outside the bathroom when she came out. She saw you then."

"Shit, if she didn't see me in the bathroom, then how does she know it was me for sure? I'm being accused of something she can't prove. It's not the first time. I'm getting a bad rep when I have done nothing."

"Just remember what I'm telling you. I don't give a damn whether you did it. But I'm telling you it damn well better never happen in my house, or you're gone, Jana. Do we understand each other?"

"I would never do that. It won't be a problem, Mr. Gresham."

"Fair enough. Let's go home."

They installed the cameras the next day. We now had a video feed on four new areas of our house. All of it was recorded and could be accessed by us anytime, even remotely if we wanted.

So Danny and I agreed to wait and see what turned up. We would have our security company review the video every day. It wouldn't be all that difficult since the video cameras were motion activated. They should only record fifteen or twenty minutes at most of action a day at any one location.

We had become the stalkers, a role neither of us was happy with.

A role which we'd never played before, either.

20

After I read all of Marcel's file memos, I decided it was time to pay a call on the Cook County Medical Examiner's office. We had an autopsy report on Amy Tanenbaum, but I always like to talk to the doctor at his office where he can spread out his chart and fill in the spots where he might have left something out.

The Examiner's building is part of the Chicago Technology Park, a tree-lined street tucked away from the hustle of the city. There was an early snap freeze overnight and the colors on the trees had turned to vibrant red and gold. The wind was blowing a brisk northwesterly, so I buttoned my overcoat and hurried inside.

Dr. Samuel—"call me Sammy"—Tsung was housed in a small, confining basement office in the Medical Examiner's building on Harrison.

"I'm Michael Gresham," I told Dr. Tsung. "I don't know if you remember me."

He smiled graciously, peering over the top of his half-glasses. "Of course, Michael. You tore me a new one on the Dunham case. I'm still bleeding down there."

I took it in the friendly tone in which he said it. Besides, if this guy, who has testified probably ten thousand times, thinks I did a good job, there's honestly no higher compliment for a lawyer.

"What brings you here, Michael?"

"I represent Jana Emerich. He's the young man charged with the murder of Amy Tanenbaum. You did the autopsy, Sammy. Do you remember anything about the case?"

"That would be the first young woman from the football field? Yes, let me bring her chart up on my screen."

He clicked his mouse and punched his keyboard.

"Yes, here we are. My, a young, young one. Too bad. Is your guy guilty?"

"Of course not. I never take cases where my client is guilty. You, of all people, should know that."

He laughs and pushes his glasses up on his forehead.

"Let me see. Strangled, carotids severed by some sharp device. Maybe a wire was used?"

I spread my hands. "Honestly, I don't know. And my client claims he's innocent, so I got nothing from him."

"Sure, sure."

He continues scrolling with his finger on the mouse wheel. "Oh, I knew there was something about this case. Have you seen the report yet?"

"Not yet. The State hasn't turned it over. What do you have, something unusual?"

"I'll say. When I went to examine her oral cavity, I was shocked to see her mouth had been Super Glued shut."

"What? You must be joking."

"No, no, no joking here. And—oh, my God. Now I remember this case. I've never seen this before."

"What's that?"

"There was a small dead mouse in her mouth. It had tried to gnaw its way out, and it chewed away a portion of her cheek."

I am stunned. Never in my professional life have I heard anything so disturbing.

"Were there any special characteristics about the mouse? Anything that allows us to trace it?"

"No. But someone has a very warped sense of... I don't want to say humor because that's not it. Just something very evil about this."

"I don't know what to say. Why on earth?"

He shrugs and pushes his glasses down onto his nose and continues reading. "Small font." When he finds his place, he continues, "Oh yes, here we are. Our biology team studied and categorized the little guy. Yes, here is the taxonomy report. It seems your man's choice was a common house mouse. This guy belongs to the Kingdom Animalia, Phylum Chordata, Class Mammalia, Order Rodentia, Family Muridae, Subfamily Murinae, Genus Mus, Species musculus. Its binomial name is Mus musculus."

"I could never write all that down on my notepad. I have no clue what you just read me."

He taps his computer screen. "Not to worry. It's all right in the autopsy report, footnote four. I'll print a copy for you before you leave, Michael."

"So her mouth contained a common house mouse. Why would anyone carry around a house mouse?"

"That's the sixty-four-dollar question. Maybe it was caught live around the house? When the weather changed, maybe someone was trapping an influx of mice coming into the house to escape the cold? Maybe someone keeps a snake and feeds it mice? Who knows? We'll probably never know."

"Unless someone confesses..." I'm thinking. "Wait. Back up. You said snake?"

"Yes. According to my quick research, this brand of mouse is bred by people who keep snakes. They call them pinkies."

I realize I've had this conversation before, something about a pinky. But where? Then it comes to me, and I know the identity of the person who did this. In fact, he's living in my guest bedroom, him and his snake with a cache of mice Danny and I probably don't know about. Oh, my God!

I am shaken. The rest of what Dr. Tsung tells me about the autopsy and his report falls on deaf ears. My mind is racing, but then it comes to me in a sudden caving in of mental walls—I have to remove him from our lives. He cannot be trusted. He's at school, right? The perfect time to evict him from my house, get him away from Danny, from Dania and Priss as well.

Ten minutes later, Dr. Tsung finishes his presentation. He stops to print me a copy of the full autopsy report. As he hands it to me, he seems to notice how my hands are shaking.

"Are you all right, Michael? Do you need a bottle of water? We keep some in our incoming coolers."

"No, no, thanks. I'm fine. Maybe a touch of the flu, but I'm all right. I cannot thank you enough for taking time out to meet with me, Sammy."

"Hey," he says with a wide smile, "I'd rather give it all up to you in here than in some courtroom down the road. You're a much more agreeable person when you're sitting across from me at my desk."

He laughs, and I join him. We are allies, at least for the moment.

I tuck the report inside my shoulder bag, and we shake hands.

Walking out to my car, the world is a blur. My heart jumps in my chest, reminding me of the exigency I'm facing. I climb into the driver's seat, turn the key, and mechanically drive home. When I arrive, I realize I remember nothing of the journey. It's like my mind has shut down and can only focus on three words that won't leave me alone: GET HIM OUT!

I rush inside my house.

Dania is just one year old and spends good portions of her life asleep. Her nanny, Priscilla, attends Northwestern at night. She is pretty and friendly and working on a degree in childhood education. Her approach with Dania is motivated by a desire to apply what she's learning in school to the sandbox world our little girl offers. A chance to put book learning into practice. Our nanny is medium height, dresses in comfortable jeans and Tees and sweatshirts, and is broad in the hips, probably a testament to her German heritage, though I don't make that remark to Danny, who is one-hundred percent pure German and has very slender hips. In fact, I've called her snake hips in the past. The memory of that tag jolts me back to the reality of snakes and their mice as I walk into the living room where I find Priscilla reading a thick book. Dania, I can only assume, is in her room sleeping.

"How's Dania?" I breathlessly ask.

Priscilla's puzzled look reminds me to slow down. No need to alarm anyone.

"She's—I checked her not five minutes ago. She's sleeping peacefully. If you listen hard, you can even make out a little snore. I call it her snorelet."

I smile. But I still walk down the hallway to Dania's room and peek inside. She is lying on her back, eyes shut, her chest unmoving to my eye. I rush to her and put my ear to her mouth. Warm breath and a sigh to ease my terror. I steady myself. There's nothing wrong with Dania, I tell myself. Settle the hell down right now before you scare Priscilla off.

While the District Attorney's office and police detectives continue to work up the case against Jana, he has remained in school at Wendover High. I had to talk with the principal there but the school's lawyers agreed that the boy should remain in school, attending classes as he normally would.

The social ramifications of that have been complicated for Jana since he's been ostracized, made a pariah by all but a few of his peers. Along with that, or because of it, I suppose, he has become very distant around the house, very morose, and very withdrawn. Danny and I have discussed the possibility of professional counseling for him, but we haven't sprung that on him yet.

Silently, without Priscilla knowing what I'm up to, I creep down the hallway past my and Danny's bedroom, past the second bathroom, and come to Jana's closed door. There is a picture of Bob Marley on the door. It came with Jana when he moved in, and the music, sometimes heard through the walls of our house, of steel drums and reggae guitar came along as well. Which led us to suspect that—with no disrespect to the musician or his music—Jana might still be smoking pot as he had been in Santa Monica. Still, we have seen nor smelled any evidence of any such thing, either by odor, physical appearance, or nodding-off—signs we know might indicate otherwise.

I try his doorknob. Locked. We had a lock installed when he moved in. The idea was to give him a sense of privacy. Well, we have succeeded, I'm now sorry to say. So I do the next best thing. I find a nearby locksmith on my smartphone and make the call. Thirty-minute service guaranteed. Rather than pass the day with Priscilla, who is studying and who I would be disturbing, I go back to my bedroom and decide I'm done for the day, meaning I get to change out of this suit and into something comfortable. The suit has been worn twice—one of my standby navy pinstripes—so into the dry cleaner's bag it goes. Slipping on jeans, a Bulls sweatshirt, and moccasins with wool socks, I steal back into my office. Here it's quiet, and I won't be disturbed, plus I can access my office network and file server from my laptop. First, though, I call Mrs. Lingscheit and tell her I won't be coming back today.

"That's too bad. Danny was looking for you."

"Put her on, please."

Waiting.

"Michael, I just wanted to hear what you learned from the M.E."

"Typical autopsy. Strangled, probably with some wire. Sharp enough to sever the carotids."

"Like a guitar string?"

She has me there. Why a guitar string?

"Possibly. What makes you come up with a guitar string?"

"Just thinking; Jana plays guitar. No reason, I guess."

I'll let that ride a minute or two.

"But here's the real catch. The doctor found a dead mouse in Amy's mouth."

"Jesus Christ!"

"I know. Her mouth was glued shut. The mouse had tried to gnaw its way out."

"Oh, my God. That is gross! Whoever in the hell—?"

"Why a mouse?" I ask. "A guitar string I can work with. But who would put a mouse in the mouth of a victim?"

"Seriously twisted, Michael."

"Agree. So, that's about it. Right now I'm waiting for the locksmith."

"What?"

"I'm breaking into Jana's room while he's in school."

"Whatever for?"

"He keeps that snake, right?"

"Right."

"Well, what do snakes eat?"

"I don't know."

"Think."

"Mice?"

"Bingo!"

"I'm on my way home. Don't touch anything until I get there. And don't give him any idea what we're up to until I get Dania in my arms. Promise me?"

"Promise. Have Marcel bring you."

"I will."

We hang up, and I'm immediately guilted by the notion we might be grossly overreacting. We've got this seventeen-year-old boy who has had a tough life, maybe smokes a little pot, but who doesn't at his age? And some Metallica and Marley. Big deal. But they saw him in the area of Amy Tanenbaum the night someone killed her. And he keeps mice (I'm guessing. I'm not in there, yet). We bought him a used Fender Strat when he told us about the guitar his mom had pawned in Santa Monica. It was only a few hundred bucks and came with a practice amp and headphones, but that was only after Amy's murder when he'd been living with us for a few days.

Twenty minutes later, Guido's Keys rolls into the drive. The brakes on the van squeak and, minutes later, the bell rings. I hurry down the hall. The guy has a toolbox and a pleasant smile.

"Is this confidential?" I ask.

"Are you the property owner?"

"Yes. Michael Gresham. I called you."

"Then only you know about it. You and your credit card company. One hundred for the call, sixty-five an hour."

"Come on in. Let's get to it."

He has the lock out five minutes later and takes it out to the van to make me a key.

Silently, I step inside Jana's room, and I am struck by how clean it is. Against the far wall on a bookshelf is where he first had the snake container when he moved in. Now, it's gone. I take a careful look around, closet, shelves, under the bed—everywhere—and the snake is gone. I shiver. At least its container is gone. *Brush that off*, I tell myself. There's no snake. Again looking high and low, even in the drawers of his chest and desk, I find no mice. I find no sign of mice ever having been in here. His guitar is leaning against the wall, the amp in between. The amp's little red light is glowing. Wasting electricity, but that's sure as hell not the point right now.

"Sir?"

I almost jump through the window.

"Sir? Here's the key. I need a credit card, and I'm outta here."

I hand him a card and turn my attention back to the guitar.

I count the strings. Six. I locate the guitar case under his bed and slide it out. I unlock four clasps and lift the top. There's a small door with a little box in the case's center. I pull at a tab to open the door.

A complete set of guitar strings. Quickly I riffle through them in their paper packages.

I count them again.

According to the box the packages came in, there should be six strings, from high E to low E. It's high E that is missing. I peer inside the packages. High E would be the thinnest string. It would be a silver, unwound string, consisting of a taut wire, if its neighbor is any indication.

A sudden chill races up my spine. I feel like I'm being watched from behind. I spin around.

He's holding out the credit card and giving me a dumb-founded look. Jana.

"What the hell, Michael?" he says. "I thought this was off-limits, dude."

"Where's the high E string from this package, Jana? It's missing."

"It's on the guitar. I broke my E and replaced it."

He's good. He didn't miss a beat. That, or he's telling the truth, and it came easy. Deceitful or truthful, what's your pick? I don't know. Discovering him behind me and his easy explanation for the errant string has me on the ropes.

"So what the fuck, Michael? You changed my lock, man?"

"What are you doing home so early?"

"No gym class today. They're resurfacing the floor for basketball season. No gym for a week."

"So they sent you home?"

"Yeah. It's only an hour early. No big deal, man. But let me ask again. What the fuck?"

"We'll talk, Jana. As soon as Danny gets home. For now, I'll ask you to wait in your room until she gets here and we can sort this out."

"Sort what out, man? Are you investigating me?"

I blanch. He's got me.

"Yes. I was looking for mice."

"What the hell for? I don't have any mice. Leonard went back to Uncle Tim's. He buys a mouse from Petco every three days. No other mice besides that."

"Why did Leonard go back to Uncle Tim's?"

"He's gonna be a mother. He is actually a she. I knew you wouldn't put up with a nest of baby snakes, so Uncle Tim came by, and we moved Leonard back to his house. He likes snakes. He's going to sell the babies to Petco."

I groan. Perfectly plausible explanations. And again, he's either lying or telling the truth. How do you ever know? How do you know if someone is merely hip, slick, and cool, or whether they're telling the truth? Simple. I'm a trial lawyer of thirty years. I know when witnesses are lying. Usually. This time, while I'm uneasy with the flow of answers, they are also entirely honest responses in their substance.

Face it, Michael, the kid is telling you the truth. And you just let yourself down a full floor of trust by breaking into his room. I'm kicking myself when I hear the locksmith's brakes squeak as he's backing out of my driveway.

"Let's get coffee," I tell Jana. "I owe you an apology."

"Don't bust a nut over it, dude. You don't know me yet. You've gotta be sure of stuff."

* * *

Danny pulls in thirty minutes later. She comes inside with a worried look plastered on her face and rushes in to check on Dania. Jana and I are sitting at the kitchen table, working on our second coffee, as Danny flashes past. She returns moments later, holding our daughter and patting her on the back.

"She was sitting up in her crib, singing. Didn't Priscilla check on her before she left for class?"

Priscilla headed out to a late afternoon class thirty minutes ago.

"She did. She said Dania was sleeping."

"I wish you'd pay closer attention, Michael. This is our baby we're talking about."

I'm chastised, and rightly so. I got lost in talking to Jana. He's a remarkable young man, I'm learning, with high hopes for a career in video journalism after college. He's talking podcasts, which I know little about, and online video reportage for some network like CNN. The technology escapes me but his enthusiasm is infectious, and I'm happy hearing him out.

"So what happened with the mouse and the dead girl?" Danny never beats around the bush. Plus, she's much more confrontational than I am.

Jana looks at me.

"Jana, I talked to the medical examiner who autopsied Amy Tanenbaum. He told me about a disconcerting discovery."

"Okay, I'm listening," says our guest.

"Someone glued Amy's mouth shut. And there was a dead mouse inside. The mouse had been alive when Amy's killer put it inside her mouth. That's why I was looking for your snake."

"Leonard's been over at my Uncle Tim's. He hasn't lived here in almost two weeks."

"How many weeks?" Danny asks. She pulls out a chair and sits on the other side of Jana. Now he's got one of us on either side.

"I was here about a week. Then Leonard went back when I figured out she was pregnant."

Out of curiosity, I say, "How did you know she was pregnant?"

"Eggs. Pythons lay eggs."

"All right. They found Amy murdered three weeks ago, give or take," Danny remarks, "so it's still possible."

"What's that mean?" asks Jana. "Still possible?"

"We can't rule you out as someone who had a mouse that might have wound up in Amy's mouth."

"Holy shit! You people are making me very uncomfortable here. I think it might be better if I move back to my uncle's."

"Not possible," I remind him. "The judge released you into our custody. You're stuck with us."

"And vice-versa," Danny says. Her eyes are sad and her voice barely audible as she says this. It's unclear whether she means for Jana to hear her negative comment or not, but he does.

"You hate me, don't you?" Jana says to Danny.

"I don't know. Sometimes yes, most of the time no. I'm just trying to understand why you were arrested for killing Amy and why you're living with us. There are moments—lots of moments—when I feel like we've made a huge mistake bringing you into our home. There are lots of times when I think you're guilty, more times than when I think you're innocent. Sorry, but that's just how I feel."

"Can you go back and ask the judge to let me stay with Uncle Tim?"

I shrug. "I don't know. Probably. But I don't know he'd allow it."

"Why not?"

"Because you were living with Uncle Tim when you were arrested. Judges are careful about putting minors, or adults even, back into questionable situations."

"So I'm stuck here with two people who think I'm a killer. That's a good way to live. Shit!"

"We're all stuck," Danny says. "It's not all about you, Jana. We're stuck, too."

The talk fades away. I get up and make another cup of coffee. Danny declines my offer to make her one. So does Jana.

"If it's okay, if we're finished, I'm going back to my room. Don't call me for supper. I'm not hungry."

"All right, if that's the way you feel," Danny says. "But if you change your mind, I'll make up a plate and leave it in the refrigerator for you."

"Don't bother."

Then he's gone, and we're left staring at each other. She hands Dania to me.

"I'm having a cup after all," says Danny. "Then we need to have a real talk, so don't go away."

"I wasn't. I'm here to the finish."

"I want him out of our house. I don't trust him for a second."

I tell her about the missing guitar string. Her face colors up and her eyes blink rapidly. "You must be kidding! She was strangled and her carotids cut and Tsung thinks it might have been something like a guitar string and our houseguest is missing a string out of his pack? Are you serious? I want him out, Michael! Now! Tonight!"

"We can't do that, Danny. There's a court order. There was no secondary placement made."

"Whose fault is that?"

I cringe. "Mine, I guess. Father Bjorn was with me, but I knew he wouldn't be a good second choice. I had no other options I could think of spur of the moment."

She hangs her head then reaches out and takes Dania back from me. "Shit, Michael. Call the judge by phone tonight if you have to. I want this kid gone!"

"I can't. But I'll see the judge and take the prosecutor with me. First thing in the morning."

"Then I won't sleep tonight. And Dania will sleep in our bed. I'm not closing my eyes while this monster inhabits our house."

"We don't know he's a monster. That's harsh, isn't it?"

She gives me a mean, questioning look. "How would you have said it?"

"I don't know."

"I rest my case, counselor. Now, you'd better trot off to your computer and come up with a motion to revise conditions of release. Figure out where he can be put and ask the judge to put him there. I'm waiting, and I want to see it."

"Will do."

"Good."

21

Judge Winifred Lancer-Burgess refused to change the conditions of Jana's release on bail. Her ruling was perfunctory, as was the in-chamber conference I requested with the judge and State's Attorney. Looking back, what I could reveal to the judge sounded somewhat superficial given I, as the boy's lawyer, couldn't talk about mice and guitar strings. To do so would have given the SA fuel for the fire, and they would have brought down a search warrant on my house and Uncle Tim's to look for mice and wires.

When we are finished, the State's Attorney pulls me aside in the hallway. He's a low-key man, modest in dress and speech, a lifer, who has always played straight with me in prior cases and has never presented with an ax to grind. Anton Melendez is average height, black hair, dark skin, and wears two small diamond earrings in his left ear, which you would have thought would be anathema to the straight arrow image prosecutors always like to present, but Melendez somehow gets away with it and, given his laid-

back demeanor, seems to fit him. He says laconically, "Have
you thought about a plea in this case?"

"Not really," I say. "We're still at the very edges of our investigation."

"I hear your investigator, Marcel, has been talking to anyone
and everyone. It sounds like you're covering all the bases."

"Yes, we're putting time in on the case. The defendant is my
priest's son. That's a long story. So I feel an inevitability
about the dues I need to pay since the priest all but raised
me when I was young."

"Got it. I had the same influence in my life growing up in
Mexico City. We were the lucky ones. So, why don't you
wrap it up and then call me? Let's see if we can dispose of
this one without trial."

I am taken aback. I am startled, in fact.

"This is the mayor's daughter. I would have thought there
would be no plea offer ever. What happened?"

"The mayor's legal staff has been privy to all our discovery.
The facts aren't a hundred percent in the State's favor,
Michael. But you already know that, and I'm not telling you
anything you don't know."

"My thinking, too. You can't place my guy with the dead
girl."

"Well, there is the muffler. It turns out your guy's DNA is all
over it."

The DNA testing on the muffler is back. He's right about it
containing Jana's DNA.

"True. For what it's worth."

"That's part of it. When you see our discovery, you'll learn more, too."

"Well, let me finish up, and I'll give you a holler."

"What's the nitty gritty on your request to change his living situation? Can you explain for me?"

I shake my head. "Not really. It's just uncomfortable for my wife, having him live with us. Not much else to say, in fact."

"Wives can be like that."

I can't mention the real reason—our suspicions—so I don't. Instead, I come off sounding vague, and that's fine. We both know there's more. He just doesn't know what else there is, and it's my job now to keep him in the dark.

I head back to my office, three blocks on foot.

* * *

Sitting in my office at my desk, I finish studying Marcel's file memos and set them aside. Then I buzz him into my office.

"This kid," I begin as soon as he walks in.

He lifts a ham-sized hand. "I know," he says. "Damned if he does, damned if he doesn't."

"Let's take them one at a time and see what we have," I say. "Catch that door."

Marcel shuts the door to my office while I buzz Mrs. Lingscheit and tell her no interruptions.

"Let me get Danny in here, too."

I buzz Danny, and moments later she comes in and takes a seat in a client chair.

"How's Dania doing in her new digs?" I ask Danny. We've taken a spare office and outfitted it with baby gear, plus made it into a toddler playroom. We did this spur of the moment because Danny refuses to leave Dania alone in the house when there's a chance Jana might be there with her. Priscilla now comes to our office to perform her nanny duties.

"Sleeping. It's quiet in there, and Priscilla's done wonders. Dania has everything she could need or even want."

"Good, good."

"Yes. But we need to talk about long-term. He's got to go, Michael."

Marcel says, "Do you want me to go out while you discuss this?"

"No, stay put," I tell him. "You're in on our protection all the way. Speaking of which, do you have any ideas how we might dislodge Jana from our home without sending him back to jail?"

"Whoa, what am I missing here?" Marcel says. "Why the sudden ejection of the kid?"

We explain to Marcel what we've found out. I show him the M.E.'s report.

"I hope she was already dead when he placed the mouse."

"You're saying maybe she was alive when he put the mouse in her mouth?" I reply.

Marcel shrugs. "Do you have any proof she wasn't?"

Danny and I look at each other.

"I guess not. I guess the thought was so revolting I just didn't go there," Danny says.

"Me, too," I add.

"Well, there you are. Weird is weird. I prefer not to rule out any possibilities when I'm approaching an investigation. It only gets as weird as the human imagination can manufacture. You both know by now that that dynamic is without limit. Until a few minutes ago, I thought I'd seen it all. Now I know *again* that I haven't."

Marcel is thoughtful for several moments. He rubs his eyes. Then he gets down to the issue. "Do you have a guest house or an apartment over the garage or something?"

"No."

"What about getting him his own apartment?"

Danny and I look at each other.

"I like that," Danny says. "That works for me."

"But the judge won't go for it I don't think," I reply. "He's not in our custody if we do, and having him in our custody was the whole point."

"Let me think about it," Marcel says. "I'll bet my devious little brain can come up with something."

"Do that." Danny smiles at him. "But please hurry."

He squeezes her arm and nods. "Sure, that."

I'm eager to get into the case proper. I say, "All right. We've got Amy Tanenbaum, who was murdered. We've got Jana at the football game that night, but his Uncle Tim says it ain't so. Whatever."

"What's Jana say?" asks Danny.

"He told me he was there," I reply. "He said he wasn't with Amy. He said he didn't kill her, either."

"Told me the same thing," says Marcel.

"That's nice," says Danny, "given he's staying in our guest bedroom."

"Touché," I tell her. She will not leave it alone. And she's right.

"So. Aren't you going to tell me how it went this morning? What did Winny say when you asked her for different accommodations for our little houseguest?"

I sigh. "Winny wouldn't hear of him moving out. She said she made her original placement with us based on many factors. And she ruled out Uncle Tim as a possible placement option."

Marcel suggests, "Did you ask about him moving in with his dad?"

I shake my head. "Moving into the priests' apartments? That wouldn't work."

Danny persists, "Why on earth not? I'm sure Father Bjorn has an extra room. If not, he damn sure has a couch where Jana could flop."

"Okay, I'll talk to him."

"And ask the judge again," Danny says. It isn't a request; it's a demand.

I blow out a breath. "Okay, moving right along. We've also received the DNA study. Jana's DNA is all over the red muffler they found near Amy's body."

"Which means one of two things," says Marcel. "Either it dropped through the bleachers or Jana was under the bleachers at some point."

"Maybe he was under the bleachers before someone murdered Amy," says Danny.

"Why would that be?" I ask.

"I don't know. Maybe someone else dropped something, and he went under looking for it? I don't know. I'm just saying it's a possibility."

"It is a possibility," I agree, "but we don't want to go there, never. We can't have Jana under the bleachers."

"You didn't tell me about the DNA," Danny blurts out. "How long have you known?"

"A few days maybe."

"Were you keeping it from me?"

"I don't think he did that," Marcel begins.

"I'm talking to my husband!" Danny snaps. "Let him answer, please."

I want to reach for her hand, but she's sitting in a visitor chair across from me with her arms crossed over her chest. She's definitely not a happy woman at this moment. "No one was keeping anything from anyone else. It just hadn't come up yet."

"Don't you think I would have wanted to know? That's our baby we're talking about, two doors down from that guest bedroom! You know what? I'm going to take Dania and move into a hotel until this gets sorted out. I'm done with all this."

I look at her, and her look back at me is a pure challenge. The glove has been thrown down. And wouldn't you know it? I can't argue with her. In fact, in a way, I'm relieved my females will be away from Jana.

"I like that idea," I say slowly. "You might not think I do, but I do."

She sniffs and finger-combs her blond hair. "See? All I want to do is get Dania away from Jana. It will work better if I move her out."

Then I'm depressed at what that means. We'll be living apart.

We'll be separated.

"Before you use a credit card," I say, "let me talk to Father Bjorn. Maybe he can step up."

"Fine, you do that. But until you have Jana dislodged, Dania and I aren't coming home. Pure and simple, so you do what you need to do, Michael."

* * *

An hour later, I've spoken with Father Bjorn on the telephone. The church won't allow a priest to have a roommate or guest living with him in the priests' quarters. It just isn't done. So that's out. The church also frowns on priests being fathers. So I decide it's not best to push the issue.

"Is it that bad?" Father Bjorn asks me.

I tell him about the mouse and the missing guitar string.

"Michael, I would never have involved you in this if I'd known. Please, I apologize to you and Danny. And Dania. I'm sorry. Maybe the best thing is to let him go back to jail. I don't want to see you and Danny living apart because of my son. That just isn't right."

"I'm leaning more that way," I say, and I surprise myself. It's the first time I've considered letting him return to jail. "I'll reach out to his mom first. I'll see if I can arrange something with her and then ask the judge if that works."

"Naomi will be tough to work with. I've spoken with her twice since the arrest. She cannot handle our son. He refuses to listen to her and tells her to go to hell."

"I wish I'd known that going in," I say. "That puts him in a whole different light."

"Yes, I think it's time for him to return to jail. Naomi isn't a solution."

"All right. I'll talk with him. Wish me luck."

"No, but I'll say a prayer for you. A good prayer."

"I need it. We all need it, Father."

"Yes, we do."

22

I don't waste any time with it. That night when I get home, Jana is already inside his room with the door closed. I can hear Metallica blasting loud and angry. It pisses me off to have him there at all now that Danny and Dania aren't coming home. Something needs to be done without delay.

I knock on his door. It opens after I knock a second time.

"Turn that down, Jana," I shout into the wall of sound that greets me.

He complies, and the song ends.

"Thank you."

It smells of pot smoke. His eyes are glassy, and there's a sloppy smile on his face.

"You're smoking in here," I say and wave my hand as if to cut the smoke. "You know the rule."

"No, dude, I'm not."

"Dude, you are," I tell him.

"All right. Busted. But it was only two hits to relax me before I crack the books."

"Jana, this living arrangement isn't working for anyone."

He flops down on his bed and places his back against the wall. He fiddles with the knee of his jeans.

"I guess," he says absently.

"I've talked to your dad, and now Danny's moved out with Dania. She's uncomfortable with you here."

"Oh, no, man, we can't have that. I'll leave."

"Where would you go? You know the judge placed you with me."

"Then what should I do?"

"I'll ask the court to modify conditions of release so you can go back to your Uncle Tim's. That's the only choice left."

"My dad won't even take me, will he?"

"The church won't allow it. Otherwise, he would take you. I think he'd love to get a chance to live with his son."

"Well, we'll never know, will we now?"

* * *

The next morning, SA Anton Melendez and I again approach Judge Winifred Lancer-Burgess in her chambers during a court recess.

It does not please her that we're here again and she speaks sharply to me. "So, Mr. Gresham, you're still unhappy with the court's placement? Do I need to return the young man to jail?"

"I'm here to vouch for his uncle, Tim O'Donnell. He's a plumber by trade, single with two spare bedrooms in his house. He is a light drinker, doesn't use drugs, and has no criminal history."

"What's wrong with the current placement, Mr. Gresham?"

"It's my wife. We have a toddler, and she doesn't like a man we don't know living with us. Plain and simple."

"She was in court when I made the original placement. She seemed happy enough with it then."

"She just didn't know what it would feel like. Now she does."

The judge blows a stream of air upward to her bangs. They move away from her forehead.

"Very well. I'm going to leave the placement as is, but I'm going to amend to give you the right to place the boy physically with Tim O'Donnell, the boy's uncle. What's the State's position?"

"No resistance, Your Honor," says Mr. Melendez.

"The order will issue this afternoon. I'm also having the sheriff verify the uncle's lack of a criminal record, Mr. Gresham. Let's hope the representation you've made to the court of a clean record proves true. If it doesn't, I'm sending your young man back to jail without further comment. Do we understand each other?"

"We do, Your Honor." It's the best we can do. If there's any criminal record on Uncle Tim, I can't help. I'm done; I want my wife and daughter back in our house with me where they belong.

"Very well, we're in recess. Please clear my office, gentlemen. I need a smoke."

We say our thanks and leave. Outside in the hallway, I clap Melendez on the shoulder and give him my sincere thanks for working with me on the issue. He smiles and nods and heads off to the elevator. I stop off in the men's room and use the urinal, wash my hands at the sink, and then cup cold water into my face.

"Traitor," I say to my reflection.

But I don't mean it. I'm glad to see him go.

Now to tell Father Bjorn and prepare Uncle Tim.

23

J ana has been returned to Uncle Tim's, and last night after work, Danny and Dania returned home. All is well, calm is restored. Danny stayed home this morning to clean out Jana's old room and open the windows with the door closed. It's cold outside, and she knows the hot air of the house will carry out the smells and smoke. It can't happen fast enough for her. She arrives in the office after one and comes into my office to check in with me.

"His pot is gone. I searched every last nook and cranny. And I cleaned up anything that needed it. It was amazing it wasn't a mess. After all, he is a teenage boy. I always thought they couldn't be bothered cleaning up after themselves."

"Well, thanks for doing that. So much for having a defendant in a criminal case move in with us."

"Did you call Father Bjorn?"

"I did. He understands. In fact, he apologized to me and asked me to apologize to you for getting us into this mess."

"Accepted. Did you get Jana's front door key when you left with him?"

I snap my fingers. "Forgot. I'll get right on that."

"Please do. I don't want any unannounced drop-ins. Or break-ins."

"Please, let it go, Danny. It's all over. You're home safe and sound, Dania is home with Priscilla, and Jana's gone. Everything's okay again. Okay?"

"Okay."

"Now, let's get Marcel in here and let's look at Jana's legal case. It's time we resolve that, too. The State's Attorney was talking to me the other day like he was open to plea negotiations, so let's figure out our bottom line."

"Excellent." Danny seems much happier now, and that makes me happy.

I buzz Marcel, and he comes right in.

"Afternoon, you two," he says. "Mrs. Lingscheit tells me they have removed the problem child. So we're ready to move ahead with his case?"

"We are."

"Okay. You've read all my memos?"

"I have. Danny?"

"I have. Damn good workup, Marcel. You talked to everything and everyone that moved."

"Thank you. You know Michael's got a rule that everything gets touched in murder cases. So I started with the police reports and went from there. If someone visited someplace or other, I did, too. If they talked to someone, I did, too, and I also confirmed that what the police have in the police report is actually what they said. I recorded their statements. All recordings are in the file and online."

"Excellent," I say. None of his speech surprises me. He always does the best-ever workups on my cases. That's ninety percent of why I'm so successful, Marcel's follow-through. "So... are there any weak spots in the State's case against Jana?"

"I've talked to all the kids anywhere near the restrooms that night. Not one of them places Jana nearby. I even showed them his picture since he's new at the school. They all recognized him as the new guy, but they all swore up and down he wasn't near the restrooms when they were using them."

"Well done. So the police aren't able to place Jana near the restroom."

"No, and CSI found her blood in the far stall of the restroom. Evidently, the string or wire had severed her carotid there, and blood spatters were up and down the walls inside the stall. And on the floor."

"What about other DNA? On the toilet seat, the floor, the sinks?"

"Only Amy's and other samples from other people. They tested it against Jana and got nada."

"What about his clothes he was wearing that night? Did they find any blood on any of his clothes?"

"You know, the kid didn't have much, but they took everything and tested everything."

"And?"

"Nothing. No blood, no Amy DNA, nothing."

"So he sounds more innocent by the minute."

"Well, there is the matter of the guitar string you found missing from his set."

"Yes, there is that. But we didn't buy him that guitar until after Amy's murder, and unless there's a nexus between the strings on his guitar and the wire or string that cut the girl's throat, Jana's missing string means zip. It's all circumstantial evidence; he might use the same brand of guitar string that killed the girl."

"What about his mice?" says Danny. "Has anyone tested the DNA of the mouse removed from her mouth with any mice Jana has? Or any mice at Petco?"

Marcel and I stare at each other, our mouths hanging open.

"No," I say.

And Marcel follows up with, "Not that I know, no."

She looks at both of us. "Well, there you are," she says, "the possibility of a smoking gun."

"Except the detectives, one, don't know Jana uses mice and, two, don't know where he gets them."

"Well, all I'm saying is you'd better hope it remains that way. This case needs to be pled out to a lesser charge before they find out about his mice. That would put him away for life."

"She's right," Marcel says.

"I know," I agree. "She's right. But damn, I'd like to see the M.E.'s mouse get sampled and compared. Who knows what might turn up?"

"What if..." says Danny, still playing devil's advocate. "What if they sampled the found mouse for Jana's DNA on its body? Has that been done?"

"We don't have any reports showing that," I say.

"Yet," she says.

"OMG," I whisper. "That could be the smoking gun if they found Jana's DNA on the dead mouse."

"Or if they matched the Super Glue to his tube of Super Glue," she says.

"Why, did you find Super Glue in his room?"

She draws a deep breath and shudders. "I did. About half a tube."

"Oh, my God," I say. "This isn't good."

"We don't have to turn over evidence of a crime to the police, do we?" Marcel asks.

"We do if we don't want to be charged with obstruction of justice if they find out," I reply. "Let me do some reading on it."

Danny gives me the stink eye. "Please do."

24

S heriff Thomas Meekins' widow, Greta, is a medium
height, large-framed woman wearing her long hair up
in a bun and her octagonal eyeglasses high on her nose. She
seems warm but is operating in a fog of shock as she enters
my office, barely speaking, scarcely looking at Attorney
Larry Glickstein, whom I have asked to meet with us. Larry
is a long-time friend, the attorney to whom I often refer civil
cases when my criminal law skills are of no use. This time
around, I intend to see him take on Mrs. Meekins' wrongful
death case.

"Mrs. Meekins, this is Larry Glickstein. Larry is Chicago's
top civil litigator in jail negligence, and I believe he is the
man who can best help you at this point."

Greta holds out her hand and makes eye contact with Larry.
She offers him a small smile in response to his warm hello.

We take a seat, and I hit the high points of the situation that
has brought us together.

Then Larry takes over, asking follow-on questions about Sheriff Meekins, the family, and any financial issues they might be facing with his sudden loss.

"We've had a visit from the county board supervisor. He's explained all of the benefits my family qualifies for. Also, I'll be seeing Social Security next week about survivors' benefits and children's benefits."

"That sounds excellent," Larry says. "I would also like you to consider allowing me to seek a pre-filing settlement with the Chicago Police Department. I say this because this is a case they will never win and, if they act forthrightly and honestly, they can avoid some of the negative publicity and expense of litigation they will otherwise be facing."

Greta shifts her weight in the seat and crosses her legs. "I didn't think of that, but I don't see why not. The main thing, Mr. Glickstein, is I want to make sure this never happens to another prisoner. He should have been medicated. He shouldn't have been allowed to have anything he could kill himself with, and so on. It's a terrible loss to a family, and I don't want anyone else to ever have to go through this."

"We'll try to impose new directives on the Cook County Sheriff in how he runs his jail. Plus, there's the medical aspect of providing inmate care. I quite agree this was a senseless tragedy that could have been avoided by the simplest of precautions. Let's you and I work together to see if we can protect the next Tom Meekins from hurting himself. I invite you to do that with me."

"We should. I accept. Also, the kids want to go to college, but who's going to send them now with Tommy gone? Who do they turn to? All I have is high school level clerical skills. I was a stay-at-home mom who was and is on-call around the clock, so I won't be able to help much. My heart is broken and so are my kids'."

"Well," I add, "I'm so glad you were both able to come here today. It sounds like you can help one another achieve some very worthy goals and provide for the children. I like what I'm hearing."

With that, the conversation drifts along and plans are made for the two of them to meet later in the week in Larry's office. There are papers to be drawn up and signed and jail reports to be obtained. After that, I am confident Greta Meekins is in the best hands possible.

I have carried Tom's water as far as I can.

It is time for me to move on.

25

A month after the initial hearing, I file to dismiss the case against Guy Lafitte. The basis for my motion is that the State has failed to provide me with the sample I requested for testing. My request was in writing, and I attach a copy with my motion. The law is unambiguous.

Two weeks later, that motion is argued, and I win. The case against Lafitte, the drug dealer of the bad bank checks, is dismissed with prejudice once the State admits the contraband is missing from the police evidence room. Evidently, they've searched the entire storage building, and Lafitte's cocaine was clocked in but then disappeared. It's simply run off on its own, we are led to believe. The judge is disgusted, and the case is over.

Interestingly enough, I get a call from my Vietnamese friend Phun Loc that same afternoon. The grand jury has declined to prosecute her. She believes it's because they have "obeyed the First Amendment and let her have free speech." She says she hasn't been back near the President's house since the grand jury call. I believe that's why she hasn't been indicted. The Secret Service subpoenas loonies and forces them to appear for grand jury testimony, and that puts the fear of God in them. It's got nothing to do with the First Amendment, and I tell her so.

Deaf ears. She's determined her First Amendment rights have carried the day.

She says she's planning to return to the sidewalk in front of his house.

I tell her that would be a huge mistake.

She laughs and chides me for being, in her words, a weenie.

I cross her off my possible client list. I won't be there for her when she comes back, her tail between her legs. And she will be back.

The Secret Service, like Neil Young's rust, never sleeps.

26

D anny and I are just sitting down to supper with Dania in her high chair mashing peas with the heel of her hand when the doorbell sounds.

"Police!" I hear a male voice call out. "Open the door!"

Danny and I trade a quick look. She shrugs as I'm standing. Then I'm moving into the hallway and up to the front door. I pull it wide open.

There, standing on our porch, is a group of six police officials, two in plainclothes, two in the uniform of the CSI, and two uniformed CPD patrolmen. The nearest plainclothes officer hands me three papers stapled together.

"Search warrant, Mr. Gresham, please stand aside."

Without waiting for my response, they enter, the uniforms waiting outside, to provide perimeter security while the search progresses. Unless I miss my guess, there are two more uniforms already around back watching the back door and yard.

As they bustle past me, I scan over the documents. What I've been handed is a search warrant signed by a Cook County Judge, directing these CPD representatives to enter my house and search for evidence of the crime involving Amy Tanenbaum's murder. The mayor has been busy, I see, motivating the cops to go the extra mile and search the home of Jana's attorney. Then it becomes clear; they're here because Jana at one time lived here. That's why they're searching.

"Mr. Gresham, I'm Detective Singh," says the first detective who has now doubled back. "Would you show me the bedroom where Jana Emerich was housed while he was living here?"

"Certainly." I lead him back to Jana's old bedroom.

He touches my shoulder so I do not enter. "Please return to the dining room table, sir. I'll take it from here," says the detective.

I do as I'm told. Danny reaches over and takes the search warrant from me and reads. Meanwhile, Dania is guzzling milk from her sippy cup, oblivious to her parents' dilemma.

"What fruits of the murder would we have?" Danny asks me. "He was only here a short time."

"Relax. It's a fishing expedition. They don't have any particular articles in mind. They're just nosing around, hoping to come across something useful."

"You seem damn sure of that," she says.

"You're angry with me? As I remember, you were in court, too, when we agreed to take Jana in. You could have told me no, and I would have moved along to some other scenario, Danny."

She nods and reaches out to brush a gob of masticated food from Dania's bib.

"You're right. I'm just really upset with this. I feel violated."

"You're not alone there. I do, too."

"Has this ever happened before?"

"Never."

My cell phone vibrates in my pocket. I answer.

"Michael?"

"Yes?"

"This is Tim O'Donnell. The cops are here with a search warrant. They want to search Jana's room. They're turning it upside down. What should I do?"

"Not much you can do, Tim. Just let them search."

"They've got Jana and me on the couch in the living room. They're going through drawers, cupboards, unzipping cushions, the whole nine yards, man."

"Yes, we've got the same thing going on over here, Tim. Just relax. They'll leave in an hour or two."

"Holy shit! They're taking the trap out from under the kitchen sink and pouring its contents into a jar."

"They'll do that. Just sit tight, Tim."

"Okay, thanks."

"We'll talk again when they're gone. I'll call you."

"Fair enough."

We ended the call. What we would later learn from Tim was that the police detectives and crime scene techs entered his house at about the same time they were entering mine. They proceeded to the room where Jana was housed and stripped it down to the drywall. Everything was removed, including carpet, quarter-round and doorway molding, curtains, books from the bookcase, snake container, mouse box, wood shavings contained in a Petco bag for the snake's bedding replacement. The mice were kept inside a metal toolbox for Leonard when he got hungry. They grabbed that box and its bedding, too. Leonard was cooperative and hid in his house while prying eyes and hands examined every inch of his abode. The three mice scurried and scampered and tried to scale the metal walls.

The Fender guitar was taken along with, presumably, the set of strings contained in the built-in box within. Jana was shoved up against the wall in the hallway and his pockets turned inside out. Then the crime scene techs spread out through the house, searching the other two bedrooms in much the same manner as Jana's, winding up in the kitchen where the sink trap was removed and its contents saved. The same was done in both bathrooms. Incidentally, Tim would tell us, the cops also didn't bother to put the plumbing back together, leaving that for Tim. Luckily, Tim was a plumber, and it was a minor task for him to reassemble the pipes and drains.

Next, the detectives searched Tim and his current lady but seized nothing from them.

While the other team was over at Tim's taking his place apart, the team in my house was likewise occupied, pulling the carpet away from the floor in Jana's old room and vacuuming the carpet and pad beneath with a small hand vac that was loud and most likely powerful. As I watched and heard what was transpiring, I knew this wasn't just a harassment search, though it was certainly upsetting. No, this search was as thorough as any the cops ever performed, always digging down to the next layer and seizing at each opportunity. They even removed the sheets from Jana's bed and took those, though I couldn't imagine why. Finally, they removed the filters from our washer and dryer and seized those contents, too.

The detectives knew it was futile when they returned to the dining room, sat down with us without being invited, and put a recorder on the table between us. We refused to make any statements. Still, it was a departmental policy they try, so there we were.

"Mr. Gresham, I'm Detective Ngo, and we have previously met. You have appeared in court with Jana Emerich and are listed as his attorney, correct?"

"That's correct."

"And what is your name, ma'am?"

"Dania Gresham. I'm a partner in Mr. Gresham's law firm and, by extension, represent Jana Emerich, so neither will I be answering any of your questions."

"And who is this?" says the tall black detective, indicating our daughter.

"This is Dania," Danny says, "As you can see, she's busy reconstructing the crime scene with her supper."

Ngo laughs, and the tension is broken.

"Well, sorry for the mess, Mr. and Mrs. Gresham, but it could have been much worse. Hope you'll forgive us."

"I might, but my wife won't," I say. "She'll be pissed when she sees what a mess you've made of our guest bedroom."

"Sorry, ma'am," says Ngo. "Sincerely sorry. Just doing our job."

"Sure you were," says Dania. "Pulling up my guest room carpet is in your detectives' manual, isn't it? Right there on the page 'get hosed'?"

"Now," I say and put my hand over Danny's.

The detective sighs and pushes up from our table.

"You'll receive a copy of the search warrant return by email," he says and leaves. Ten minutes later the team is gone from our premises.

I read the notice contained on the second page of the search warrant he's left behind, outlining what happens next:

Sec. 108-10. Return to court of things seized.

A return of all instruments, articles, or things seized shall be made without unnecessary delay before the judge issuing the warrant or before any judge named in the warrant or before any court of competent jurisdiction. An inventory of any instruments, articles, or things seized shall be filed with the return and signed under oath by the officer or person executing the warrant. The judge shall upon request deliver a copy of the inventory to the person from whom or from whose premises the instruments, articles, or things were taken and to the applicant for the warrant.

Danny reads it over next. "So that's what he means when he said we'll receive a copy of the search warrant return by email?"

"Yes, we'll be told what items they seized while they were here. We'll also receive those from the court to our office file as the attorneys of record."

"Shall we go look at our guest room?" Danny says.

"Let's do it."

Danny brushes off Dania with a damp cloth and hikes her up onto her hip. The three of us proceed to Jana's old room.

"Oh, my God!" Danny exclaims, and then she turns her face into my shoulder and cries. Dania, meanwhile, is sucking at her fingers, her head bobbing around as she ignores the pandemonium we have found ourselves within. In cops' parlance, the room has been tossed, which is an understatement. It looks like a bomb was set off. The carpet was peeled back and left doubled up against the wall. The underlayment, the rubbery mat, has been cut and taken away. The moldings and quarter-round wood pieces were pulled out and left hanging. The bed was stripped, and the bed covers and sheets seized. Every book in the bookcase had been pulled out and riffled. Some older volumes came apart, and their pages lie scattered on the rubber matting. These were my college yearbooks. We open the closet door and find all garments missing, and the extra blankets that Danny kept on the upper shelf.

"These guys are very serious," I say under my breath, and Danny, from behind me, stifles a sob.

"Oh, Michael! What will we do in here?"

"Well, first, we'll get carpet people in. Hell, maybe this is a good time to re-carpet the whole house."

We had hardwood floors until just before Dania's birth but switched to carpet to soften those head-first landings that kids take.

"The carpet we have is still new. Let's think about just our guest room."

"They might not be able to match it," I caution her.

"Whatever. I'll call them in the morning."

We spend another half hour going through things, trying to figure out what's missing.

Then I call Tim back as promised.

"It looks like a tornado went through here," he says.

"Yeah, same on our end. How's Jana holding up?"

"Fine. A bit sour for all his things they took."

"Yeah, that's to be expected."

"Craziest thing. They took all of Leonard's bedding. And the mouse bedding."

"What's that mean?"

"You know, the sawdust he crawls around in. They took all that. The stuff in the cage, the new stuff in the bag, and the stuff Jana had dumped into his wastebasket. Same with the mice, all their bedding."

The memory of the mouse comes to mind. Hair. They're looking to match mouse hair with mouse hair. The mouse in Amy's mouth had hair. Match that to hair left behind in the snake's bedding or mouse bedding, and there's the smoking gun. The mouse had to have come from Jana's menagerie.

I feel like someone has struck me down. The roof is caving in, and I see it coming. If there's a match between the hair on the mouse removed from Amy's mouth to any mouse hair found in Jana's room, he's going away for a long, long time.

"Why take the bedding?" Tim asks.

"We'll just have to wait and see."

"Sons of bitches," says Tim.

"Just doing their job," I remind him. "You would do the same if you were a cop."

"I'm glad I'm a plumber. I dismantle people's stuff, but then I put it all back together again before I leave."

"Yeah, well, cops don't. You're fair game to them."

"Can't I sue them for the mess or something?"

"You can try it in small claims but, trust me, you'll get nowhere. Just suck it up and clean."

"Okay, Michael. Thanks for calling."

We say goodbye and disconnect.

I find Danny in the kitchen where she is pouring herself a glass of port.

"Dinner is cold," she says.

"I'll order something delivered," I tell her. "Put your feet up. Where's tiddlywinks?"

"She got crabby, so she's in her bed, singing to herself and kicking her legs at her mobile."

"Sounds good. I'm going in to kiss her goodnight."

"Kiss her for me, too. I doubt I'll leave this chair again tonight, Michael."

"Be right back."

"Michael, one other thing."

"What's that?"

"They found the Super Glue."

"Jana's Super Glue. Where was it?"

"In my briefcase. I was keeping it there."

"They took it?"

"It's not there now. It's got my prints all over it. And maybe Jana's, too."

On my way back down the hallway, I can think of nothing but mice.

Mice, dammit, big, fat mice.

Then thoughts of the Super Glue take hold, and I know we're in trouble. Danny has inadvertently injected herself into the case.

I enter Dania's room and find her sound asleep. I turn her onto her side. Her breathing is deep and steady.

I hold my hand on her shoulder, and I know that, for the first time, I have found the pure innocence my clients never have.

Not Jana, not Tom Meekins, not Guy Lafitte, not Phun Loc.

And now, not Danny, either.

27

The search warrant returns come by email four days after the searches. The number of items seized from my house and Tim's is nothing short of astonishing. All told, there are at least fifty items seized from my house, and it looks to be over one hundred from Tim's.

I shut my office door and sit back to digest the list of items. There is one thing that I search for on the list of items from my house and that is the tube of Super Glue. They state its location as ISP crime lab. They're comparing the glue in the tube to the glue that held the victim's lips together that required the medical examiner to cut into the oral cavity to get inside. It was a mess and disfigured the young girl. The funeral was closed casket, but it would have been even without that, given the hemorrhages in her eyes and the terrible cuts on her neck where she was garroted. When someone is strangled, it is common for their eyes to hemorrhage. Even a deceased loved one presented to the family with her eyes closed by the mortician is no guarantee that her eyes remain that way, given how people might touch a loved one. Some people, I have been told by morticians over the years, even take pictures of their dead loved ones in remembrance of their last moments on earth. That one escapes me, but I try not to judge such things.

At any rate, the Super Glue has been scraped away from the victim's lips and samples preserved for further testing. I am confident that both the batch number of the Super Glue in the tube and that from the skin samples are being tested for a match. But the bad part is that if there is a match, then Danny's having possession of the tube of glue constitutes an ethical violation.

"An attorney is required to turn over evidence of a crime," I tell her when she comes into my office and we review the lists together.

"I agree. It's not confidential."

"It's not. What is confidential are statements made by the accused to his lawyer. That is protected, and you must keep that confidential. What is not confidential are items you receive from your client that constitute evidence of the crime. That must be turned over by you. Failure to do so is both a crime and an ethical impropriety."

"So I will be charged with a crime?"

"Not likely. Your response is that you meant to turn the glue over and were taking it with you to the office to do that. That's why it was in your briefcase in the first place."

"But that's not why I had it."

"Why did you have it?"

"I was planning on testing it."

"What was your thinking?"

Her hands shake, and she pulls at the scarf around her neck.

"I was going to obtain a sample from the DA and have it tested against the tube I removed from Jana's room. Then I was going to decide."

"Decide what?"

"Decide what to do with it. I was confused. We're defending Father Bjorn's son, Michael. That's got to mean something to us. Imagine how horrible it would be if we turned over the one item that got him convicted, like the tube of Super Glue? We couldn't ever go to church again."

I edge around my desk and then pull her to her feet and hug her.

"No need to ever do something like that," I whisper. "Next time, tell me. Let me make that decision about how to handle it. Okay?"

"Okay."

"Good. Now let's go over the rest of this list."

28

I t is now late November and trial is slated to begin the seventh of January. One month, more or less, until we take Jana back to court. We have received the crime lab reports, and we have received a list of the State's witnesses and their probable testimony. Marcel has been busy taking the statements of those witnesses who would speak to him. Smooth as he is, and as understated as he can be, there were still several students whose parents had told them not to speak with Marcel. Someone had told them to speak with no one except the police and the DA's office. Which is entirely legal and entirely within their rights. In the U.S., witnesses have no obligation to speak with the defense or its representatives. Open and shut.

Then a strange thing happens. The police return to Tim's house with a second search warrant. They come in the evening when he is home. Straight to the hall closet they go where they seize his winter coat and an army surplus work coat. Then they search the other closets in the house. Within ten minutes, they finish and are walking out the door when Tim complains to them about the loss of his coats. Without answering his questions and complaints, they abruptly leave. So he calls me.

"Tell me about the coat with the scarf. Does Jana ever wear that?"

"Well, sometimes. When he moved back here from Santa Monica, he had no cold weather gear. So he wore some of my stuff a few times until I got paid and could get him a coat of his own. I'm sure he's the one who lost my red muffler on one of his jaunts here or there."

"Like maybe to a football game?"

Tim is silent for several moments.

"I told you, Mr. Gresham, Jana wasn't at that game where the Tanenbaum girl was killed. Why don't you believe me?"

"I'm having trouble with it because they found a red muffler that Jana was seen wearing at the game near the girl's dead body. You should be having trouble, too!"

"Well, say he sneaked out that night without me knowing. And say he wore my coat. What's it about that coat that would make the cops make a special trip out here to grab it?"

"Mouse hair."

"What in the hell are you talking about?"

"They found a dead mouse at the scene."

"What the hell has that got to do with my coat?"

"Does Jana keep mice?"

"Sometimes."

"And if he took a mouse to the football game, wouldn't it make sense if he hid it inside a pocket of the coat he was wearing? Your coat?"

"Oh, holy shit!"

"Now you see where they're going with this?"

"Oh, my God! Are they gonna think I was there and killed the girl?"

"Hold on, slow down. You were home with Ruby, your dispatcher. Ruby can establish that. Plus, someone saw Jana at the game wearing the muffler, not you. Several witnesses will testify to that. You're clear. It's Jana you need to be worrying about, not yourself."

"I didn't mean I was worried."

"Like hell you didn't, Tim. You were worried, but you were worried about the wrong guy. Jana wore your coat and your muffler to the game that night, and you might as well get used to that idea. A bunch of people saw him there. And you didn't have your eyes on him all night because you thought he was upstairs in his room. Well, he wasn't. He went to the game."

"Why wouldn't he tell me?"

"Why would he take a mouse with him?"

"Because he planned to use it for something?"

"Now you're getting warmer, Uncle Tim. Very warm."

29

According to an entry of appearance I have received in today's mail at the office, Jana's case has now been assigned to State's Attorney Trey Dickinson. I run the name through an online list of biographies and find out Mr. Dickinson is the third in a long line of Chicago attorneys. His grandfather founded one of Chicago's premier criminal law firms in the 1940's, and his father practiced law in that same firm from the 1970's to present. Trey evidently went to work for the Cook County State's Attorney right out of law school, and he chalked up a record of 65-0 over the first three years of his term as a career prosecutor.

On Thursday, we meet in the office of Judge Winifred Lancer-Burgess. We are thirty-eight days out from trial, and it is time for the regularly scheduled status conference on the case. Attending are me, Danny, and Mr. Dickinson.

Judge Lancer-Burgess is a feather of a woman with a huge, deep voice. It's pretty clear she's still smoking cigarettes even though she's in her sixties and should know better. Her skin has the sallow, grayish sheen of a smoker, and I can see a hint of nicotine-stained fingers on her right hand. She brushes the comma of gray hair from her forehead and examines the file briefly. Then she looks up. "Gentlemen and lady, I set this case for trial January seven. Have you had any plea negotiations to date?"

I begin, "Your Honor, Mr. Dickinson and I have spoken by telephone. Some time ago I thought the State wanted to discuss a plea, but now it seems they don't. That's the sum and substance of what I know as we sit here today."

Her gaze swings to her left. "Mr. Dickinson?"

"Your Honor, early in this case we thought we had a problem linking the defendant to the victim at the football game. Now we have discovered other evidence that makes that link for us."

"What evidence is that, counsel?"

Dickinson flips through his notes. It is clear to me he is planning how he will say what he will. It's obvious to me that the State has been hard at work on the mayor's daughter's case. I will not like what I'm about to hear.

"Well, we have discovered physical evidence at the scene that links the defendant to the scene."

"Counsel," says the judge, "you're playing hide-the-ball with the court. Please come out and tell us what you mean?"

"Mouse hair, Your Honor. We have mouse hair."

The judge's lips curl into the beginning of a sneer.

"Yes, Judge, mouse hair. A mouse was taken from the victim's mouth at the medical examiner's autopsy. The hair on that mouse was compared to hair samples seized from the defendant's mouse cage, bedroom, and clothing. There is a definite match between the two hair samples, which, we will argue, implicates the defendant as the killer. Plain and simple."

"Mr. Gresham? What's your position on this?"

"Your Honor, until this very minute, I wasn't aware the State had any such evidence. My position is that I would like the court to direct the State to provide me with hair samples so that I can arrange independent testing for my client."

"Counsel," she says to Dickinson, "I want samples in defense counsel's office by close of business today. Do you understand me?"

"I will do it, Your Honor. And there's more. We also have a tube of Super Glue seized from the briefcase of Ms. Gresham here. That batch of Super Glue matches the batch taken from the victim's mouth."

Danny begins, "I was about to turn that glue over to the police. That's why it was in my briefcase."

"I'm sure you were, Ms. Gresham," says Judge Lancer-Burgess in a low voice. "Not to worry."

Danny's face relaxes. The judge is taking her side on any possible argument that she might have been obstructing justice by keeping evidence away from the police. Score one for the defense, anyway.

"So, Mr. State's Attorney, where does that put us concerning plea negotiations."

"First-degree murder, Your Honor," says Dickinson, "with the possibility of parole."

"Mr. Gresham?"

"That's impossible, Judge. We might just as well go to trial. The defendant has nothing to lose."

"Except that he might be sentenced to life with no possibility of parole," says the judge, insinuating that she might do just that. I have no response for her. That sentencing provision is entirely within her discretion, and we will argue against that if I refuse the State's offer and lose the case.

"There won't be a guilty plea," I tell the judge, but I am instantly struck by the realization I have zero idea what my defense will be for Jana. The mouse hair, the glue, the muffler—he is one hundred percent guilty, according to most of the juries I've ever worked with. I can already hear the testimony in my mind, and I have no idea at all what questions to ask in response. Research is indicated as well as the investigation of other possible witnesses. Why no plea? Jana has told me he's innocent. I can't plead an innocent defendant to any crime. So there won't be a guilty plea.

"Very well. Are there any issues with evidence or witnesses?"

"No."

"No."

"Good. I don't want any last-minute *in camera* motions, is that clear?"

Meaning, she doesn't want last-minute day-of-trial motions that would slow down the jury trial, motions that could have been filed days or even weeks before. Jury slow-downs are anathema to judges. One would think their re-election constituency is composed entirely of those who have sat on juries in their courtroom, so anxious are all judges to keep their jurors happy. It goes with the territory, and as a defense lawyer, I always try to file motions well ahead of the trial.

Judge Lancer-Burgess, "If there's anything else, file a motion, and we'll jump right on it. Motion practice ends seven days before the trial except for emergencies. And I mean *emergencies*. If you file inside the cutoff, you better damn well be able to convince me it's some emergency or you'll be looking at sanctions. Any questions?"

"Does that mean all discovery has to be exchanged thirty days before trial?" I ask. "That's a good way to avoid last-minute motions. Otherwise, the Cook County State's Attorney Office is notorious for dumping discovery items on defense counsel the day before or the day of trial. That's a practice I hope we're avoiding here."

"It is, counsel," she says. "All discovery by December eight. I'm marking this case-ready status. That should do it. We're adjourned, lady and gentlemen."

We gather our papers and leave the judge's chambers.

In the hallway, I'm hopeful Dickinson makes a sudden offer that reduces from first degree to second.

But he doesn't. After all, it's the mayor's daughter.

Time to prepare. Time to do jury instructions, prepare opening statements, prepare direct and cross-examinations.

The ball is in play.

30

Priscilla's in tears. She is angrily stuffing her textbooks into her book bag as she prepares to leave.

We are in the family room. Dania is seated in front of the TV in her Tinkerbell chair, watching a cartoon while Priscilla and I are full-bore into the discussion of what exactly has prompted her to quit her job and leave our house.

I was at the office when I got her call. Danny was in court, so I'm the one who came rushing home. This is what I found out: Priscilla's alarm didn't go off at five a.m. this morning, so she was late to her workout. She arrived at her gym and worked out for the full hour nonetheless, and then skipped her shower, planning to shower here at our house. She came here on time and settled into getting Dania's breakfast. She then jumped into the shower for a quick rinse-off while leaving Dania in her playpen with a favorite book and toy. It would not take even five minutes.

While she was rinsing, she felt cool air coming in from outside the bathroom and heard the bathroom door open and close. Someone had entered, and she instantly knew it was Jana. She saw his form outside the shower curtain but kept rinsing off. Slowly, the end of the curtain was peeled back, and she suddenly stared eye-to-eye with Jana, who was having a quick look at her nakedness.

She screamed; Jana fled, slamming the door behind him. He did not try to close it quietly. He slammed it, and she felt the blast of cold air. She toweled off and shrugged into her underwear, jeans, and T-shirt and rushed into the family room to check on Dania. Dania was lying on her back, holding her book overhead, flipping through the pages. All good there. So then Priscilla rushed to the phone and called me. I told her to put Jana on the phone. She went to his old room and knocked, but no answer. She then searched the house, but he had evidently left.

So now she's in tears, we're losing our nanny, and I am furious with Jana. Enough is enough.

"You never got his key back," Danny says to me when I get her on the phone.

"You're right," I respond. "It escaped my mind. I'll call the locksmith."

"So now he can come and go whenever he wants until the locks are changed? That's great news, Michael. I want him arrested."

"God no," I say, "not right now. That could seriously impact his trial."

"So you don't think this is just as serious? That your daughter's nanny was assaulted by this little asshole?"

"I don't know. I only know I don't want the cops laying their hands on him right now. Trial begins in a week. Let's see how that turns out."

"Call the security service, Michael. Have them study the video. I want evidence for when I go to the police if you're not going to do it."

"Please. Hear me out, Danny. I'll have the locks changed today. He won't be able to gain access again."

"That little bastard," she says. "I could tear him a new one."

"I know, I know. So could I. But a first-degree murder case is a thousand times bigger deal than a Peeping-Tom case."

"Not to mention the burglary, also a felony when he came into our house."

"I'll call the security service right now."

"And you're sure Dania's okay?"

"She's right here on my lap, pulling my necktie."

"Okay, then."

We hang up, and I kiss my baby's forehead.

It's that innocence we all crave.

That's why we yearn to be children again.

31

Priscilla has agreed to stay on until after the trial. At least one issue had a solution. As for *State vs. Jana S. Emerich*, I'm still searching.

Jana came to me a day after the Priscilla Peeping-Tom incident. He was contrite and maybe embarrassed, but determined. Determined that I allow him to use another attorney and for me to "get off his case." I said that would be fine, but he would need to speak to his father first. He wanted to know why. Because, I told him, you don't have the money to hire another attorney. I stop short of telling him I haven't been paid for his defense and I'm defending him because of my love for Father Bjorn. He was confused by the time he left, saying he will see his dad. Which he did. Father Bjorn called me and begged me to stay on, which wasn't necessary. I wasn't planning on going anyplace, anyway. So, here we are, Jana and I, a team comprising a less-than-thrilled attorney and a distant, withdrawn client. A team in name only.

Father Bjorn and Danny arrive at court early and commandeer two front seats in the gallery. He looks pallid and sleep-deprived; Danny and I have discussed what a terrible toll this whole thing is taking on our friend. He frequently calls, sometimes just to ramble and express his regrets and seek reassurances that everything is being done for his son that can be done. Danny and I take turns assuaging him though we would need ten more clones to entertain the show of force his doubts crave.

Like the priesthood, one dedicated actor can make a huge difference in the practice of law. While one is designed to save souls, the other is designed to save corporeal beings. How very different they are not. And so now I understand his angst over the unconfessed sins of his congregants. I have the same worries about the young man I am defending and his apparent lack of remorse. We are brothers, Father Bjorn and I, far more than we are priest and penitent.

32

W e have been selecting a jury for three days now. We have twelve jurors in the box, and we are exercising peremptories and challenging for cause until we, like the armies of the Spartans and Trojans, lay exhausted upon our shields and our swords and accept the inevitable when our objections have all been spent.

The State's Attorney has just used his final challenge. The departed juror was a middle-aged mother of three boys who all were arrested for underage drinking. The eldest served a week in juvie, which still rankled the mother and skewed her vote to favor the defendant. And so, at last, we have left ourselves with spice-free, tasteless vanilla. A jury of peers without important opinions, that have no relations in law enforcement, have never been arrested, have never been the victim of a crime, have never committed one, and weren't smart enough to come up with some bias or ailment that would have sent them home to watch Bonanza reruns and play hooky from work. The American jury system at its very best. And when they screw up the verdict in the case, which they too often do, the appellate courts will hold sacrosanct what that tribe of twelve has done because, after all and thank God, they were the almighty, all-knowing, all-wise, and judicious jury. Their findings will go untouched. Only the law itself will be questioned. In that regard, the law will have on its side only law-school-trained advocates who will use every skill and cunning to pervert it. That is the American judicial system I have come to know and fear.

But maybe I overstate. And maybe not.

So we are ready to begin.

Media comes bursting into the courtroom once the jury is sworn and seated. They were not allowed to broadcast jury selection for anonymity purposes. This is Mayor Tanenbaum's daughter we'll be talking about. Judge Lancer-Burgess has allowed one TV camera inside. The jury cannot be displayed publicly. Court TV will receive and broadcast the feed. The other news channels collecting in the galley will get their soundbites from Court TV's feed, but are here to write up their assignments. I recognize a few of the reporters from other cases and other days. They know better than to approach the attorneys at counsel table on the north side of the bar, so it is a safe zone where the attorneys, and defendant, police, and court personnel can work in peace.

Giving the first opening statement is Assistant State's Attorney Trey Dickinson, who now finds himself surrounded by two junior attorneys who will review his every strategy and will catch him should he fall. Mr. Dickinson begins with a diatribe against crime, but knowing he must offer more statement and less argument, switches gears to cover the case the jury will hear. He talks about Amy Tanenbaum and her place at Wendover High, the leader of the spirit squad, the freshman class vice-president, a student who aspired to be a pediatric surgeon and her commitment to all the science and math classes the school had to offer. She was a mild-mannered girl, Dickinson tells the jury, a girl less willing to speak out in a group setting and more apt to share on a one-on-one basis. She was active in her synagogue's Rosh Hodesh: It's A Girl Thing! for teen girls. Why anyone would choose to murder this particular angel (Dickinson's words) was beyond his, the prosecutor's, imagination, and he promised the jury they would soon fall in love with her, too, as they learned more about her.

Dickinson describes the finding of the dead girl's body by the groundskeeper: filthy and covered with a film of frost by morning since it dipped below freezing the night before. He describes the detectives and CSI and gives thanks for their efforts and their handling of the corpse. Then he goes onto to describe the terrible task faced by the medical examiner who, upon opening Amy's mouth, made a horrifying discovery. He talks about the importance of the Illinois State Police crime lab, its efforts and findings.

On the other side of the street, as Dickinson tells our jury, lurked the devil himself in Jana Emerich. The defendant was the embodiment of evil, a pot-smoking, devil-worshipping transplant from California. He murdered our Amy with a coiled guitar string and then besmirched her dead body with a live rodent glued inside her mouth. The jury visibly recoils at this disclosure. Several turn away and close their eyes. Dickinson walks up to our table and points at Jana. He tells them the killer is a monster with homicidal tendencies and a dysfunctional family that has betrayed him, so he took up the sins of his peers.

I glimpse the jury looking over at Jana who is sitting beside me and working up a pen-and-ink rendering of the judge on a legal pad I'd provided to him for notes. Their look is one of distaste, at first, trailing off into various degrees of fear and loathing by the time Dickinson takes his seat and smolders under the terrible burden of grabbing justice by the neck and wringing it into submission for Amy.

Dickinson's words have sucked all sound out of the room by the time I take my feet and offer my opening statement on behalf of Jana. But how, really, do you un-ring the bell that has just been rung? By telling the jury that the police arrested the wrong man? That the virtuoso work of the crime lab might prove specific facts, but that it fails to create the bridge between the dead girl and Jana that is needed to convict?

I decide to begin slowly and keep it low key. I don't have facts to argue except that the cops have nailed the wrong person and many people keep snakes and mice and scarves and glue and Jana shouldn't be convicted on that weak tie-in alone. Then I shift into second gear as I realize that, as overwhelming as Dickinson's presentation has been, the only physical evidence tending to incriminate my client is the mouse hair and the Super Glue batch number. But how many tubes of that Super Glue have been sold in Chicago? I wonder aloud for them. Surely, not just one single tube was sold in this city out of the thousands of the same batch produced and distributed.

Then, shifting into high gear, I begin the refrain I will come to over and over during this trial, the refrain that argues a jury cannot convict on circumstantial evidence alone. Not in a first-degree murder case where so much is at stake. Then it's into overdrive as I hammer home the duty upon the State's Attorney to convict not with circumstantial evidence but with evidence that proves beyond a reasonable doubt that Jana killed Amy.

When I take my seat, I have made circumstantial evidence into a dishonest tool of prosecutors who know they don't have a real case. And that's how I leave it with them, hopefully wanting and demanding more than what they have been told thus far.

When I was speaking, maybe half of the jury made eye contact with me. And only one, maybe two, showed any buy-in to my view of the case. That would be a woman who grabbed the last chair in the jury box even though she had a son who was cited for possession of marijuana. The State couldn't rid itself of her, and I wanted her. She nods as I mention abuse of power by police agencies generally and continues to nod after I mention abuse of power by the Chicago Police Department in particular.

Largely, my presentation is ineffective and wins no converts. As I sit and prepare to begin, I wonder whether my client wouldn't be better off if I had just waived opening statement until it was my turn to present his defense.

The judge takes the morning break.

We refill water glasses, and Danny comes forward and clasps me on the shoulder. She squeezes, letting me know she's there for me. Jana sits, head down, adding shadow to the judge's inky features. So this is it, I think. This is my defense team: a lawyer (me), who probably just came across as slightly befuddled and bewildered, joined at the hip to a teenage boy who refuses to look at the jury despite my admonitions to him to do so early in the trial when any of them might want to make eye contact with him. But now his fledgling art skills are working into a full-time experience for him, an experience to replace the reality of sitting in on his own first-degree murder case. Perish the thought that he should help his attorney out. I'm feeling sorry for myself but haven't even cringed and dissolved emotionally like I will when the jury speaks as one: WE FIND THE DEFENDANT GUILTY. So I put on my big boy pants and resolve I will come out swinging when it is my turn to cross-examine the State's first witness. And its second, third, and so forth, until I am convinced I have done all anyone could do to defeat their testimony and exhibits.

"How are you feeling?" Danny asks me with another squeeze of the shoulder.

"Am I looking that bad?" I ask in reply.

"You look peaked."

"Wouldn't surprise me. It's the mouse and the glue. Who would've thought?"

"Hey, man, lots of my friends have snakes," Jana says without looking up. "And probably every house has a tube of Super Glue somewhere in some drawer."

"Hey, we covered this before. I asked you if any of your friends keep snakes."

"No, you didn't. You asked whether I had any friends who raised snakes. I don't."

"Who else among your friends keeps a snake?" I ask half-exasperated. I didn't realize he was such a hair-splitter.

"For one, that fucking Rudy Gomez."

"He's a suspect in the Franny Arlington case," Danny says.

"Has Rudy ever seen your snake?"

"Sure. Lots of times."

"When?"

"He brings his snake over after school. We let it fight with Leonard. It's gnarly watching them go at it. But we don't let them hurt each other."

On my feet now, I'm beginning to see the reasonable doubt that all criminal cases have.

"He comes to your house? Has he ever taken one of your mice with him when he leaves?"

"Sure. We trade mice when we run out. Sometimes I give him three pinkies, and sometimes he gives me three pinkies."

"Pinkies?" asks Danny.

"You know. The little ones. Just born."

"Do they have hair?"

"Some. Not much."

"But some."

"Yes."

After he drops his head back to his pen and ink, Danny and I look at each other for a long moment.

"Well?" she says to me with a shrug.

"I've got nothing better," I tell her.

"It gives you something, for God's sake."

"But there's still the glue."

"Ask Rudy if he uses Super Glue," she says and smiles slyly.

"Come on. This is damn serious."

She shakes her head. "I know. I'm sorry. But there is the batch validity. Chicago probably distributed thousands of tubes out of the same batch."

"Get Marcel working that up."

"He already is. He's out in the hall making calls to the manufacturer and distributor. We'll have answers for you by the noon break."

"Bless you two. Thanks, Danny."

"Eat 'em alive," she says and gives me a caress on my cheek before turning and resuming her seat in the gallery. Danny isn't second-chairing the trial with me because she has other duties, other hearings on her calendar. You can't have attorneys coming and going in a trial; it's unsettling to a jury that always wants consistency. That's why real trial lawyers never cut their hair or style it during a trial. It can distract a jury from the important stuff.

Any little thing can.

33

J udge Lancer-Burgess calls us to order.

Edward Ngo is called by SA Dickinson as the State's first witness. Ordinarily, the State wants to set the scene at the beginning. It wants to give the jury the twenty-thousand-foot view. Ngo will be perfect for that. As he goes through his name, age, business address, and employment, he comes across as a sincere, well-spoken, and a man who doesn't tend toward embellishment, even when asked about the studies and exams he underwent to earn his detective's shield. Some police officials love to add merit badges to their history at such times, but Ngo doesn't.

"After you received your detective's shield, what was your assignment?"

"Burglary. Four years working residential burglaries."

"Are there also commercial burglaries?"

"Yes, but at the time, our bureau handed those off to a team that specialized in commercial."

"And from Burglary, where next?"

Dickinson is standing at the lectern, his right leg balanced behind him on the toe of his shoe as he lays down the man's history and credentials. He is rock solid, veering neither right nor left, adding pebble after pebble to the case he hopes to build into a monument that convicts Jana Emerich.

"After Burglary, they promoted me to Robbery-Homicide."

"In what capacity?"

"Detective, the night shift at first."

"Did you go out on robbery calls?"

"Hundreds."

"On homicides?"

"Hundreds, too."

"What do you do when you go on a homicide call in your present position?"

"Assess the scene. Decide what workups I want. Examine the victim or victims. Make a preliminary determination of the cause of death. Instruct the CSI to obtain cameras, videos, trace and transfer, fiber and hair, blood and fluids, DNA, and fingerprints. Plus, I'll direct a ballistics crew when there's been a shooting. They'll dig slugs out of walls, locate and photograph spent bullet casings, take control of any weapons at the scene, those sorts of things."

"Tell us about the Amy Tanenbaum case. How did you become involved?"

"Rotation assignment. It was my turn. My partner and I rolled out to the scene and took command."

"Who is your partner?"

"Andy Valencia. He is my same grade."

"Who drove to the scene?"

"Andy. I handled the radio."

"Did you run code three? Lights and siren?"

"No. No need. The uniforms had control at the scene. They would touch nothing before we got there."

"Tell us where and when you arrived."

"We arrived at the Wendover High School football field at eight-thirty-two a.m. It was Friday morning."

"What did you do first?"

"We parked, badged the uniforms, and took over the scene. The crime scene was underneath the bleachers at Wendover Field at Wendover High School. The uniforms had already strung crime scene tape all around, and we didn't cross it beneath the bleachers. Unlike what you see on TV where the detective walks up to the body and turns it to see better, we don't do that. We take pictures and measurements first."

"Why is that?"

"Less risk of contamination. Your CSI's can locate the tiniest bits of evidence, including hairs and fibers and who knows what, as long as the scene is a virgin."

"Did you and Andy have a name for that?"

"Yes. Entering a scene, we pop its cherry when we duck inside the tape. Not a pretty expression."

"But we get the idea," says Dickinson, speaking for the

whole of the courtroom but shooting a quick smile to the jury. Several jurors return the smile then drop it when the solemnity of the moment returns.

"Where was the body located?"

"About thirty-five feet underneath the bleachers. She was lying face-up, her head toward the west and her feet almost due east. She was fully clothed, lying on top of her right arm and her left arm flung out to the side. One eye was partway open, the other eye closed. There was a ring of blood around her throat as far to the rear as we could make out without moving her. She was very obviously dead."

"Had another officer made that determination?"

"Yes, the first-on-scene officer had checked her wrist pulse. He didn't touch her carotid because of the injury to her throat. Didn't want to disturb any latents."

"Latents?"

"Sorry. Fingerprints. He didn't want to smudge any fingerprints she might have on her neck where she was garroted."

"By the way, have you ever located the item used to murder her?"

"We have not."

"What did you do after observing Amy's body?"

"Reviewed CSI assignments. I told them I wanted the entire scene vacuumed."

"You vacuum the ground?"

"We do. That's something else you don't see on TV. Then we check the bag for hair and fiber. Those things can be very revealing."

"Did you find any hair or fiber?"

"Not on the ground underneath her."

"On her body?

"Yes."

"Tell us about that."

"The killer left a mouse in her mouth. Her mouth was Super Glued. The medical examiner had to cut into her oral cavity, and there was the mouse. It had tried to gnaw its way out and did serious damage, then it died. We got mouse hair from the autopsy."

The jury recoils. Hands tighten on purses, pens pause from note-taking, several people in the front row cross their arms on their chests. It isn't pleasant to see. But it's having a huge, emotional impact, and I hate that. Still, I'm powerless to do anything about it. It is what it is.

"Died inside her mouth?"

"Died inside her mouth, yes."

Beside me, I can feel Jana stiffen and inhale sharply when the mouse details come out. He stops doing his art.

A hand shoots up from the jury box, and juror number eight rushes toward the restroom door without getting the court's permission. Judge Lancer-Burgess takes a ten-minute recess. The other jurors file out of the courtroom. They are in shock, and it shows.

Once the judge disappears through her door in the wall, the courtroom erupts in pandemonium. This is the mayor's blessed daughter we're discussing here. Phones are produced, and frantic calls made to media outlets and offices. Voices are raised: "Yes, a mouse in her mouth! Yes, you heard me right!"

When we return from recess, and after another dozen questions about the scene and tasks undertaken, State's Attorney Dickinson begins asking questions about Jana's involvement in the second murder at the school.

"Did you have a chance to interview the defendant?"

"We asked some questions, and he gave some answers."

"Was he under arrest when this happened?"

"No. We were down at the station, but there was no arrest. We were just investigating."

"Investigating what?"

"We were investigating the murder of Franny Arlington. This investigation happened two weeks after Amy was killed."

"Was Jana Emerich a suspect?"

"Objection!" I cry and leap to my feet. "Relevance."

"Sustained," the judge drawled. "Counsel, you know better."

"Was Jana Emerich a person of interest?"

"Same objection!" I shout. "This is purposeful and grounds for reversal, Your Honor."

"Counsel," the judge says to Dickinson, "let's move it along. Ask something else."

"What else did you ask him?"

"Does it matter? All he would say is he wanted to see his lawyer."

"Did you then cease asking questions?"

"Yes. We took him with us to identify another person of interest."

"In the Franny Arlington case? Not this case?"

"Correct. It had nothing to do with Amy Tanenbaum."

"Very well, I think that's all for right now, Your Honor."

"Counsel? You may cross-examine."

I stand and step up to the lectern. Laying my yellow pad on the wood surface, I immediately ask, "Detective Ngo, isn't it true you know of no evidence linking my client to the death of Amy Tanenbaum?"

"No, that's not true."

"Well, tell the jury what links you know about, please."

"Mouse hair. Mouse hair in her mouth that matched mouse hair taken from your client's mouse cage."

"Could that mouse hair also have come from Rudy Gomez's mouse cage?"

The detective shoots a look at the State's Attorney. Knowing he is being watched by the jury, the SA makes no move to suggest an answer.

"Without looking at the State's Attorney, please answer my question."

"Would you repeat it?"

"I asked whether the mouse hair removed from Amy's mouth might also have matched mouse hair at Rudy Gomez's house."

"I don't know."

"Did you investigate that possibility?"

"Yes. We searched Mr. Gomez's house."

"Why did you do that?"

"He admitted being present when Franny Arlington hit her head and died."

"Did he admit killing her?"

"Killing her? No, you couldn't say that."

"What could you say?"

"He was there when she fell and struck her head."

"Did he cause her to fall?"

"She wouldn't obey him so he pushed at her. She fell back and hit her head on the bleachers."

"Do you believe he killed her?"

"We have a working hypothesis. We always do."

"Which is what?"

"That he was with her under the bleachers and he killed her by pushing her against the bleacher metal. She hit her head and died. We also believe he held a knife to her throat."

"Why do you believe he held a knife?"

"We seized a knife when we frisked him. We had it tested. Franny's blood was found on its blade."

"Detective Ngo, I want to suggest another hypothesis to you. What if you worked up the Amy Tanenbaum case from the same starting point as the Franny Arlington case? What if you went in with the idea that Rudy Gomez killed them both? After all, he admitted the second, so why not the first, too?"

"I don't know. Because your client's muffler turned up near Amy's body."

"Speaking of which, the muffler proves what, exactly?"

"That it was near her body. He might have been under the stands with her."

"He might just have easily lost his muffler when it fell through the bleachers, correct?"

"Correct."

"Did Jana Emerich ever admit killing Amy Tanenbaum?"

"No."

"But Rudy Gomez admitted being with Franny Arlington when she died beneath the same bleachers as Amy?"

"Yes."

"Do you see a pattern there?"

"I knew you would see one. That's your job."

"What about you? Do you see a pattern?"

"Maybe. Maybe not."

"Well, doesn't it seem supremely coincidental that two high school boys would suddenly go off on killing sprees in the same month of football season?"

"I don't know."

"I mean, what are the odds of that happening?"

"I don't know."

"Have you ever known it to happen before?"

"No."

"And how long have you been a cop?"

"Fifteen years, give or take."

"And during those fifteen years, you've never seen two murders at the same spot like we have here by two different assailants?"

"No. But that doesn't mean it didn't happen. It could be a conspiracy."

"But you have no proof, correct?"

He draws a deep breath.

"We have the muffler, the mouse hair, and the Super Glue that sealed her mouth shut."

"Would it surprise you to hear that my investigator will testify the company that manufactured that tube of Super

Glue was sold along with twenty thousand other tubes in Chicagoland over the past two years?"

"It wouldn't surprise me."

"So your Super Glue theory has twenty-thousand ways it's possibly wrong, true?"

"I guess."

"What proof do you have that my client and not Rudy Gomez murdered Amy Tanenbaum?"

"I've said what our investigation uncovered."

"Asked and answered," says the State's Attorney, arriving late to the party.

"Sustained. Please move along, counsel."

The remainder of the morning is spent with me covering and recovering the same arguments, favoring my client as much as possible, given that the second time around, the State's Attorney is on his feet objecting that I'm re-asking the same questions. I am, but I'm enough of a trial lawyer to phrase them just differently enough the second and third time that his objections are mostly denied. Good on me.

When I, at last, take my seat, I am feeling much better about our defense.

The next witness is late in showing, so we break for lunch.

34

Hector Rodriguez is the groundskeeper who found Amy's body the morning after the football game.

The State's Attorney calls Mr. Rodriguez as his second trial witness when we take up after lunch. Mr. Rodriguez is a short, dark Mexican national who was working at a job that generally had no involvement with police authorities. But this time around it did. Big time.

He testifies that he went beneath the stands with a wheeled trash barrel just after eight o'clock that morning. He was alone when he went under, the other three members of his crew handling the restrooms, parking area, and sidelines. As he was walking to the far end of the bleachers to begin, he noticed the body maybe ten feet off to the side of the under-passage. Leaving his trash bin behind, he crept close enough to get a good look. He couldn't tell whether the girl was asleep, unconscious, or dead. But he had seen enough TV to know he shouldn't disturb or try to move the person. He pulled his cell phone out of his pocket, found he had no bars underneath the bleachers, and hurried back out to the open side where he dialed 911. In ten minutes, a police cruiser came roaring into the parking area, nosed up to the chain link fence, and parked. The driver and his partner hit the ground running to where Hector directed them.

Hector watched as the police officers checked the body for signs of life. He watched as they carefully followed their footsteps back out of the high grass under the stands. Then he was told to leave the area, and he never went back. That was the last time he saw the dead girl and the crime scene.

There is no tactic available on cross-examination so I pass on the witness and he is excused by the judge.

Next up is Erin Caulflo, a freshman girl from Amy Tanenbaum's homeroom at Wendover High. She is a sprite of a girl, barely five feet tall with a developing body and long, black eyelashes. Her fiery eyes flash when she describes what happened to her friend that night.

"Tell us where you were sitting," the State's Attorney directs.

"About five girls, Amy included, were in the stands watching the boys straggle in. We had all come in one car and were excited because it was homecoming and there would be a huge dance the next night."

"Why was your game on a Thursday night?"

"The other team had several players whose holy day is Friday. So they arranged their entire schedule around that. All their games were on Thursday. We didn't care, except there were lots of absences from class the next day because lots of kids slept in."

"You were on the home team's side of the bleachers?"

"Of course. About two-thirds of the way up in the bleachers. There were people all around, young and old, and lots of other students. But we were a clique, and we kept to ourselves."

"Describe Amy that night."

"What do you mean? How she was acting?"

"Yes. Whatever you can remember."

"She was in a great mood. She was showing off a bar mitzvah outfit. It was cute and showed off her figure."

"Was she upbeat?"

"Yes. We listened to some hip-hop on her iPhone. We shared earbuds.

"Did you eventually pair off with boys?"

"More or less. Boys came and sat with us. But no one was dating or anything. We were mostly freshmen and sopho-mores, and everyone knew everyone else since, like, grade school. Except for Jana Emerich. He was from California and a senior, so he was kind of mysterious. I know Amy liked him lots and talked about him sometimes. She sat with Jana."

"Did she ever date him?"

"Like *date* date? Not that I know."

"What did you see happen between her and Jana that night?"

"They just watched the game and talked like all the rest of us. There was lots of talking. A popcorn fight broke out just before halftime. All the girls left for the restrooms. We always left early to beat the crowds. Amy came, too, naturally."

"What happened next?"

"Next? We peed. I mean we all went to the bathroom and used the facility then washed. Except some girls wouldn't wash. They didn't want to touch anything. No one did."

"Did Jana Emerich accompany your group to the restrooms?"

"Not that I know of. Later on, I heard he trailed behind us, but I never saw him."

"What happened after going to the bathroom?"

"We talked quite a bit. Some of us fixed our makeup in the restroom mirror. But the light was so bad it wasn't easy. Next thing we knew, the game was going again."

"How did you know that?"

"Our team scored a touchdown, and the crowd began stamping their feet in the bleachers and clapping and whistling. So we came running out of the bathroom to see what the uproar was all about."

"Was Amy with you then?"

"I don't know. I don't have a memory of who was there."

"Then what did you do?"

"Ran back over to the snack shop. I bought an Almond Joy and a Mountain Dew. My girlfriends bought their drinks and food, and we all went back up the steps."

"Back up the bleachers?"

"Yes."

"Who did you see at the snack shop?"

"I don't remember."

"Who went back up the bleachers?"

"Everyone except Amy."

"Did you think there was anything wrong at that time?"

"No. In fact, we laughed. We laughed because we thought she'd snuck off somewhere with Jana Emerich. We knew she would if he asked her to go somewhere to talk."

"Did you see Amy again that night?"

"I never saw Amy again period."

"Now, this is important. Did you see Jana when you went back up the bleachers?"

"Honestly? I can't say I did."

Tears start rolling down the schoolgirl's cheeks, and she wipes at them with a tissue from the box on the shelf before her. She dabs carefully around her eyes as if to preserve her makeup.

"Have you talked to your friends about that night, Erin?"

"Lots of times."

"Did anyone else see Amy after the restroom?"

"Objection. Calls for hearsay."

"Sustained. Counsel, ask it another way."

"All right, Your Honor. Erin, did you ever become aware of any person who saw Amy after the restroom that night?"

"No. No one saw her again."

"Did you ever discuss that night with the defendant, Jana Emerich?"

"No, why would I? They arrested him right away. Everyone's parents called the school board about getting him kicked out of school, but they wouldn't. So my parents ordered me to stay away from him no matter what."

"Have I failed to ask you anything that might better help us understand what happened to Amy that night?"

"Objection. Vague and ambiguous."

"Overruled. You may answer."

"You've asked me everything. I don't know anything else."

The witness is turned over to me for cross-examination.

35

E rin Caulflo eyes me suspiciously as I step up to the lectern for her cross-examination. Her long black eyelashes flutter, and her eyes dart from the State's Attorney to the jury then back. She grips the rail of the shelf in front of her as if to lean against a coming storm.

I am anything but stormy.

"Good afternoon, Ms. Caulflo. May I call you Erin?"

"Sure, Erin is fine."

"I am Jana Emerich's lawyer. Jana has pleaded not guilty in this case. He says he had nothing to do with Amy's death. Do you understand this?"

"I understand. I may not agree, but I understand."

"Why do you say you may not agree?"

I know better than to ask a witness an open-ended question on cross-examination, but I do. I do because her direct examination has yielded nothing damning, so I will take this opportunity to shoot down any theories she may have. This will impress on the jury yet another way of thinking of Jana's innocence.

"I don't agree because he was with her. I saw how he was looking at her."

"How was that?"

"Not normal. He looked like he wanted to jump her bones right there in the bleachers."

"Jump her bones?"

"You know. Make out with her."

"But you're not saying he looked like he wanted to murder her?"

She looks helplessly at the State's Attorney, and it becomes clear she is here to help her friend Amy.

"I don't know how someone looks when they want to murder someone. So I don't know if he was looking like he wanted to murder her or not."

So. That makes her feel safe. Here we go.

"Well, let's talk about his look. Did he appear angry?"

"No."

"Was he frowning?"

"No."

"Did he look threatening?"

"No."

"Was he raising his voice to Amy?"

"No."

"In all truth, he looked like he was enjoying being with Amy, didn't he?"

"I guess so. I didn't watch them all that much."

"But you did see enough to be able to tell us today that Jana looked like he was enjoying being with Amy, correct?"

"Yes."

"And while we're at, let's talk about Amy's look. Was she frightened?"

"No."

"Did she raise her voice?"

"No."

"Did she cry out for help?"

"No."

"On the way to the restroom, did she come to you and complain about Jana?"

"I didn't talk to her on the way to the restroom. She was walking up front of the group so I can't answer you."

"But for what you did see of her on the walk over, you didn't see her trying to get away from Jana?"

"No."

"And you didn't hear her complain about Jana?"

"Not to me."

"To anyone? Did she complain to anyone?"

"Not that I heard."

"After leaving the bleachers and heading for the restroom, did you see Amy and Jana together again?"

"No."

"Did you see Amy again after leaving the bleachers?"

"No."

"Did you see Jana?"

"No. Somebody told me Amy stopped at the snack shop to give Scott his ring back."

"Who is Scott?"

"Her old boyfriend. They were an item since eighth grade."

"Why give him his ring back, if you know?"

"She broke up with him that week, and he wanted the ring back. It was his class ring."

"So she left your restroom procession and stopped by the snack shop?"

"That's what someone told me."

"Objection. Hearsay."

"Exception to the hearsay rule—doesn't seek to prove the truth of the matter asserted but only that it was said."

"Overruled. Please continue."

"Now, Erin, how long did you know Amy Tanenbaum?"

"Since first grade."

"Were you classmates that entire time?"

"Yes. Except we have different classes in high school. She wanted to be a doctor, and I didn't."

"So your curricula didn't match up?"

"That's true."

"Did you spend time at each other's houses in high school?"

"At least one night a week."

"You were good friends?"

"Best friends."

"You want whoever killed your friend to be convicted and brought to justice, don't you?"

"Yes."

"Is there any other reason you think Jana Emerich might have been Amy's murderer?"

"No."

"And you were with her all that night?"

"Yes."

"Rode with her in the same car to the game?"

"Yes."

"Sat with her the entire first half?"

"Yes. Except when she sat with Jana."

"You observed her, and she appeared fine?"

"Yes."

"Observed Jana, and he appeared normal?

"Yes."

"You witnessed nothing that might suggest Jana was her killer?"

"Well, not exactly."

"Then what?"

"Nothing, I guess."

She is crying now, her shoulders shaking, and I step away from the lectern, back toward my table. "Your Honor, that is all I have."

There is no re-direct examination. We are through with this witness.

She flees the witness stand, leaning against an adult who must be her mother, wiping her eyes with a tissue as she walks up the aisle to the door.

My confidence is building. I am seeing some light.

But we haven't gotten to the tough witnesses yet. The medical/technical witnesses. They will be hardened veterans and will out-dance me if they can because they know all the steps.

But so do I.

It is Thursday afternoon, two o'clock when the first CSI takes the witness stand. This is the first of the technical witnesses. Crime scene techs are professionals, usually with a degree in biology or other applied science. They have been trained in their specialty, certainly, but also exhaustively trained at the police academy in witness methods and testimony formulation and withstanding cross-examination. They are professional testifiers: they make and keep eye contact with the jury, keep a patina of seriousness on their testimony, and they can bury your client and look pleasant and innocent while they are doing it.

She is a black woman, average height, wearing her hair close-cropped like Halle Berry and dressed in the uniform of the Chicago Police Department Crime Scene Investigation unit sans the hat. Wearing a hat in court is a sign of ignorance and disrespect. Taking the witness stand with grace and ease, she is the picture of confident competence.

"Your name?" asks State's Attorney Dickinson.

"Angie McClelland."

"Occupation?"

"Crime scene investigator two, Chicago Police Department."

"How long have you worked for CSI?"

"Thirteen years and six months."

"Ms. McClellan, please tell us about your education. Do you hold any college degrees?"

She smiles and looks directly at the jury, warm eye contact already in play.

"Bachelor's degree in biology, Loyola University. Master's degree in forensic science, National University."

"Finally, please tell us about your departmental training in crime scene investigation."

She goes on and on for several minutes, detailing this and that experience beginning with the Chicago CSI Academy and weekend courses and conferences around the country. She has also published ten different papers on the DNA practices of police departments around the world, including Scotland Yard, Interpol, the LAPD, and CPD. She is well-versed, well-trained, and to hear her speak and exude her knowledge, I know she will be an implacable witness. A tough cookie.

"Were you involved in the investigation at the Amy Tanenbaum crime scene?"

"I was. I headed up the CSI team that day."

"Please tell us your responsibilities at her scene."

"My primary responsibilities are, one, to secure and preserve the scene and, two, to task different team members with their roles at the scene."

"What does that last part mean, tasking team members?"

"That's just departmental speak for assigning different jobs to each CSI at the scene. Some did fluids, some did hair and fiber, some did trace and transfer, including fingerprints and handprints, some did DNA. Of course, the same worker might do two or even three things. My third job was to make sure any contact by our team members to the crime scene met departmental and professional standards."

"Do you recall particulars about the Amy Tanenbaum scene?"

"Of course. And I also have my case notes."

So do I. Through the discovery process, all CSI notes and workups and reports have been made available to the defense team. I am well-versed in what she did, who she spoke to, and conclusions that devolved from her investigation. Ms. McClelland spends the next forty-five minutes describing what she heard, saw, and discovered about the death scene.

During her testimony, she describes finding the red muffler and the DNA testing. Jana's DNA is, of course, lifted from the muffler. So is the DNA of other individuals, unmatched since they haven't been sampled and don't exist in any database. But Jana was last seen wearing the muffler, so its presence at the murder scene rests with him. Jana loses this point.

She also talks about the lack of fingerprints. They have examined her entire body for a latent print from someone other than Amy herself and have found nothing. Jana wins this point.

The entire body depression left in the tall grass was vacuumed, and the vacuum's contents studied under a microscope. This has yielded human and animal hairs that cannot be matched to Jana's hair, thank God. Jana wins this point.

There is no instrument of death found as Ms. McClelland puts it. Meaning no wire or garrote was found that might have been used to strangle and sever the carotids of Amy Tanenbaum. This point is neutral although the search warrant that later turned up a missing E string from the package in his guitar case could make this a point for the prosecution. I'll give it a half-point, their favor.

Then come the endless photographs of the scene and the body. There are over fifty in all, and they are identified by Ms. McClelland and introduced into evidence one by one, at which moment they are passed to the jury. The rest of the afternoon is gobbled up by this process, and by the time we quit at five-fifteen, we are all dizzy with horrendous images of death. A smart move by the prosecution to send the jury home for the night with horror dancing in their brains. And there's nothing I can do to sap away the sting. It's a *fait accompli* when we all pack up.

Detective Ngo spots me and approaches my table. The courtroom is empty but for the two of us. His black face is twisted in a rage, and the whites of his eyes are red-veined with anger.

"How can you defend this man?" he hisses. "He killed an innocent child!"

He places his hand on the side of his waist, purposely displaying the gun on his belt.

"It's my job," I say. "It's nothing more than that. I don't vouch for these people, don't know all that much about them. But the U.S. Constitution says they're entitled to a lawyer. I'm just providing that service."

"I was at Amy Tanenbaum's autopsy. I watched the mouse being pulled out of her mouth. It was covered in black blood. Amy's blood. They couldn't have an open casket because of the terrible damage done to her face by the autopsy and by that goddam rodent your client put in there."

He moves around my table and sits down on the end of it, the end nearest me. If I reached out, I could touch his side.

He glares down at me. "You and I are going to meet someplace again. I guarantee it. It may not be tonight or tomorrow. It may not be until next month or next year, but we will meet again. And you will be alone and so will I. You are going to feel pain, friend. You are going to feel serious big-boy pain. I'm not going to kill you, but I am going to fuck you up." He stands and remains nearby. "Remember this when you see me again. Remember that I told you so."

"I will."

I make the elevator minutes later and hammer the down button, praying that it closes before Ngo comes onboard. The door whooshes closed, and I ride down to the lobby alone.

Then I am outside, and Marcel is waiting with my car.

We are gone.

37

I arrive at court to find Judge Lancer-Burgess has vacated the trial today and continued us until Monday. When I stop by her office, her secretary tells me on the down-low that the judge wanted to avoid any prejudice or inflamed emotions from the murder last night. Evidently, the entire courthouse—the entire city—is stunned. Wendover High has closed its doors, as have all other schools in the Chicago Public Schools System.

What I can piece together about last night from what I hear is that Wendover High hosted the Triton basketball team at the Superior Field House on the Wendover High campus. The game began at seven o'clock. Security and CPD uniforms were everywhere—at the entrance, at the exit, at the restrooms, in the stands around the basketball court proper—everywhere. So how it could have happened is unknown. But it did happen.

A high school sophomore girl, who had spent the last three years of her life in a wheelchair following a tragic auto accident, was murdered in the girls' restroom. Even with security posted at the door leading in and out. The theory is that the assailant, dressed and made up to look like a woman, entered the restroom and strangled the young student, again with a thin wire that severed her right carotid artery so that she bled out in the accessible stall and was found slumped sideways in her wheelchair. It was only when her brother noticed she hadn't returned to her spot courtside that a hue and cry arose and a search quickly located the victim. Her name was Scarlett Newson, and she had just turned fifteen.

A stylish dress and plain black flats were found stuffed inside a large trash dumpster behind the building shortly after the discovery of Scarlett's body. Evidently, the courtroom deputies are postulating this morning before court that the assailant, after murdering Scarlett, then dodged around to the back side of the field house, changed back into men's clothing, washed away the eye makeup and lipstick, and left the area.

To say that I am astonished would be to understate. I step outside the judge's chambers to tell Danny. She is equally shocked and rushes back to the office to see what else can be learned. She is doing this because, of course, the death of another young female student at Wendover High tends to exonerate Jana Emerich from the death of Amy Tanenbaum because Jana, last night, spent the evening with his father, the priest, at a movie at the Cineplex. There could be no better alibi witness in all of Chicagoland than Father Frederic Bjorn.

I've heard the cops already contacted Jana and attempted to question him, but he referred them to Father Bjorn, who swiftly dampened their enthusiasm by confirming the time he and Jana spent together last night, even going so far as offering to produce two admission tickets validated for last night's seven o'clock showing.

Marcel tracks me down just as I am exiting Judge Lancer-Burgess's chambers. He wants to go straight over to Rudy's house and question the boy about last night. I consider whether this might be regarded as interfering with an official police investigation—a crime itself—but again fall back on the excuse that I am doing whatever I can to defend Jana. It's not unreasonable for us to follow up on the boy who admitted pushing Franny Arlington when she died. We've heard there's a plea pending in that case to voluntary manslaughter, and we also know he's out on bail and has been attending school at Wendover as if nothing has happened. Not so dissimilar from our own Jana's continued matriculation.

We walk back along the sidewalk to the parking lot and agree we'll take Marcel's Ram truck. It's freezing this morning, snow flurries blowing bursts of white flakes across the asphalt and snow-covered sidewalks of this part of Chicago. I walk with my head down, against the wind, my hands stuffed inside my overcoat's large, warm pockets. Marcel easily outpaces me, and I feel him holding back his gait to enable me to stay beside him.

"So," he says as we make our way, "what the hell is going on at Wendover?"

"All I know is that it wasn't Jana. He was with Father Bjorn last night."

"Well, thank God for that."

"Agree. And this Rudy Gomez kid...I can't imagine him pulling off another. I mean, why would he even want to? He's made it to his senior year, and all of a sudden a switch gets thrown inside his brain and he starts killing classmates? I'm sorry, but that doesn't stack up for me."

"Maybe it's a conspiracy."

"How would we ever know?"

"So where does that leave us? There's a third killer on the loose? Or just a second, the same one who murdered Amy Tanenbaum?"

"Bingo. I think that's our argument. The phantom killer. We argue that Rudy was a copycat or just an aberration, and there's a serial killer on the loose that has now killed twice."

Marcel turns to me as we walk. "What if we put Rudy on the stand, too, just to give the jury the possibility that he might be a suspect in all three cases?"

"I like that. We can suggest a two-and-one by two assailants or a three-victim by one assailant. Either one holds water."

"And the two-and-one allows for the possibility of a serial killer if it turns out Rudy's got a strong alibi for last night."

I like what I'm hearing. As horrible as it is, the death of Scarlett Newson gives rise to the possibility of a serial killer being on the loose. The fact that Jana has an airtight alibi takes him out of the running for those honors. So we get a new phantom plus we get a suggestion it's Rudy on all three. Nice and neat. It's terrible for a person to have to think this way. And it's even more appalling for a defendant's attorneys to have a happier day because yet another young girl has died. But that's the way of the lawyer game. And it is just that, a huge frigging game. With the losers attending their own funerals and the judicial system culling out who goes to jail. It's not pretty, but it's what I do. It's where I spend my days. No wonder my alone times are troubled and conflicted. It's time for a couple of days on my boat. Lake Michigan can't thaw out soon enough to suit me.

Rudy's father is a top-flight oral surgeon and in the OR today. His mother is at yoga class; Rudy doesn't want us to come inside. He says the cops have already been there, and his lawyer has told him not to speak with anyone. He starts to close the door.

"One more thing," I interject, "about your snake."

The door stops.

"What about my snake?"

"Is it true he's friends with Leonard?"

"Jana's snake? Yeah, they've met."

"You guys trade mice back and forth sometimes, too, isn't that right?"

He rubs his eyes. He looks beyond us, then says, "Why are you asking me about my snake? Is that really why you're here?"

"It is," I tell him.

"We'd like to see your setup," Marcel tells him, all innocence. "I'm thinking of getting my kid a snake. Do you mind if we have a look at what you've got?"

The door opens a couple of inches.

"I guess. I mean, if you want. But don't ask me any questions about last night. My lawyer says I'm not to discuss my whereabouts last night."

"Sure, sure," Marcel says. "I just want to see the snake setup. My kid is bugging me to no end for a snake."

"What kind's he want?"

"She. She's a freshman at St. Elizabeth's."

"What's her name? I know some kids over there."

"Mary Ellen. She's small, about five-one, dark hair, still wearing braces. But she gets those off next summer."

"Doesn't ring a bell," says Rudy. He pushes the door wide open. "I guess you can come in and look. But not you," he says, meaning me. I stand back.

"Fine, fine, I don't like snakes. I'll wait in the truck."

"Fine," says Rudy, and he steps aside so Marcel can enter, which he does.

I turn, walk back across the circular drive, and climb back into the Ram. The key has been removed, so I stuff my hands in my pockets and shiver in the cold. Meanwhile, I can only imagine what Marcel is doing inside. Ten minutes drag past. Then fifteen.

Finally Marcel emerges. He shakes Rudy's hand, gives him a big smile, and then turns and heads for the truck. He is keeping his right hand tight against his North Face parka pocket. When he climbs inside and turns the key, I understand why.

"In my pocket, sir, is a half a pound of bedding."

"Out of the snake's container?"

"Nope. Out of the mouse cage."

"What? That's beautiful!"

"So I'm driving over to the lab. Let's get this tested and compared to the hair from Amy's mouth."

"Drive on, genius," I say. I'm warming with anticipation way before the heater kicks in.

"Let's think this through," he says. "We've got the sample of mouse hair from her mouth."

"And we know from the reports that the hair matches hair from Jana's mouse cage."

"But what about DNA? Can they compare animal DNA to animal DNA?"

"What would that prove? That the same mouse was in both places? I highly doubt we're going to get that. Way too much time has passed."

"Did you have the DNA tested between the Amy mouse and Jana's mouse?"

"Yes. Inconclusive."

"Okay, so we've ruled out Jana."

"Well, let's say the State can't rule him in. According to microscopic study, it's the same type. But so are a million other mice in Chicago."

"Agree. So maybe we're still close enough in time to last night's murder. Do we know if there was a mouse?"

"Too soon to hear. That news hasn't hit the street yet."

"Okay, so we need to subpoena the lead detective on that case."

I nod. "And have him testify about a new mouse in the Newson girl's mouth. We'll use him if there is one."

"We should use him in either case."

"Agree. Whether there is or isn't one."

"I'll give him a call. But I know he won't talk to me."

"No, he won't. Especially not with our trial still underway."

"What's his name?"

"You know how that works. No need for me to tell you, Marce."

Meaning, Marcel can merely call the CPD tip line and get connected to one of the detectives working on the new case. Then he hits him or her with a subpoena. Simple.

"Did you get anything else out of Rudy?"

Marcel looks out the window and taps his fingers on his leg. "It's not so much Rudy said but what he has."

Here it comes. "What?"

"Rudy also owns a guitar. A Gibson electric was perched on a stand in the corner of his room."

That's good to a point. It means Rudy had easy access to guitar strings. But anyone could buy guitar strings these days, in a shop or just as easy online.

"Anything else?"

"Nope. He listened to his lawyer."

"Too bad for us."

We drive over to the lab and submit our samples for testing. DNA, hair type, the whole nine yards. It's expensive but must be done.

It's all in the name of my priest. No skimping there.

38

D r. Samuel Tsung is called to the stand by SA Dickinson as his first witness Monday morning. The medical examiner looks calm and sounds smooth as he answers the standard foundational questions including education, training, licenses and certificates, work experience, teaching experience, published writings, professional organizations, and previous times and cases where he qualified as an expert witness in a Chicago court, state or federal.

Then the SA gets down to our case. "You have previously examined victims of strangulation?"

"Yes, thousands."

"Are you familiar with the signs and symptoms of strangulation?"

"Yes."

"Please tell us about strangulation. For example, are there types of strangulation?"

"Yes. Strangulation is defined as a form of asphyxia or lack of oxygen. Strangulation is characterized by closure of the blood vessels and air passages of the neck."

"Why would those be closed?"

"Well, as a result of external pressure on the neck. The three forms of strangulation are hanging, ligature, and manual. Ten percent of violent deaths in the U.S. each year are due to strangulation, six females to every male. Ligature strangulation is strangulation with a cord-like object, also referred to as garroting, and may include anything from a telephone cord to articles of clothing."

"Is Amy's death a ligature strangulation death?"

"Yes and no. I say yes and no because her carotid arteries were also severed. The severing of even one carotid artery always causes death if untreated."

"Were you able to determine what caused Amy's strangulation and carotid cuts?"

"A thin wire."

"Could a piano wire do this?"

"Definitely."

"Could a guitar string?"

"Absolutely."

"Or even common baling wire?"

"Without a doubt."

"Tell us more about the carotid artery involvement, please."

"Carotid arteries are the major vessels that transport oxygenated blood from the heart and lungs to the brain. These are the arteries at the side of the neck where persons administering CPR check for pulses. Jugular veins are the major vessels that transport deoxygenated blood from the brain back to the heart. The general clinical sequence of a victim who is being strangled is one of severe pain, followed by unconsciousness, followed by brain death."

"Describe Amy's death."

"Well, assuming she was attacked with a thin wire, the wire, of course, destroyed her carotid arteries and she would have bled to death within minutes. Or she would have died from lack of oxygen. Either or both killed Amy Tanenbaum."

"Was it a painful death?"

"Extremely. There was great suffering."

"Please describe the injuries to Amy's neck."

"Of course there was the ligature line. A complete circle around her neck that cut into the flesh all the way around. Also, I observed and filmed scratches, abrasions, and scrapes. These would be from the victim's fingernails."

"She was struggling to free herself?"

"Yes. It was a very violent death as she flailed and fought to free the noose from her neck."

"Describe the scratches first off."

"Three types of fingernail markings occurred, singly and in combination. These were impression, scratch, and claw marks. Impression marks occurred when the fingernails cut into the skin. They were shaped like commas or semi-circles. Scratch marks were superficial and as long as the fingernail itself. Claw marks occurred near the end of Amy's struggle when the skin was undermined. These are more vicious and dramatic appearing."

"So she scratched and clawed to free herself?"

"Her skin and some flesh were removed from beneath her fingernails and examined. There was no foreign skin or flesh, indicating to me the assailant attacked her from behind and she wasn't able to reach around to him."

"Dr. Tsung, please allow me to back up with more general questions."

"That's fine."

"For the record, are you a medical examiner?"

"Of course."

"How long have you been a medical examiner?"

"Fifteen years."

The doctor explains what happens in an autopsy and the reasons we do autopsies. He has performed more than ten thousand autopsies himself. He then goes on to describe the role of the pathologist and how the pathologist and medical examiner will work together and complement each other. Finally, he describes Amy's autopsy in detail. The court takes a break at the midpoint, and the jurors file out of the courtroom, visibly stunned with what they have just heard.

Upon taking up again, Dr. Tsung describes photos of her wounds. He denies any internal injuries secondary to physical trauma. Then, for the record, he says the cause of death was strangulation coupled with exsanguination or bleed-out.

The State's Attorney is gearing up for what I know will come next. "The last area I want to cover, doctor, is the area of extraordinary findings by you. Were there any extraordinary findings?"

"Yes. The assailant had put a live mouse in Amy's mouth then glued her mouth shut."

"Was the mouse alive when you performed the autopsy?"

"No."

"Had the mouse damaged Amy's oral tissues?"

"It had chewed almost completely through her right cheek."

The State's Attorney turns and walks to his table for a glass of water, which he pours and slowly drinks down. Then he returns to the lectern. The moment is a high one for him. The jury is stupefied: what they were told earlier by Detective Ngo did, in fact, happen, and the mouse chewed her cheek then died.

"Now. Tell us about the glue," the SA continues.

"Someone had applied Super Glue to Amy's lips. I had to use my scalpel to visualize the oral cavity."

"You had to cut into her mouth?"

"Yes, unfortunately."

"Have you ever, in your ten thousand autopsies, seen anything like this before?"

"I have seen everything. But not this. Ever."

"Thank you, doctor."

The SA abruptly breaks off, and it's my turn to cross-examine. He has caught me just a bit out of rhythm, and so I ask the judge for a ten-minute recess. Granted.

Marcel comes forward through the bar with Danny close behind.

"How horrible!" Danny says.

"That was the worst ever, boss," Marcel agrees. "That son of a bitch should get the electric chair."

"Well, lucky for him, Illinois no longer executes. So we're good there. Was it that bad for the jury?"

Danny's look is grim. Her lips are ringed with white anger lines. "Several women were crying. Even the men were having trouble holding it together. One man became visibly ill and was swallowing bile over and over. Poor Amy! The secrets girls keep!"

"So, are we hurt?"

"Well," says Danny, "it sure as hell didn't help."

When we resume, my cross-examination takes no more than five minutes. Why allow this expert to keep repeating what the jury has already found so repulsive? That's my thinking. The girl is dead, the death was violent, and the mouse and glue inexcusable. There, it's over and done. Time to move on.

Hopefully without dragging all of this behind. Unlike Amy, who is gone and now cries out for justice.

But it hangs on anyway. The afternoon air in the courtroom is polluted by what we've all just heard. We have inhaled it, and it has become a part of us. A nightmare that will never die.

The face of every last juror says so.

39

Colleen Takaguchi from the CSI team is telling us about hair and fiber. The jury is somewhat tuned in, but the forensics are slowing the State's momentum from the overdrive of the medical examiner to the less exciting testimony of this technician who spent over six hours at the scene collecting evidence and over forty hours examining and testing what she found.

"Tell us about the hair in this case. What do we need to know?" asks SA Dickinson.

Takaguchi, a strapping thirty-something with the arms of a world-class weightlifter, reaches and adjusts the rectangular eyeglasses on her flat nose.

"In my workup, I used a comparison microscope to view known and unknown hairs side by side."

"What hairs did you compare?"

"I compared the hairs taken from the rodent removed by Dr. Tsung from Amy's mouth to the hairs taken from the mouse cage belonging to the defendant."

"The hairs taken from the mouse cage of Jana Emerich?"

"Yes."

"Your findings?"

"Well, there are common characteristics in the study of hair. My checklist of comparisons includes color and width, distribution pattern of the medulla, color and distribution pattern of pigment in the cortex, and cuticle pattern."

"We'll hold off on describing those things. Did your comparisons of these two hair samples result in a laboratory finding?"

"Yes. The hair in her mouth was the same as the hair from the defendant's cage."

"You mean it was the same type."

"The same type of hair, yes."

"Are you saying it's the same hair or just the same hair type?"

"Hair type. Hair type only."

"Now, let's go ahead and describe the hair types you compared."

"Rodent hair contains coronal scales. Coronal or crown-like scales give the hair a mosaic surface appearance. Human hair rarely has these scales, but they're common among rodents. So, for openers, I knew I was dealing with rodent hair."

"What else?"

"The characteristics I've previously mentioned. They all matched up."

"So hair of the same type of mouse was found in the mouse cage and the decedent's mouth?"

"Yes."

"What about transfer evidence? Any fingerprints, for example?"

"No, and no DNA samples, either. Not from the rodent where the killer might have handled the mouse and not from Amy's skin where the killer may have touched her. No DNA to study."

"What about mouse DNA? Did you try to establish whether the mice in the defendant's cage were the same family as the mouse in Amy's mouth?"

"Inconclusive there. I cannot say."

"Very well, then, that's all I have. Counsel, you may cross-examine."

I am immediately on my feet and stepping up to the lectern. "Ms. Takaguchi, you've told us about the defendant's mouse and the Amy mouse. But isn't it true you also did a study on the mouse hair taken from a second individual?"

"Yes."

"Who would that be?"

"Rudy Gomez."

"Who is Rudy Gomez?"

"Another student at Wendover High."

"And what did your comparison of Rudy's mouse hair to Amy's mouse hair tell you?"

"They matched. Same kind of hair."

"So at least one other person in Chicago keeps mice like the one in Amy's mouth?"

"Yes. At least one."

"And there could be thousands more, correct?"

"I'm sure I wouldn't know."

I knew that. It was the question I was after, not her answer.

This next one will get me in trouble, but I ask it anyway because defense lawyers should never fear trouble with the judge. Not in a criminal case, and certainly not in a criminal case as serious as this one.

"Ms. Takaguchi, wouldn't you agree, being that there is at least one other source of mice in Chicagoland with the same hair, that therefore reasonable doubt has been established to the defendant's guilt?"

"Objection!"

"Sustained! Counsel, you know better. The jury will disregard the last question."

"That is all I have," I say meekly, seriously contrite as far as anyone can tell.

But inside I am singing the praises of Marcel Rainford, my investigator who obtained the Rudy Gomez mouse hair sample.

Thank you, Marcel.

We have raised a reasonable doubt whether the court wants me to ask about it or not.

Now to do the same with the Super Glue.

If I can, Jana has a chance of walking out of here a free man.

Just then he looks up and says, "What are my chances, Mr. Gresham?"

I look down at him and whisper, "Eighty-twenty."

"Eighty-twenty?" he whispers back. "That's fantastic!"

"No. The eighty is at the other table. The twenty is you."

"Oh. Eight times out of ten I'm dead in the water."

"In a manner of speaking, yes."

"Well, do something, man. Do something!"

I reach down and pat his shoulder. I do it for the impact it has on the jury. They like me, and the theory among defense lawyers is that some of that will rub off on the defendant when I touch or pat him.

That's the theory.

Had the jury not been there, I never would touch this young man.

I just wouldn't.

40

We take our afternoon break and, just as we stand and stretch, Danny returns with a Starbucks for me. My nectar. I take a sip and smack my lips. It's the little things that get the trial lawyer through the trial. Always the little things.

Ordinarily, on our breaks, Jana will disappear. I think he's going outside on the sidewalk to smoke, and I couldn't care less. His help to me in the trial has been worthless. I'm even thinking he knows nothing of use to me because he's not the killer. He has personal problems galore, like spying on Priscilla in the shower, but I'm almost a hundred percent certain he's not a killer to boot. I have been wrong before, but always find out too late after I have gained freedom for someone who goes back out to kill, rob, assault, or drive drunk again. It's happened many times over my thirty years.

We launch into the final session of Monday afternoon, and the SA announces he will call his second to last witness. He calls Mira Kendricks, a gaunt image of a once-beautiful

woman who has spent her life inside laboratories and courtrooms, without sun, without exercise, and without personal
care. Her hair is stringy and different lengths, her eyes look
flat and lack makeup, and her tight lips and small chest give
her an almost childlike look that makes me think of an
angry high school boy.

The State's attorney asks the witness the usual foundational
questions, and we discover she's a chemist with the crime
lab. If it's got any chemistry, she does it. This time around,
it's the Super Glue. She has tested what was found and
seized from Danny's briefcase in our home, admitted by
Danny that it had come from Jana's room, and she tells us
it's the same batch of glue that was used to seal Amy's
mouth.

But we knew that, and I'm ready for it. I cross-examine her,
making a big point out of the fact there are thousands of
other tubes of Super Glue in downtown Chicago alone that
would have come from that sample. She limps from the
courtroom, having been bitten several times by me.

Hopefully, that put an end to the Super Glue connection.

Now to wait for tomorrow's final witness. I can guess that it
will be Amy's father, our esteemed mayor, but I can't know
for sure. Whoever it is, the State's Attorney has exhausted
his list of expert witnesses.

We are done with the technical portion of the trial. The
science has been handed off to the jury for its consideration.
Good riddance, I think as I ride the elevator downstairs,
exhausted. I close my eyes and visualize my boat and the
lake. We are a good team; we have our own special blend of

chemistry. Now that's some science I could spend some time with. Like I said, it's the small things that get a defense lawyer through their trials. Even if it is only a daydream. But it will be a few more months before the ice melts.

Then I'm all in. I'm gone.

41

We're off and running at 9:03 a.m. the next day.

Our mayor is a Jew and a damn smart one. He came up through Yale and Wharton and worked for a stint at Goldman before returning to Chicago and buying a seat on the Exchange here. He amassed a fortune, sold his seat, and turned to politics to bleed off the incredible energy he generates. He is a cultured man in his Savile Row suits and shirts and neckties. He is understated in mood and manner and will not countenance drama in the mayor's office. He wears his white hair parted on the side, and his black eyebrows give him a conflicted look as if he exists somewhere between young and old. It is a look many his age have and, like everything else he does, he wears it well.

Amy Tanenbaum, he tells the jury from the witness stand, was a late-in-life child who grew up with the "only child" syndrome because of the ten years between her and her nearest sibling. By the time she reached high school, her older brothers and sisters, two of each, were gone and either settled down with children of their own or pursuing medicine or Ph.D. Programs.

She was a charming girl, he says, an astute observer of people and the degree of sincerity with which they communicated, and so, the mayor assures the jury, the man who murdered her was not someone with whom she would venture far from the stands, as in going down the sidelines and into the dark to the restrooms. She just wouldn't have done that.

"So what are you telling us, Mr. Mayor?" SA Dickinson asks.

He hand-brushes his dense hair. "What I'm saying is, Amy was surprised in the restroom. Someone she trusted had caught her off-guard."

"So you believe the man who murdered her was someone she knew."

"That's exactly what I'm saying."

"So we can rule out strangers as potential suspects?"

"Yes. My point, exactly. She took great care in choosing who she let come near."

"Were you familiar with Amy's circle of friends?"

"Very. We hosted a sleepover just about every weekend. Our pool is heated and covered, there's a pool table in the game room, and the refrigerators and pantries are always well stocked with teenager food. We've done everything possible to encourage Amy to bring kids home with her. So, yes, I would say I knew them all. More than most parents, I would venture."

"Was she friends with the defendant, Jana Emerich?"

"Never heard his name before his arrest. Never saw him at our house. He was never there."

"Had you ever seen him before?"

"Never."

"Have you spoken to her friends about Mr. Emerich?"

"Yes."

"What have you learned?"

"Objection," I say, "hearsay."

"This is preliminary, counsel," says Judge Lancer-Burgess. "I'll allow it, but only so far, Mr. Dickinson."

"Please answer," SA Dickinson tells the witness. He takes a sip of water from his glass on the lectern.

"I never heard her speak of the boy and wouldn't have had any idea whether he could be trusted. I've learned since that she did talk to a couple of her friends about him."

"It's true he was a newcomer at the school?"

"He started Wendover in September with the new semester. Before that, I believe he was in the Los Angeles area."

"Mr. Mayor, shifting gears now, are you acquainted with the detectives who have taken the lead in this case—Detective Ngo and Detective Valencia?"

"Yes. I have spoken with them numerous times."

"And you have asked them to find your daughter's killer?"

"No more so than any other homicide file on their desk. But I have asked, yes."

"At any time have these two detectives exhibited any doubt as to the identity of Amy's killer?"

"Never. They have been certain all along that Jana Emerich is the man who killed my Amy."

"Objection! Opinion testimony, prejudicial. Strike."

The judge immediately agrees. "The jury will disregard that last exchange. It is improper, and it is stricken from the record."

The State's Attorney then goes on to establish what the mayor knows about the investigation, the standard departmental procedures that were followed, and the like. When it comes to my turn to examine, I know better. Leave the family members alone. The jury will filter out what is useful and what is not. Their bullshit sifters are always at work.

So I have no questions for His Honor.

At which point, the State rests the prosecution's case against Jana Emerich.

There follows the usual motion for a directed verdict, made by me to Judge Lancer-Burgess, as is the standard procedure in criminal and civil cases at the close of the prosecution and plaintiff's cases. These motions have never been allowed, but I plunge ahead anyway, out of the hearing of the jury, with what will amount to my closing argument. It's a good time to hone my words and my logic and get my ducks in line for the time when we argue to the jury.

My motion for a directed verdict is denied.

The defense case must now begin.

42

Tim O'Donnell—Uncle Tim—arrives at court wearing gray Dockers, a white shirt with a wide tie from the Seventies, and a blue blazer that is frayed at the wrists and threadbare at the elbows. He looks hungover and probably is with his venous red sclera and two-day growth of facial hair. His appearance isn't anything like what I asked for. But like with so many things that happen in courtrooms, it is what it is. So I call him to the stand, and they swear him in and then he takes his seat.

He is restless and drums his fingers on the shelf at the front of the witness chair. I catch his eye and give him the briefest head shake. He looks at me with a question mark on his face, apparently without a hint of what I'm driving at.

Anyway.

So we launch right into our discourse.

"Please state your name," I say.

"Timothy J. O'Donnell."

"What is your business, occupation, or profession?"

"I'm a plumber."

"Where do you work?"

"Out of the back of my Ford truck."

"So you're self-employed?"

"I am."

I pause in my questions and appear to be reading through my notes. What I'm doing is giving him a chance to relax and acclimate to his surroundings. I don't want what he's about to tell the jury to be tinged with fear or trembling. I want him rock solid.

"Your nephew is Jana Emerich, correct?"

"Jana is my sister's boy. That makes me his uncle."

"How long have you known Jana?"

"Known him only since last summer when my sister and him moved back here from L.A."

"They'd been living in Los Angeles?"

"Santa Monica, to be exact."

"How old is Jana?"

"Seventeen. Eighteen this coming summer. July twenty."

"How close are you to Jana?"

"Well, he eats my food and sleeps under my roof. That's pretty damn close where I come from."

"Is there an emotional connection?"

"I like the boy a lot. He helps me on weekend emergency calls."

"Plumbing emergencies?"

"Yeah. Water heaters, overflowing toilets, clogged sewers, burst pipes. The usual."

"He goes with you in the truck?"

"Sure, and he goes to the truck and grabs things when I'm on my back under a sink. That kind of help."

"Do you pay him to help you?"

"Room and board."

"Does he have any source of income?"

"His mother is on Social Security Disability as of a month ago. Jana's now getting benefits because of her."

"How much?"

"Objection. Relevance."

He's right. I'm only relaxing Uncle Tim, getting him into the flow, letting the jury see him for the decent man he is.

"It is rather tenuous, counsel. If you don't have a particular objective in mind with this line of questioning, please move on."

"Mr. O'Donnell, do you recall the night of the football game when Amy Tanenbaum was murdered?"

"It was October twelfth. I remember."

"Do you recall what you were doing that night?"

"Thursday night? Probably watching Thursday Night Football. It was the Bears playing."

"You're a Bears fan?"

"Isn't everyone?"

A smile from the jury. They just might be warming to him.

"Where was Jana that day after school?"

"He came home from school about three-thirty. It was cold outside, and my truck cab was a mess. I had him clean out the Ford."

"Why was the cab of the Ford a mess?"

"Because it was the end of the week. Or almost. Soft drink empties, fries on the floor, packages, and wrappers. I hate a dirty truck, so Jana keeps it clean."

"Room and board?"

"Exactly."

"Do you recall what time it was when he cleaned the cab of the Ford truck?"

"Well, he would've changed clothes, so I expect he started in around four o'clock."

"So he was outside?"

"He was in the garage. The trash barrel's in there, too. Pickup's on Friday. When he finished, he rolled the barrel out to the curb. We put it out on Thursday night."

"You saw him roll it out?"

"Not so much as I heard it. Plastic wheels make a racket on the concrete driveway."

"What happened next?"

"He came back in the house and sat down on the couch. He wasn't wearing a coat, and I chewed him out about that. It's flu season, and I don't want him coming down sick and missing school. I'm supposed to be his overseer, you know."

"So he sat down on the couch about what, five o'clock?"

"Give or take twenty minutes. Something like that."

"What happened next?"

"He went upstairs and took a shower. I told him he smelled bad. Teenage boys."

"I thought teenage boys his age kept themselves very clean and smelled good in case they met someone."

"Not this one. He had to be told."

"So what happened?"

"I heard the shower pipes upstairs. They pound in the wall. Air in the pipes."

"What time did the shower noise stop?"

"Five-fifteen, five-thirty."

"What were you doing?"

"Watching ESPN and clipping my toenails. I had my work boots off because they hurt my feet when my toenails get too long. Should I say that here?"

"Sure. We want to know what happened, and that's part of it. What happened once the shower ended?"

"He came downstairs. He was wearing baggies and a Chargers sweatshirt. He knew I hated it, so he wore it to piss me off. Sorry."

"Chargers football team?"

"Yep."

"And you're a Bears fan?"

"Who isn't?" he asks again with a short laugh, like when you're poked in the ribs unexpectedly.

"What happened next?"

"I made some money that day, so I had him call for Chinese food. We both ordered Kung Pao Chicken. It came about forty minutes later."

"So now we're talking maybe six-thirty?"

"Yep. So we eat and I grab a shower. By this time, he's inside his room with the stereo blasting. I can hear it through the walls even from downstairs."

"Did you see him later that night?"

"No. I watched the game until I fell asleep in my chair, then I hit the hay."

"Was Jana in his room all that night?"

"Sure."

"How can you be sure if you didn't see him again after your shower?"

"Because I had told him no football at the high school that night. It was a school night, and I wanted him to study for his math test the next day."

"But you didn't see him again?"

"No. But he didn't leave. I'm certain of it."

We then go into the arrest the next morning, the move-out of the defendant to my house, Jana's return to his uncle's and a brief explanation for that, and then I turn him over for cross-examination. With all of my witnesses, I instruct them to listen to the questions on cross and answer only what is asked. They are specifically instructed not to embellish and not to explain. I tell them that if an explanation is called for, we'll get it done on re-direct examination when I'm controlling things.

"Mr. O'Donnell," says SA Dickinson, "I'm the attorney for the State. My job is to put your nephew in prison. Do you understand my role?"

"Yes."

"My job is also to bring charges against witnesses who commit perjury. Do you know what perjury is?"

"I grew up on Perry Mason. I know perjury."

"Have you committed perjury here today by telling this jury you're certain that Jana was in his room all that night of the football game?"

"No. I told the truth, sir."

"How can you be sure he was in his room when you didn't see him again? I mean, couldn't he have snuck out of the house while you were in the shower?"

"He could, but he didn't."

"How can you be sure of that?"

"I know my nephew. He's a good boy. He does whatever I say."

"Yet you didn't actually see him?"

"No."

"Or hear him?"

"Heard his music."

"But you didn't hear him?"

"No."

"So we could say you're only guessing he was in his room all night?"

Uncle Tim turns to me. I am busy with my head down. I can't be seen telegraphing an answer to the questions. Especially not this one.

"I didn't see him. I didn't hear him. But I knew he followed my orders, and my orders were to stay home and study."

"Did you speak to the police when they came for him the next morning? The police report indicates you were very uncooperative."

"Who the hell's gonna cooperate when their family is getting arrested? I didn't jump in and help them take him away. Hell no!"

"You swore at the police?"

"Sure did. They put the cuffs on way too tight. I thought he was gonna cry any second."

"Isn't it true you told the police you didn't know for certain that Jana was in his room all night?"

"I told them he would've had to have wings to get out without me seeing."

"And you also told them you were certain he was there?"

"As certain as I could be. I'm not running a jail, sir."

"So you weren't certain?"

"Did I do a head count like on California Avenue?"

"Yes."

"No. Like I said, my house isn't some jail."

"I am left with the impression you don't know where your nephew was the night Amy Tanenbaum was murdered. Is my impression accurate?"

"I don't know nothing about your impression. I don't even know what the hell you're talking about, your impression."

He's riled, and I decide not to re-direct when the State's Attorney breaks it off. Sometimes it's best to leave an agitated witness alone. Emotion too often brings out the truth. The last thing I need right now.

So the witness is excused, and we all have the same impression.

He didn't know for sure on October 12th, and he doesn't know for sure now.

43

It is eleven a.m. when Father Bjorn takes the stand. He has come to court wearing a black suit and white shirt and white collar. He is a diminutive man in stature though a giant in accomplishment and community regard. Everyone loves Father Bjorn including, evidently, the mayor himself, who has stayed to watch our trial and gives a friendly smile to his friend, the priest.

I ask him questions about his education, his training, and his work history. He entered the priesthood at a very early age and has maintained a steadfast love of the Lord and Church ever since. Except, he says, for one time when his faith was weak. He was in his late twenties, and he just lost his parents in a car wreck.

"How did that loss affect you?" I ask him.

"It devastated me. I felt as if God had turned his back on me. There was no real connection there, and I became rootless."

"How did you meet Jana's mother?"

"She was a long-time congregant of our parish. She came in for counseling when her fiancé of two years abruptly left her for another man."

"So she was vulnerable?"

It is a sore point with him. It is probably the only time in his life this man has ever taken advantage of another person, and he isn't proud of it.

"She was vulnerable, and I was lonely. We talked several times and prayed for her. I heard her confession. On perhaps her fourth visit to my office, it happened. I crossed a line, and she didn't resist. Quite the opposite. We were extremely attracted to each other."

"What happened?"

"We began a sexual relationship that lasted six months. Then she informed me she was pregnant. I don't have to tell you the Church's position on abortion. So, there we were. I couldn't leave the priesthood, and I couldn't even think of ending the pregnancy. She was a devout Catholic and wouldn't think of it either. So we made the best of a dire situation. I had money saved, and after Jana was born, I helped her move to California and get set up there. Then the years passed, and my son grew up without a father."

"But she married at some point?"

"She did. But she would tell me when we spoke each Christmas that her new husband was anything but a father. He wouldn't countenance even throwing a ball around with my son. But I was in no position to criticize him."

"Because you were never a father to him yourself?"

"Exactly. The pot calling the kettle black."

"Did you ever see your son before he moved back to Chicago last summer?"

"No."

"What kind of boy is Jana?"

"Objection! Foundation."

"Sustained."

"Your Honor," I begin, "he's the boy's father. He's known him only a short time, it's true, but this is his son, and he is an expert judge of character."

"You haven't laid a foundation for how he might know about the boy's character counsel. The objection is sustained."

"Father Bjorn, how many times have you seen Jana since he moved here?"

"Four. Twice in my office, once at the movies, and once at the jail. Plus, in court, but those weren't visits."

"During that time, have you been able to form an opinion as to your son's character?"

"I have. He's—"

"Objection! Foundation."

The judge nods and gives me a fierce look. "Counsel, I will not allow his opinion about his son's character. There just isn't foundation enough for that."

Meaning, the priest doesn't know his son well enough to comment on his character. Which was my whole point in putting the priest on the stand in the first place: to anoint the boy with the priest's blessing in court. That has failed.

I then tread water on unrelated issues for ten minutes and finally break it off. On a one-to-ten basis, I would give this witness's effectiveness maybe a four. Maybe less.

There is no cross-examination. Dickinson doesn't want to insult the Catholics on the jury, and it's a wise move on his part. Neither would I, and I hope I haven't. I was reaching, though, and they could very well have seen right through my ploy.

44

It is the twilight of the trial, and the question has come up again, as it always does.

Does the defendant testify? Does the defendant take the stand, impart his story, and undergo decimating cross-examination by the prosecutor?

I say no, but the defendant, Jana Emerich, insists otherwise.

"Who are you to say?" he complains noisily after the priest has returned to the gallery and the jury is out of the courtroom during our recess. "It's my case, dammit!"

Which is correct. Jana has the final say in the matter of defendant testimony. It is not my or any other defense attorney's decision to make, not ever. We can cajole, threaten, forecast devastation and dozens of years in prison but, in the end, it's Jana's call.

And so he takes the witness stand and swears to tell the whole truth. As I knew they would, the jury is looking at him askance. They expect him to lie on his own behalf; they would do the same if it were them. It's human nature, and that's how the game is played. Everyone knows it. So, they are wary.

We hurry through the background without much detail. The more I leave for cross-examination, the better. The theory is that the prosecutor can bring out fresh detail, but he can't trap Jana with detail that I introduced. It's a cat-and-mouse back-and-forth, and we're both expert at it, Dickinson and I.

Then, "Directing your attention to October twelfth. Were you here in court when your uncle Tim testified about your activities that day after school?"

"Yes."

"Is there anything about his testimony that you need to correct?"

"No."

"Uncle Tim told the jury you didn't leave your room that night. Is that true?"

Keep in mind he previously told me and Father Bjorn at the jail that he had been at the game that night. No questions about it at that time, a definite yes, he was there.

"Yes."

"Yes, he's wrong?"

"Yes, he's right."

I am stunned. He has just lied. No, he has told the jury something different from what he told Father Bjorn and me at the jail. However, my professional affect doesn't change. I keep a straight face. I do not grimace, and I do not telegraph how upset I am with Jana and his answer. I plunge ahead.

"So you weren't at the game that night?"

"No. I went over to the field the next morning and climbed up in the stands."

"Why was that?"

"I wanted to get a look at what was going on down below. Bobby Knupp called me and told me there was a dead body under there."

"And—and—so you went to look?"

"Yes. I climbed up in the stands. The cop was over in his car talking on his radio. That must have been when I dropped my muffler."

My mind is whirling. My hands twitch as I leaf through my notes, buying time. Where do I go with this? It's unethical for an attorney to put false testimony on the witness stand. But there is a saving grace here for me: I don't know that it's false. I only know that it's different from what he told me at the jail. At the jail, he said he'd been at the game. Today he says he wasn't at the game. Which one is true? I wasn't there, so I have zero way of knowing. And this is how lawyers get into serious trouble with the Bar Association. They do it unwittingly or, like me, they do it half-assed, backing into a situation where they don't belong. I should call a recess now and talk to Jana out of the hearing of the jury. But to do so would send up a flag that something was wrong. So, in the interests of preserving my client's veracity (or lack) with the jury, I move it along.

"The night of the game. What were you doing in your room?"

"Listening to rap and doing my physics homework. We had a test the next day."

"Uncle Tim said it was a math test."

"He just didn't know. It was physics."

"So he did get something wrong when he testified?"

"I guess so."

"Have you gotten anything wrong?"

"No. I know what I was studying that night. It's only been three months."

"Do you know Rudy Gomez?"

"Yes."

"What is your relationship with Rudy?"

"Just a friend. We both have a snake."

"Does he come to your house?"

"He did last semester. A few times, I think."

"Did he take any mice from you?"

"I gave him three mice one time. He was out, and his guy was hungry."

"His guy?"

"His snake was hungry."

"Jana, did you murder Amy Tanenbaum?"

"No."

"Were you with her the night of the game?"

"No. I already told you I wasn't even there."

"Did you know her from school?"

"No. She was a freshman, and I'm a senior. We don't mix."

"Was she in any of your classes?"

"Maybe homeroom. I don't know for sure."

"Have you spoken with the police about this case?"

"Yes. Twice."

"When was that?"

"The morning after it happened and the morning after Franny was murdered."

"Both times, the police have talked to you about those girls?"

"Both times."

"Were you involved in any way in either of those tragic crimes?"

"No, I wasn't."

"Do you know anything about them?"

"Only what I've heard and read."

"But you didn't see anything yourself?"

"No."

"And you weren't there?"

"No, I wasn't there."

"That is all, Your Honor."

Judge Lancer-Burgess is looking at Jana, but I can't tell by her expression what she's thinking. "Very well. Mr. State's Attorney, you may cross-examine."

Unlike some prosecutors, Dickinson doesn't run to the lectern as if he's ready to eat this man up and spit him out. No, Dickinson saunters, for want of a better term. He is casual, almost friendly, as he approaches my client and shoots him a small smile. Jana, damn him, smiles back. I don't want him smiling and loose. I want him uptight and mute right now.

Dickinson flips a page on his yellow notepad and then flexes his right hand. He looks directly at Jana and purses his lips. Now there is no smile.

"You want this jury to believe you didn't kill Amy even though your muffler was found near her dead body?"

"Yes."

"So you were at the football game?"

"No."

"Why not?"

"I was studying for a physics exam. I want to be an engineer, and I need good grades."

"A snake engineer?"

"I don't know what that is."

"Tell us what physics you studied for your test. Oh, before you do, I had a police officer contact your physics teacher to obtain a copy of the physics exam you told this jury you took on Friday, October thirteenth. Guess what? He didn't give an exam that day. Do you still want to stand by your story?"

Jana nods. "I didn't say I took the exam. I said I was upstairs studying for it. We got to school the next day, and the exam was canceled. You'll have to ask Mr. Augsberger about that."

Dickinson appears to suppress a smile. It is an act. He's good, very good.

"You also said you know Rudy Gomez. How do you know Rudy?"

"Everybody does. The cops picked him up for killing Franny Arlington."

Bingo. That was a setup, courtesy of Michael Gresham. We had talked and talked about how to get in the bit about Rudy killing Franny. I instructed Jana to wait for any question of whatever nature from the SA referencing Rudy and to slip it in then. He did, right between Dickinson's ribs. Now I get to come back to that question on re-direct examination because the prosecutor opened the door. What a great game, trial law.

Dickinson quickly moves on. "Speaking of Franny, since you mentioned her, are you telling us you didn't have anything to do with Franny's death?"

"Objection!" I explode, coming up out of my chair. "Prejudicial, no such charge pending! Defense moves for a mistrial, Your Honor!"

"Motion denied," Judge Lancer-Burgess says summarily. But then she addresses my objection based on the prejudicial matter being injected into the case by the State's Attorney. "Objection sustained. The State will not go there again, Mr. Dickinson! The jury will disregard the question and disregard all references to any case except the one involving Amy Tanenbaum."

"You said Rudy Gomez has been to your house?"

"Yes. Maybe three times."

"And you gave him some mice?"

"Yes."

"Are you aware that a mouse was found in the mouth of Amy Tanenbaum?"

"I heard that."

"Are you aware that the hair from that mouse matched the hair from your mice?"

"Yes. And matched the hair from Rudy's mouse."

"And you say your muffler was found by Amy's body because you were there the morning after and dropped it through the bleachers?"

"Yes."

"So let me see if I understand you. Your same mouse hair was found in Amy's mouth, your muffler was found near her body, and the Super Glue in her mouth was the same batch as your Super Glue. Isn't that just a little too coincidental to be a coincidence?"

"I don't understand you."

"Too many things that tie you to Amy make you appear to be her killer. Don't you agree?"

"I didn't kill Amy. I don't know who did. What else do you want me to say?"

"Mr. Emerich, were you ever in trouble in California?"

"Objection. Relevance," I say.

"Sustained."

SA Dickinson continues with barely a hitch, "Were you ever arrested in California?"

Judge Lancer-Burgess looks at the SA over her glasses. "The court objects to that question, and I am going to admonish, you, Mr. Dickinson. That question is improper, you know it is improper, and if this happens once more in any form, you will be looking at a mistrial. I might even revisit the defendant's motion for a directed verdict."

"Yes, Your Honor. Thank you."

I am relishing this, of course. Moreover, I'm wondering how I might trigger such an impropriety again by the State and win a mistrial or dismissal. But I know I can't do it without Dickinson's help, and by now he's been chastised enough. So he shakes his head as if he's been treated poorly and takes his seat.

"That's all I have," he tells the judge.

If nothing else, his being called up short two or three times has rendered his cross-examination almost useless. I also know better than to play the Rudy Gomez-Franny Arlington card again. It would rebound and possibly open the door to extremely damaging questions by the State. So I back off, too.

Jana is dismissed and takes his seat beside me once again.

I then stand and rest the defense's case.

My team could have presented Rudy to suggest he was a serial killer of sorts, but we ultimately decided against that. Why? Because it was a cheap shot. More importantly, though, I didn't sense that we needed it. Plus, it could have backfired, angering the jurors for attempting to point the finger at some kid without an attorney. Knowing Rudy's father, though, he would have had an attorney, an outstanding attorney, and our poking and prodding would have been fruitless and even come across as foolish. So we did the next best thing and pulled in our horns and rested.

It was time.

Judge Lancer-Burgess then gives the jury their instructions. This eats up ninety minutes, and when she finishes, it is two o'clock. Plenty of time for closing arguments.

State's Attorney Dickinson gets to go first.

45

Trey Dickinson, Assistant State's Attorney, walked in here five days ago with a win-loss record of 65-0. As we're waiting for the jury following the judge's jury instructions and ten-minute recess, Dickinson leans across the four feet separating his table from mine and says with a smile that becomes a smirk, "So, I'm gonna start calling you Ol' Sixty-Six."

I give him an empty look.

"What? You don't get it, Michael? I'm just a few hours away from my sixty-sixth win before a jury."

"I'll bet that means more money in your pocket, right, Dick?" I say with all the sarcasm I can muster.

"Fuck you and fuck that liar sitting next to you." He leans forward and looks at Jana. "I'm talking about you, boy. You're going away for a long time. Bubba's Bitch. That's your new name."

"Hey, easy, Dick. You're personalizing," I say.

"Yeah? Maybe that's because I stood in at Amy's autopsy, eh? I saw the mouse in the mouth. I observed the half-eaten cheek. Then you know what? Dr. Tsung opened her eyes. They were eyes of terror."

He suddenly laughs and leans back to his side of the aisle. He waves at me as if waving me off. "You had to be there," he says, finished.

And five minutes later, he's making his closing argument to the jury. The same anger and rage that he spewed at us only minutes ago comes spilling out into the space separating him from the jury and ignites those people. Honestly, he has them and carries them for the next thirty minutes. At some point during this discourse, every head nods along with him and refuses to look at Jana. Or at me.

I know we are finished. Dead in the water.

Unless I can put something together that surpasses where Dickinson has taken them.

He sits and draws a deep breath. The judge looks at me, so I proceed to the lectern. I have a prepared closing argument with notes on a yellow pad, but I set those aside. The energy in the room seeps into me, and I step up to the jury.

"A killer walks among you," I begin. "So when you head off to bed tonight do double-check your door locks and window latches. Count the noses of your loved ones. Batten down the hatches because he is coming for his next victim."

A look passes among the jury. They stir. They are uncomfortable. Press on.

"What nobody has talked about, and what this case is really about, is the fact there have been three homicides at

Wendover High over the past six months. We've been here in this courtroom day after day discussing a third of that killer's work. One homicide. And we are being asked by the State to blame that one on a young man who, no one doubts, had nothing to do with the subsequent two murders."

They lean forward in their chairs, not much, as imperceptible as a buckle in the wind on a fall day. But they have reacted; I push on.

"A student named Franny Arlington has died since Amy Tanenbaum. Was that the work of Jana Tanenbaum? No one has said it is. No State's Attorney has indicted him for the crime. A third student has died as well. Her name is Scarlett Newson, and she was a young woman who spent most of her life confined to a wheelchair. Without regard to her disability or her desire to live, the same killer who killed Amy and Franny also killed Scarlett. But have they charged Jana with that crime? No. Nor will they."

Two jurors are nodding with me now. A third has uncrossed her arms and her frown has relented somewhat.

"And please remember. The police force in Chicago is thousands strong. The prosecutors in the Cook County State's Attorney's office are hundreds, maybe thousands, strong as well. And how many of these thousands of America's best prosecutors and law enforcement officials have pointed to Jana Emerich and said, 'Young man, you've killed three now, and you're done'?"

Another juror and yet another nod. They continue nodding as I press on.

"Let there be no mistake," I tell them, chopping at the air with my hand. "There is a killer loose among you, and he hasn't been brought to justice, not yet.

"And what? Are we to believe the State that Jana Emerich killed Amy Tanenbaum, and this somehow inspired another killer to kill Franny and then Scarlett?

"Nonsense. While the State's case is inviting at its cellular level, when viewed as a whole, we all know it has entirely missed the point. The overview, the big picture, cries out for justice. Yet, the overview isn't your responsibility. It is the State's responsibility to come in here and present you with a coherent view of your world, the world of Wendover High, the world of Amy, Franny, and Scarlett. And guess what? The State has failed utterly to do that. Instead, it has pursued a boy whom was an outsider and whom no one knew very well and was thus fair game. Until his father, a priest in Chicago, heard what was happening. And he said, 'Enough! Enough! I am going to go before the people and help my son.' So I was retained to come here and defend him against this wrong-headed attack."

Now the Catholics are with me. I hate to be so base about it, but there you are. We win these cases one mind at a time. A pebble at a time, never an avalanche.

On, I continue, building to a review of the facts in the case, which I don't spend much time on since the jury knows all too well the simple facts of the State's case against Jana.

Then I discuss reasonable doubt and go through the judge's instructions on the law. When I am done, I have covered the facts and the law. Plus, I have covered what so often is forgotten in these rooms: the jury's need to do justice. All

juries have it, and there is the secret to winning—help them
do justice.

"So bring what has been so sorely lacking in this courtroom.
Bring it because you can. I am talking about justice. Only
you are allowed to do justice. Only you are burdened with
doing justice. I am trusting you with it. Jana trusts you, too.
Vote not guilty. Go in there and vote and come back and tell
this young man he is free to live his life, to go out from here
relieved of the terrible burden placed on him by this detective and this team of prosecutors. Give him justice and be
done with it. Thank you."

It is silent when I am done and silent when I take my seat.

The judge sends the jury to the jury room and, when they
are gone, bedlam erupts. The press, too long quiet and
respectful, suddenly are talking animatedly among themselves, phones are produced and connections made, and the
TV camera, in violation of the court's order, pans the courtroom, sweeping east, west, north, and south.

Danny makes her way through the crowd and reaches us.
Then comes Father Bjorn. He sweeps his son into his arms
and hugs him, a first for them both. Danny throws her
arms around me and lays her head on my chest and
breathes. "It's over," she whispers above the bedlam. "It's
over."

Two hours later, there has been no word from the jury, so
the judge calls them into the courtroom and recesses the
trial for the day. She admonishes the jury: they are to avoid
all TV and newspapers and radio stations that are beaming
out any news of the trial. They are to refrain from discussing
it with anyone. They are to tell the judge immediately if

anyone approaches them about the trial and tries to influence their vote.

Then we are gone.

Marcel drives us north to our home and pulls my car into our garage. His truck is parked in the driveway where it's been all day since he came and drove us in this morning.

Then we are alone. Me, Danny, and our baby.

I lock the doors and check the window latches that night before bed.

I finally know I am right: the arrest of Jana has solved nothing.

The killer is out there loose, searching out his next victim.

46

The next morning, I swing my Mercedes into its underground parking slot. I am climbing out when I turn and find myself suddenly confronted by the larger-than-life seven-foot frame of Detective Ngo. He towers over me and smiles at me. I dart my gaze around the parking garage. There is no one else around. Is this it? I wonder. He warned me that our time would come. What was it he said? That he was going to fuck me up?

During the trial a year ago of James Lamb, I took to wearing a gun. Not because of James Lamb, but because of the husband of Lamb's victim, a federal judge. Marcel taught me how to use that gun, and I shot at least a thousand rounds through it before he was happy with my knowledge and skill. I don't wear that gun every day as I did back then, but today I've decided to wear it. In fact, ever since Ngo cornered me in the courtroom and threatened me, I have been wearing my gun.

He sees me move my hand inside of my coat, and he steps back. He is wary, watching my hand, watching my eyes.

I turn and pull my briefcase off the seat and lock my car. Then I return my free hand inside my suit coat. Ngo is still watching my every move.

"Did you have something to say to me?" I ask him.

"I'm not here to talk. I'm here to observe."

"Observe what?"

"Observe where you park. Observe where you work."

"I'm filing a complaint against you."

He laughs. "Be my guest. Spell my name correctly."

He spells his name, but he's moving backward, allowing me to pass beyond my row of parked cars. I head off toward the elevators. He doesn't follow, but I keep my hand inside my coat.

Then I realize. This man respects only force.

So I am glad I'm wearing my gun. I decide I won't stop wearing it this time.

I remain in the office that morning, trying to concentrate on other cases and kidding myself into thinking I'm successful. I'm not, of course, no more than any other trial lawyer with a jury out deliberating.

It is a difficult time, too. My breath comes and goes sharply in and out. Danny made sure I had a substantial breakfast this morning before leaving home. She remained behind, her day to spend with Dania. In a way, I envy them, but not too much. There is no better in-your-face experience than waiting for your jury. My pulse pounds and my sight flickers as I look beyond my office windows at Lake Michigan. Seagulls float and rise and descend in time with the music of the wind. Spreading their wings and drawing their feet to their bodies they are free—I think an astronaut said—from the bonds of the earth. In a few months, I will keep them company from my boat, my Sundancer, *Condition of Release*. Just like when the court says to the defendant being admitted to bail, "Here are your conditions of release." While I am very concerned, deep down I am at peace because I know I have done my best for my client. That is all a trial lawyer can ask of him or herself. Do your best and leave it all in the courtroom.

At eleven-thirty, Mrs. Lingscheit comes into my office with the news. They're back. The judge is waiting.

Marcel drives me to court on California Avenue where we park and hurry inside.

When we push through the door, all heads turn to watch us, then just me, walk up the aisle and come through the bar. I nod at the judge and take my place next to Jana who sits slumped in his chair. For such a monumental moment in his life, he looks indifferent, one could even say blasé.

"We have a verdict," the judge says flatly, and she nods at the bailiff. He disappears into the short hallway that leads out of the room to where the jury deliberates. Within minutes, they are following him back into the courtroom, twelve serious-looking citizens who have also done their best.

"Ladies and Gentlemen, have you reached a verdict?"

"We have, Your Honor," says the CEO of a software startup in the Union Station building.

"Please pass your verdict to the clerk."

I am scanning jurors' faces, looking for a hint, some indication. But they all look away, and I take that as a warning of bad news to follow.

The clerk hands the verdict to the judge who reads it quickly. She hands it back to the clerk. "Ladies and gentlemen, is this your verdict?"

All jurors indicate that it is their verdict.

"The clerk will read the verdict," the judge pronounces.

With a flourish of the wrist and a clearing of the throat, the clerk reads simply, "We the duly impaneled jury do find the defendant, Jana Emerich, not guilty."

I am jolted alive, but I force myself to remain motionless.

Final ministrations of gratitude are passed by the judge to the jury in a short speech thanking them for their service, telling them they are free to go, telling them they may now talk to the press, but only if they wish.

Then we are adjourned.

Mayor Tanenbaum bursts through the gate and heads straight for the prosecutor. Trey Dickinson begins talking, folding his arms over his chest and giving the mayor defeated looks as he listens to what can only be a scathing diatribe. Voices are raised, completely ignoring those of us nearby. Marcel comes forward, prepared to walk us through the press and spectators.

Jana turns to me. He looks into my eyes.

Then he turns away. Without a word, he is gone. Father Bjorn catches up to him just beyond the gate and attempts to talk, but the boy apparently brushes him aside with a querulous look and a quickening step. Then Father Bjorn is swallowed up by the press as it surges up the aisle to get a statement from the man whose life has been restored. Whether they are successful, I do not know as they all disappear through the courtroom's double doors, propped open now by the bailiffs as they stare grimly at the throng passing through.

Father Bjorn makes it through the gate and up to me. "Well," he says, "thank you, Michael."

"You're welcome."

"Well done, boss," says Marcel.

Dickinson breaks away from the mayor and begins packing his bag. I step over and try to shake his hand, but he keeps his back to me.

Then, in a snarl, he turns his head. "Sixty-five and one. Enjoy it, Gresham. It will never happen again."

Then he is gone.

I return to my small group, and we all grab a stack of books or a stuffed briefcase and move through the gate and up the aisle.

It is finished.

Outside the room are TV cameras and crews. One mic and then another is jammed in my face.

I nod. "A killer walks among us. The Chicago Police Department needs to step up and tell the citizens they are at risk. He must be found and brought to justice. It awaits him inside that courtroom we have just vacated. It is waiting."

When I turn, Marcel shoulders our way through the crush of reporters and gawkers, and then we are on the elevator with a handful of occupants and are sailing down, down, down.

Free at last.

47

A week later, things are finally settling down again. Business has picked up at the office following the front page profiles I received on the *Trib* and the *Sun-Times*. New referral attorneys are calling to introduce themselves and prospective clients. Mrs. Lingscheit doesn't get to do much anymore but operate the phones. Marcel is working up a dozen cases and talking to me about adding a second investigator to our roster. Danny has a full caseload and is supervising several associate attorneys in pre-trial motion practice, plea negotiations, and client management. But yesterday was Priscilla's last day, and we're still calling nannies in for interviews, so Danny will be home with Dania starting Monday. Again, we are a bustling practice and a relatively happy place to work.

Saturday, Danny and I attend a church social at All Saints-St. Thomas Catholic Church, Father Bjorn's church. Everyone is there who we usually hang out with, and we mix in the church's basement and share potluck. The barbecue chicken is superb, and I overdose on that and potato salad. My faves.

Father Bjorn mingles and laughs with a steady coming and going of his parishioners. Around eight o'clock, during a lull after prayers and blessings, who should come down the stairs but Jana himself. He is wearing black Dockers, gray sweater, and a North Face parka that looks new. There is no muffler, I observe, and I begin to chastise myself for even thinking that but then let it go. There hasn't been sufficient time yet between the trial and tonight that I can consider myself disengaged. Father Bjorn goes directly to his son and throws an arm over his shoulders. He maneuvers him through the crowd, introducing him here and there, and then talks to him while Jana fills a plate.

They come to the table where Danny and I are sitting, talking to a rotating group of well-wishers, receiving congratulations on our victory and just being neighborly. Jana is his usual sullen self as I speak his name and tell him hello. Danny tries to engage with him, but her efforts are quickly deflected. We back off and try not to watch as he gorges himself on the church's bounty. As is customary, his eyes flit to Danny several times as he chews and I catch him staring at her breasts. Father Bjorn notices none of this. He carries on conversations with everyone around him, three or four topics at once, as people with public roles do, always to my amazement. Then Jana finishes his plate and begins picking at pecan pie, removing the pecans and putting them to the side of his paper plate. *Why on earth would he choose that?* I wonder as he busies himself with the de-nutting process.

As he wipes his hands on a napkin at the close of the eating business, I finally ask, "How have you been?"

"Fine," he says without making eye contact with me.

"How does it feel to be a free man again?"

"Great, but I'm leaving Chicago."

"You are? Where are you going?"

"Joining the Coast Guard. As soon as I turn eighteen this July."

"Well, congratulations on that. I'm sure you'll make a great sailor."

"Yeah, well, I remember the day we went out on your boat. That was sick, man."

Sick as in really cool.

"I'm so glad you remember, Jana. We did have fun that day."

"Do you ever need help cleaning that boat? I can do it from bow to stern for twenty bucks."

"I'll keep that in mind. When would you be available?"

"Anytime. Especially now with winter blowing ice and rain and snow all over."

"It's in a covered slip."

"Yeah, but still..." His voice trails off as Danny stands to refill her coffee. Again with the eyes.

"I'll make a mental note. I'll call you."

"Super, man. Thanks."

"Have you heard any more about Rudy or the third case?"

"Nope, not a word. He's still in school with us, so I don't know what the hell is going on."

"My guess? The mayor's got his police department regrouped and went after the real killer this time."

He smiles slyly. "The real killer," he whispers. "I like that."

"What do you mean?"

"Nothing."

"Hey, the guy's a real threat. He's out there, and he'll kill again if he's not stopped."

"You're right." He gets up and stretches and yawns. "Well, call me about the boat, Mr. Gresham. I'm your boy."

"Yes, you are."

He walks off. We both know I'll never call him. We both know there's nothing between us.

We are disconnected, and it feels more than right.

48

M onday afternoon I receive a cell call from Danny. She sounds flustered and upset. She sounds scared.

"Michael, Jana's here."

"What? What the hell!"

"He says you told him to come by for the key to the boat. He says you're paying him to clean it. Is that right? Did you hire him?"

"No. Don't act alarmed. Give him a soft drink. Make him a sandwich. Suggest it's time for him to leave, but if he doesn't get the hint, just don't force it. I'm on my way."

"Okay."

I can't make it downstairs on the elevator fast enough. Marcel is off somewhere staking out police detectives as they stake out one of our clients. We need to know whether they're planting evidence, which we suspect. I try his number. No answer. I climb into my Mercedes and back out of my slot, squeal up the curve to the exit arm, and flash my pass. The arm lifts, and I am out.

Lake Shore Drive takes ten minutes in traffic. Then I am headed north. Traffic is sluggish and slow when it's normally quite speedy. I fall in behind an eighteen-wheeler even though trucks aren't allowed on this stretch. I pound the steering wheel and curse. Speed dial is trying Marcel again. Still nothing.

My schoolboy mind urges me to call the police while my tough lawyer mind says to keep them out of it. Cops rushing in with drawn guns where my wife and baby are being held is the last thing I want. So I will think about it a few minutes as I drive.

Today is March 1st. I will remember this day forever as the day some asshole took my life hostage. I resolve this will never happen again. No client will ever have access to my private life again. Danny will have to find another job, something like civil litigation where the risks are significantly reduced. Or maybe probate and writing wills and setting up trusts. In fact, perhaps that's where I belong, in a world unpopulated by crazy sons of bitches who might take a liking to your wife, your kid, or your property. Never again, I vow. I'm cleaning out my files, giving everyone their money back, and closing down for good. I have enough money after a case I filed against a Mexican utility company that I never have to work again. I pound the steering wheel. "What have I done to myself?" I cry out against the windshield, but no one hears. They know nothing about my oath as an attorney to help even the evilest son of a bitch on earth that even he deserves a fair trial and a competent lawyer to stand up for him. But I'm done with all that. As of March 1st, put it on your calendar.

I dial Marcel again. No answer, it goes straight to voicemail. I tell him to call me asap and come to my home immediately when he gets the message. Finally, I'm able to swerve out and gun it around the truck in a no-passing zone. Rules of the road be damned. Nothing matters to me right now except my family.

Nothing else matters.

I floor it, and the car lurches into passing gear, and I'm again facing oncoming traffic as I pass a slow-moving SUV in a no-passing zone. The woman flips me off.

So be it.

49

Danny returns to the family room and asks Jana to join her in the kitchen. Without being asked, she pours him a Coke. He drinks it down and holds out his glass. He doesn't ask; he just holds out his glass. She refills it and drops in two more ice cubes. Then he sits back in one of our captain's chairs.

"So," Danny asks lightly, "how's the world treating you?"

"I never got to tell you this before, Danny, but when I was living here, I used to watch you in the shower."

"Jana, I'm going to have to ask you to leave. That's inappropriate."

"I totally like when you drop the soap, and I can see your breasts. You turn me on, girl."

"Leave right now, or I'm calling the police."

She pulls her phone out of her jeans pocket and begins punching numbers. Her eyes never leave his except to make the call. 911 rings once, twice, when he suddenly lunges at her. He doubles up his fist and swings at her head. She remembers the phone ringing twice, and then she finds herself on the floor of the family room, bound on her side with clothesline rope. Her legs are pulled up behind her as they would have been if she were crouching, then the rope travels up her backside to her wrists, which are also tightly bound together. She is at his mercy.

He pulls a circular silver object out of his pocket and steps over her, positioning himself behind her. "I'm going to place this E string around your throat."

"No! Please, Jana. My baby!"

"Please Jana? Does that mean you would rather please me than die just now? Because either way, you're going to die."

"My husband will kill you. If he doesn't, Marcel will."

"Let them. I will die knowing I've had the best woman in Chicago. Whattaya say, Danny? Care to buy yourself another ten minutes?"

"Yes, I do. Whatever you want, Jana. I'm willing to bargain it out. We could have sex every time you come over if that's what you want."

He begins laughing—*laughing.* And then she feels the very thin, high-tensile wire loop drop down over her neck. Then it tightens.

"I had another girl like this once. What was her name? Oh, yes. Amy something. Tanenbaum? That seems about right. Does that seem about right to you, Danny?"

Danny says, "You murdered that poor baby. I've always known it was you, Jana. You're lucky you had Michael defending you. Anyone else, and you'd be sitting in prison today."

"You say that like I owe him. He's a grunt. I don't owe him a goddamn thing."

Danny's fingers claw at the knots behind her back where the rope encircles her wrists. Unable to get purchase on the knot, her efforts break away fingernails.

He is watching her. He points to her hands. "Your fingers are bleeding."

"That's just a sign of how much I hate you."

"What? Do you hate me? Okay, darling girl. Here I come."

50

I can't locate Marcel, so I call the cops. They are warned that it's a hostage situation. They promise to wait until I arrive so I can talk to my "client" as I describe him. Most likely I can talk him down as one would a jumper from a rooftop, I explain to the 911 dispatcher. He's my client, and he respects me, and I guess that he's mental today. He gets that way.

A duty sergeant comes on the line. "Michael Gresham? This is Sergeant Hollingsworth. Your wife is being held against her will?"

"Yes, and my daughter."

"How old is your daughter?"

"A little over a year."

"Okay. What else can you tell me?"

"You need to understand the man is my client. He's probably just upset. Please let me arrive and speak with him before anything else. Will you agree to that?"

"We have to, I'd say. All right."

"Good, then I'll give you my home address."

"Does he carry a phone?"

"Yes."

"Give me his number."

I have to scroll through the phone log as I'm driving along the lake, but there it is, a call from three weeks earlier. I give it to Sergeant Hollingsworth.

"I'm contacting the Evanston PD. We're going to ask you to stop at Channel View Road and wait there for a cruiser to bring you on up. What are you driving?"

"Mercedes 500. Black."

"Park on the northeast corner please. And wait."

It's probably another ten minutes away. I press the accelerator, and my high-powered car lurches ahead. On the spur of the moment, I dial Jana's phone myself. No answer. Then I kick myself. I should have stood back and let the police make that call.

The rest of the way up, there's no passing anyone. The traffic is tightly knitted together while I stew and curse. Finally, I make it to Channel View Road, drive across the intersection, and immediately park in a red zone. I shut down the car and climb out. Within moments a police cruiser, EPD, comes wailing through the intersection and swerves to the curb. His window lowers. Two cops, a huge shotgun dividing them.

"Climb in."

The back door opens and in I go.

And we're off.

51

The noose still around her neck, Jana has unbound Danny's feet so he can pull her down the hallway. She is crying. They pass by the sleeping Dania's room, and he stops and peers inside. "Good baby," he says. "Except you're a Gresham. That's three strikes right there, kiddo," he says to the sleeping child as though the mother isn't around.

Then he pulls, and the tightening wire causes her to lurch onto her toes and tap-dance behind him as they reach the end of the hallway and enter her bedroom.

He unties her hands. He tells her to strip off all clothing and jewelry, and she complies.

"Yes, the wedding ring, too," he says with a set smile. "We'll just pretend you're a virgin." He laughs. "Going in, at least."

When he has spent himself on her, he rousts himself off Danny, off the bed, and stands.

"You wait here. I'll see about the little biscuit."

Danny lies there in shock, unable to move for what has just happened. Her chest has constricted and she can barely breath. Her throat also tightens and her nostrils flare with the tears building behind her eyes.

But then she hears Dania in her room waking up. She is squeaking and squawking, the build-up to an all-out wail if she isn't picked up soon out of her crib. Danny is gripped by the instinct to rush to her daughter's side and protect her from Jana. The guitar string is still loosely coiled around her neck, and she gingerly lifts it off and flings it across the bed. It hits the wall on Michael's side and falls to the floor, straightening out in its tensile flex as it falls out of sight. Then she is moving toward the door and edging down the hall.

She hears Jana talking to Dania.

She peeks through the doorway and there is Jana, seated in the rocking chair, rocking and holding Dania on his lap. The little girl sits upright, her back to Jana, and when she spies her mother's face, she reaches out toward the door with both arms. Jana looks up and sees Danny.

"Come in," he calls to Danny. "We were just deciding what to do with this little bitch."

"Give her to me. Please."

Danny approaches the man with her arms extended as if to receive her child. Jana abruptly stands and is out the door, whisking the child down the hallway and into Danny's room, where he sets the child on the bed and turns around to face Danny.

"Where is it? Where's the guitar string? Or do I just snap her neck right now?" As he says this, he places a hand on the back of the little girl's neck. He squeezes until the child looks up with tears in her eyes.

"No," Danny says. "Don't!"

He squeezes harder.

"The string is on the floor on the far side of the bed. Let me get it for you."

She edges around the bed and retrieves the string. She comes back around and passes the string to Jana. He takes it in his hands and refashions a loop, passing the end through the tiny washer meant to anchor the string at the guitar bridge. He holds it up, admiring his work.

Then, "Whose neck first? Mother or child? You tell me, Danny. Do I cut your throat with the string first? Or second? I'm waiting for your answer. Five-four-three—"

"Me! Do me first," she cries and reaches for the string.

"That's it. Drop it around your neck."

Danny complies, moving the loop down around her neck.

"Now come closer. Let's see how it works."

She steps to him and leans down as he motions with his hand to do so. He seizes the end of the string and yanks. The string snugs up around her throat, and she can feel it bite into her flesh. A pain impulse rushes to her brain, and she cries out.

"No!" she yells. "Not my baby, please, Jana!"

"Hush, sweet Danny, hush and shut your eyes. It won't hurt as much if you relax."

She shuts her eyes and waits.

He wraps the loose end around his fist and pulls the noose tighter.

52

When we turn off the main drag onto Moors Road, we are nearly to our house. The officer is running with his lights flashing but turned off his siren five minutes ago. He has told me he is doing that so we don't alert Jana of our approach.

I am sitting belted into the backseat, praying as we rush along. I have heard from Marcel, and he is on the way. I have called Father Bjorn and told him what's happening, and he is in the vestry in prayer for our situation.

When we arrive at my house, two other police cars are already there. Their occupants have remained inside the squad cars at my earlier request. Good, I am thinking, as I decide what comes next.

Then I phone Jana's number. It rings once. Twice. Then it goes to voicemail.

I check my gun, ensuring the safety is on and it's loaded and ready.

The police officer protests, but I have no patience with his point of view. "Look, officer, I don't have time to argue with you. Jana Emerich is inside my house with my wife and daughter. You can't expect me to go inside unarmed. He'll be armed, so please."

The police officer remains adamant. I remind him that as an officer of the court, I have a permit to carry and, as the homeowner, I have a right to defend my property and family. Then I make my decision. I've got to offer myself in place of Danny and Dania. Most likely I'm who he wants anyway.

I walk boldly to my front door and try to open it. It's locked. I ring the bell since I don't have my car and the garage door opener is with my Mercedes as are my keys in the center console. I should have thought, but in such a panicked state, I rushed in head first without thinking things through.

No answer, so I ring again.

Still no answer.

I circle to the back of the house and try the patio sliding door. It opens a crack, but then the twist lock secures it against entry. It is locked from the inside. So I step down to the guest bedroom window and try sliding it open. This is the room where Jana was lodged while he was staying with us. This is the room in which he probably smoked his pot, and Danny might have left it unlocked when she aired out the room.

I lift against the window frame and, to my relief, it slides up and opens. I lead with my upper body inside the room and then leap forward, coming through the window head-first before I arch down onto the floor. I am as quiet as I can be and collect myself once I am inside. Then I stand.

I can hear voices coming from my bedroom. So I peer out into the hall. My bedroom is off to my left. I creep down the hall, my back pressed against the wall as I go.

I am not a physical person. I have never been in a fight, have only been hit by a man's fist maybe two times in my life—while conscious, at least. My gun is out. I decide it will just have to be me against him.

I freeze. Jana's voice can be heard coming from my bedroom. He is talking gibberish as if he's speaking to Dania.

Without my okay, the police are pounding the front door. I am alarmed beyond saying. They have ignored my demand they allow me to speak with Jana before they act. Then I hear the front door flying open after a loud crack and the sound of feet hurrying inside. I am beside my bedroom door when Jana's head suddenly protrudes, looking away from me and down the hallway toward the front room. Just as he retreats into the bedroom, I swing my gun with every muscle against the back of his head.

I discover I'm much stronger than I thought. He jerks forward and his head slams into the doorframe. He slumps down to his knees, gripping the back of his head. Without knowing it will happen, I launch my body on top of his and pummel him with my fists. He loses consciousness under my blows, and I am still screaming at him and punching him when the police approach me from behind and pull me away. His face is bloody and his eyes wildly askew in their orbits. Have I killed him? I don't know and don't give a damn.

Then I am on my feet. Danny is sprawled half on the bed. Her feet are on the floor, but her back is on the bed cover. She is nude and her neck is bleeding profusely down one side.

Then I hear paramedics scrambling into the room around the remains of the altercation in the hallway, and I am pleading with them to save Danny's life. Then I see my little girl, seated on the rocking chair, gently swaying back and forth and watching the activities in her parents' room.

"What about her carotid artery?" I plead with the EMT who is holding what looks to be a gauze pad to the wound. "Is she going to die?"

I am frantic beyond control, and the EMT is busy. Others are doing the ABC's: airway, breathing, and circulation, listening to her heartbeat.

The EMT with the pad at the neck wound looks up at me. His words are like music to my ears. "Luckily, we have two internal carotid arteries and a thing called the Circle of Willis that can redistribute the blood flow. So if one carotid is cut, there will be a pressure loss distal to the cut. Then, blood from the other internal carotid will flow around the Circle of Willis and perfuse vessels distal to the cut in the carotid."

"What's that mean?"

"It means she should survive, all else being equal."

"Breath sounds bilateral," says an EMT with a stethoscope plugged into his ears."

"Good BP and vitals," says a third, a woman maybe half my age.

Then I am swaying on my feet, and the arms of two police swing up to steady me. The room spins, and they lead me to the bed and sit me down. I take Danny's hand in my own.

"You need to let her go, sir," says the female EMT. "We're transporting now."

A gurney has appeared, and Danny's inert body is lifted onto the bed and covered while the first EMT continues to apply pressure to her neck.

Someone says to ride in the ambulance with Danny so I leap up and go around the bed to scoop Dania into my arms. When I jerk the covers off our bed, the wool blanket comes away, and I wrap Dania into a warm cocoon. We hurry after the gurney as it rolls through the house. Jana is restrained face-down on the carpet in the hall. Handcuffs bind his hands together and a uniform has a knee pressed against the back of his head, pinning him to the floor where he has ceased struggling.

We are in the ambulance, careening around corners and rushing down streets and back roads until we screech to a stop beneath the overhang of our local hospital's ER entrance. Danny's gurney is lowered to the ground, and she is rushed away. Dania and I follow. We come to a closed door through which Danny, evidently, has disappeared. The orderlies guide me to a chair in a small waiting area, and I sit with my daughter snuggled up and held close to my chest. Now we can only wait.

It is several hours before a surgeon in green scrubs comes out through the forbidden door. A surgical mask is hanging half off his face and he is rubbing his hands on his pants.

"It's good," he tells me. "She's going to pull through just fine."

"Can we see her?"

"Sure. Give us about thirty minutes to move her from recovery to a room. Someone will come for you, okay?"

"Okay."

"Incidentally, we did a rape kit and exam."

"What did it—"

Marcel rushes into the waiting room and takes a seat beside my daughter and me. I update him on Danny. He remained behind at the house to give the police detectives a full run-down on Jana: who he is, why he had lived with us, and my defense of him at a murder trial.

"I came as fast as I could. An officer ran interference for me. So you're sure she's okay?"

"That's what I was told. Thank you."

Dania has been asleep in my arms through it all. I ask a passing nurse for a bottle of milk. She will send someone with one, she says.

Tears come to my eyes, and I lower my head. My shoulders shake as it all comes pouring out. Marcel sits down beside me and drapes a heavy arm across my shoulders. We sit there like that for a good five minutes. Dania finally stirs and blinks her eyes. A bottle of milk appears with a cafeteria worker wearing a hairnet and, with a gracious smile, she hands it off to Dania. We talk in our strange pidgin, and I tell her that mommy's okay, that we're going to talk to her in just a few minutes. She goes to work on her bottle.

Two police detectives find me and Marcel and Dania before we are allowed into Danny's room.

"Ah," says Marcel in recognition of the two men. "Michael, these are the gentlemen who gave me three minutes alone with Jana in your bedroom."

The detective with the long hair and the gold watch says, "It was amazing. Your guest confessed. It was a miracle how Marcel must have sweet-talked him."

Marcel is smiling ear-to-ear. "Something like that," he says. "We were alone, and I said, 'Hey, how about telling me the truth about Amy Tanenbaum? They can't do anything with you now, and I want to know.'"

"What did he say?"

"He says, 'I did her. Rudy and I planned them all out. The guitar strings, the mice, the glue—we made a plan. I did Amy, he did Franny, and we both did Scarlett.'"

"He was with Father Bjorn," I say. "He couldn't have killed Scarlett. But conspiracy, yes!"

"That's right," says the detective with the long hair. "We're charging him with sexual assault on your wife and conspiracy to murder all three girls. Your boy is going away for three life sentences. Plus the aggravated sex assault time. Maybe twenty-five years on that."

"And Marcel, you just asked Jana nicely?"

Marcel gives me a wicked grin. But I know. I know Marcel and how he works. But no one else needs to know. Besides, he's not a cop. A citizen can beat a confession out of someone, and it's still a good confession. I nod ever so slightly at him.

"So..." says the one with the gold watch. Along with his long hair, he is wearing a natty sports coat and gray slacks. His partner is impeccably dressed in a navy suit. They make quite a duo. "Are you up to giving us a statement?"

I'm not, but I want to get it over with. "Okay."

They then take my statement with a recorder and advise me they'll return tomorrow to speak with Danny. We all shake hands and, for the first time in a long time, I am glad they are there. Marcel and the first detective lapse into a chat about firearms while I rock the baby in my arms. She looks up at me, guzzling her milk down. The second detective says he's going for coffee and wanders off.

It takes twice as long as the doctor said, a full hour, before I'm allowed into Danny's room. I hand Dania off to Marcel and go inside alone. To my great surprise, the head of her bed is elevated, and she can look into my eyes when I approach her. I lean down and kiss her on the mouth. Her neck is remarkably free of dressings, just a small four-by-four taped over her surgical wound. An IV is plugged into the back of her hand, and a heart monitor is clipped on an index finger. Other than that, she's doing remarkably well and her color is back.

"Hey," I say, "I'm so glad you're going to be okay."

"Hey, yourself," she says hoarsely. "Did you get him?"

"I did."

"He heard the window slide up in his old room. That's the only reason he didn't finish strangling me with the wire. He let go and waited at the door. I passed out then. When I came to, we were in the ambulance, and I heard the siren. You and Dania were with me. Is she all right?"

"Yes. Marcel has her right outside the door."

"Bring her to me, please."

I step out into the hallway and return with Dania. Danny outstretches her arms and takes Dania to her chest. She kisses the top of her head and lays her cheek on our little girl's head. "This is good, Michael."

"No more criminal law," I suddenly blurt out as tears rush into my eyes. "I cannot tell you how sorry I am!"

"Nonsense. We'll go on doing what we do. We just won't invite any more of our clients to move in," she says with a smile.

"We'll talk about it."

Marcel sticks his head inside and tells us he's going to get going. But first he comes to Danny's bedside where he leans down and kisses her forehead. He takes her hand in his paw and squeezes it. Then he turns and is gone.

"Love that guy," Danny smiles.

"I know. I love him, too."

"So, I know they arrested Jana. What else?"

I spread my hands. "He confessed to conspiracy to murder all three girls. He's going away forever."

"My God!"

"Oh, yes. We missed the call on that one."

"Where does that leave us?"

"He's going away for many years for what he did to you, too."

"You know what he did?"

"You've been examined. We know what happened."

Just then, Father Bjorn comes rushing into the room. "Marcel called me," he says breathlessly. "How are you, Danny?" He takes her hand and holds it to his chest before she can reply. "Let's pray."

He says a short prayer, and while he does, Danny's eyes find mine.

I return her look, but she is suddenly gone. She is asleep as the pain pump has delivered another dose through her IV. I study the delicate blue veins of her eyelids, then take Dania back.

Father Bjorn steps away, then lays a hand on my shoulder. "Thank you, Michael."

I reach up and touch his hand. Words are unnecessary, but still I want to tell him about Jana. He should hear it from me.

I turn, but he is gone.

With the baby in my arms and a silent room all around me, I back into the visitor's chair and find that it is a rocking chair. I breathe against my daughter's hair. Her head carries a smell like no other in the world.

I hold her, hold on tight, just me between her and the world.

Just me, and I am a better man for it.

EPILOGUE

Six months pass and, at last, an answer.

When we meet for coffee in his diocesan office, Father Bjorn is looking like a man who has spent too many nights waiting up for the adolescent who's stayed out beyond curfew. Having a son who has been thrice-convicted for first-degree murder will do that times one thousand. Under the best conditions, parenting an adolescent is an exercise guaranteed to exhaust and drain even the most hardened player. Parenting a serial killer while serving in *loco parentis* to an entire congregation must be somewhere on the road to sainthood for Roman Catholics. We'll see what the Pope decides to do for Father Bjorn, whether he'll recognize the merit and grit of our priest and commence the search for two miracles or whether his sainthood will be the other kind, the kind that isn't celebrated, the kind that happens once a month through prison Plexiglas. Time will tell, I think, as my priest pours our coffee.

"This time I called you," I mention to him. "I called you because in my heart of hearts I am struggling with a personal problem involving us both."

"Both, meaning you and me?"

"Yes. You see, Father, your son impregnated Danny when he assaulted her."

Father Bjorn slumps in his chair, closes his eyes, and mutters a long prayer. Then he looks up at me, meeting my eyes again.

"God's pursuing grace is what's needed now, Michael."

"I know that."

"How can I make this right, Michael?"

"Father, it isn't your wrong to make right. So you can't."

"But still—"

"No, let me tell you why I'm here. It's not about guilt or responsibility or sin or repentance—none of that. The simple fact is, your son has made you a grandfather, a grandfather to my wife's son."

"Sweet Jesus!"

"Yes. I will be the father to my wife's son. I don't know how else to conceive of this except by the common terms we all use in our everyday language."

"Oh, oh, oh!" he exclaims, tears in his eyes. He produces a folded handkerchief and wipes at his eyes.

"But we are going to want this child christened. And we will dedicate him to the Church. We will want you to perform the service. Would you be able to do this for us?"

He shuffles his feet uncomfortably as he struggles to right himself in a world that must be swaying at all four corners. I am struck that it is too much at once for this dear man. His tragedy continues to lap at him, his youthful sin refusing to extinguish.

"Of course, I will do it. The only reservation is that I first go to the Church and seek its guidance."

"How long will that take?"

"Months. Maybe a year."

"We wanted to have him christened sometime in his first ninety days."

"Maybe you should select a different priest."

"Maybe we should."

We both sit there, watching the cloud of motes dance between us in the morning shafts of sunlight separating his chair from my own.

I lean forward and rest my elbows on my legs. "But here's the saving grace for us all. We are going to list me on the birth certificate as the child's father. He will take my name, Michael Gresham. He will grow up as my son because I will not see him suffer even a jot or a tittle of shame for what his biological father has done. That slate will be wiped clean. There will no longer be any reason for you to be known as the child's grandfather, and there will be no reason for the child to know you as his grandfather. The thread will be severed along with his umbilical cord, and it will be concluded."

"That would be the best thing."

"We're Catholic. The second best idea was to adopt him out. But he's Danny's son. She can't do that. She is torn apart by this because, for her, there's no good answer."

Again we study the dust floating in the light.

"One thing..." he begins slowly. "How are you sure the child isn't your offspring?"

"You've seen those ads on TV? The ads for erectile dysfunction?"

"ED?"

"Yep. That's me. And my prescription was awaiting refill at the time this child was conceived. Which was the exact day your son raped my wife."

"Sweet Jesus! Why did I ask?"

"Because you're a good man, and you would have guided me free of all this if you could have. But you can't and I can't. What's done is done. It's our work now to confirm and protect innocence, no matter the price."

"Then I join you in that. I will have no claim on your boy."

"That's what I came here to know."

"Well, you have my joinder in this."

"Your lineage will end with you, Father."

"So be it. As it turns out, it's a win for the world."

Now it's my turn to sit uncomfortably, my mission concluded. The child's genetic code, which in other circumstances would have placed him with Jana, has been interrupted and changed.

Peace spreads over me then, and I am calm as I visualize a baby boy turning right, taking a new path.

I have hope, new hope.

It will have to be enough.

THE END

UP NEXT: THE LAW PARTNERS

"WHAT A RIDE THIS BOOK TAKES YOU ON! "

"This is a thrilling legal adventure made even more so by Ellsworth's long career as a lawyer having experienced similar courtroom situations. "

"The Law Partners by Mr Ellsworth is one of the best legal thrillers I have read in a long time. "

"The story is good, the characters are believable and the suspense is addictive. "

"Fantastic book! John Ellsworth at his best in this Michael Gresham thriller. "

Read The Law Partners: CLICK HERE

ALSO BY JOHN ELLSWORTH

THADDEUS MURFEE PREQUEL

A Young Lawyer's Story

THADDEUS MURFEE SERIES

The Defendants

Beyond a Reasonable Death

Attorney at Large

Chase, the Bad Baby

Defending Turquoise

The Mental Case

The Girl Who Wrote The New York Times Bestseller

The Trial Lawyer

The Near Death Experience

Flagstaff Station

The Crime

La Jolla Law

The Post office

SISTERS IN LAW SERIES

Frat Party: Sisters In Law

Hellfire: Sisters In Law

MICHAEL GRESHAM PREQUEL

LIES SHE NEVER TOLD ME

MICHAEL GRESHAM SERIES

THE LAWYER

THE DEFENDANT'S FATHER (THIS BOOK)

THE LAW PARTNERS

CARLOS THE ANT

SAKHAROV THE BEAR

ANNIE'S VERDICT

DEAD LAWYER ON AISLE 11

30 DAYS OF JUSTIS

THE FIFTH JUSTICE

PSYCHOLOGICAL THRILLERS

THE EMPTY PLACE AT THE TABLE

HISTORICAL THRILLERS

THE POINT OF LIGHT

LIES SHE NEVER TOLD ME

UNSPEAKABLE PRAYERS

HARLEY STURGIS

NO TRIVIAL PURSUIT

LETTIE PORTMAN SERIES

THE DISTRICT ATTORNEY

JUSTICE IN TIME

ABOUT THE AUTHOR

For thirty years John defended criminal clients across the United States. He defended cases ranging from shoplifting to First Degree Murder to RICO to Tax Evasion, and has gone to jury trial on hundreds. His first book, *The Defendants*, was published in January, 2014. John is presently at work on his 31st thriller.

Reception to John's books have been phenomenal; more than 4,000,000 have been downloaded in 6 years! Every one of them are Amazon best-sellers. He is an Amazon All-Star every month and is a *U.S.A Today* bestseller.

John Ellsworth lives in the Arizona region with three dogs that ignore him but worship his wife, and bark day and night until another home must be abandoned in yet another move.

johnellsworthbooks.com

johnellsworthbooks@gmail.com

EMAIL SIGNUP

Click here to subscribe to my newsletter: https://www.
subscribepage.com/b5c8ao

AMAZON REVIEWS

If you can take a few minutes and leave your review of this book I would be very honored. Plus, by your support you will be helping me write more books.

Made in United States
North Haven, CT
29 September 2024

58083699R00202